With so many people not what they seemed, how could I possibly know who to trust...

Just as the van was pulling up to me here comes the Grinch who stole Christmas. Andy the cop looked like he hadn't slept in weeks, but I'd only known him a few minutes, so maybe I looked that way, and I just put it on him. Either way, he was fast approaching, and I had nowhere to run.

My sister-in-law, the lawyer, intercepted him. "What do you want?" She stood there in black high-heeled pumps and a black shark suit to match. Though she was tiny, her stance would have made most sumo wrestlers turn and run.

Yet, he was still trying to go around her to speak to me. "I need to speak to her."

She shadowed his every move. It almost looked like they were dancing. "She's not up to talking to you right now, Officer..." She was waiting for his surname. Truth be told, I had no idea what his last name was. I had been questioned all week by many different policemen, and one sort of blended with the other. Still, Andy stood out and not just because he was a hottie...well, maybe a little because of that.

"I'm her lawyer, and she isn't speaking to anyone on the street."

"I need to speak to her, miss..." So two could play that game, aye? He smirked at her. "Will you move over, please? This is an official police investigation, Counselor."

Ooowee, he could really play it.

"Officer D'Souza, please come here," a strong voice boomed behind him, and there stood a man in a large coat that sported a fur-topped hood pulled over a massive head. A certain haze hung around him. "Detective, this is not your investigation right now."

Did I smell sulfur?

Two Weeks before Christmas....

Finding a red weave pocketbook—containing a passport bathed in a creepy, glowing plasma—in a Goodwill and being followed around by the murdered woman to whom it belonged is just another day in the life of Theresa Lillian Lewis. The plucky war widow and mother of a twelve-year-old is all too used to the weird.

Theresa communicates with ghosts—they mostly want her to find lost items—but after she buys the red pocketbook, things get complicated fast. She collides with a hot cop named Andy, gets shot, finds out that the devil has a serious bone to pick with her because of something she did as a four-year-old, and gets to meet Santa and a mischievous nymph named Barney. Now, all Theresa has to do is to resolve some mysteries about her childhood and her parents, learn what she has to do to put the world back in order, and escape from the devil in hell...

KUDOS for *Goodwill*

In *Goodwill* by Arcey Dear, Theresa sees dead people. When she goes to the Goodwill to do some Christmas shopping, she sees a dead woman standing by a rack of handbags. A sucker for a deal, Theresa grabs a handbag of the rack with the price tags still on it. But there's a spectral green goo inside, along with the passport and birth certificate of the dead woman standing beside her. Concerned, Theresa decides to do the right thing. She heads for the parking lot, where there's a police cruiser parked, and tries to give the documents to the cops. And that's where things start to go wrong. It's bad enough there are two teenage spirits in the back seat of the police car, but when a van full of nymphs start shooting at them all, Theresa wonders if her good deed will turn out to be her last. Cute, clever, and zany, the story is full of fascinating characters, a number of plot twists and turns, and an intriguing mystery. I thoroughly enjoyed it. ~ *Taylor Jones, The Review Team of Taylor Jones & Regan Murphy*

Goodwill by Arcey Dear is the story of Theresa Lewis, who is still in mourning for her husband Paulo, killed in Afghanistan two years ago. Now, as a single parent of a twelve-year-old daughter, Theresa lives with her husband's extended family. They're Greek. And she isn't. They're all gorgeous, confident, gregarious. And she isn't. But when she finds a red handbag at the local Goodwill while doing some Christmas shopping, her world is turned upside down. First she finds a passport and birth certificate inside the purse, which would be bad enough, but these belonged to a dead woman, one who is standing right next to her. Theresa is not surprised to see a dead person, she sees them all the time. Usually, she just finds lost items for them and returns them to the deceased's family. But something tells her that this time is different. Maybe it's the green plasma slime covering the passport, or the fact that the two cops she tries to give it to have two dead people in the back of their car—not the bodies, just the spirits. Or could it be the nymphs who attack them in the parking lot? Whatever it is, Theresa is about to get more than she bargained for—a lot more. While the story is fast-paced, tense, and exciting, it's also fun, witty, and intriguing. Combining mystery, suspense, humor, and a hint of sweet romance, *Goodwill* is truly a delightful read. ~ *Regan Murphy, The Review Team of Taylor Jones & Regan Murphy*

I laughed until I cried, and then I chuckled all the next day, even after I finished. It was so much fun, I couldn't put it down. Marvelous." *Pepper O'Neal, author of the award-winning Black Ops Chronicles series.*

GOODWILL

ARCEY DEAR

A Black Opal Books Publication

GENRE: URBAN FANTASY/HUMOR/WOMEN'S FICTION

GOODWILL
Copyright © 2017 by Arcey Dear
Cover Design by Jackson Cover Designs
All cover art copyright © 2017
All Rights Reserved
Print ISBN: 978-1-626948-27-3

First Publication: DECEMBER 2017

Published by Black Opal Books **http://www.blackopalbooks.com**

DEDICATION

It is my great privilege to dedicate this book to my parents. Most people have one set I have had the honor to have had two sets to annoy most of their adult lives. Sorry folks.

Mom and Dan
Dad and Joan

Also, I wanted to give an honorable dedication to my own set of 'DEAR' children, who took my role over most of my adult life.

Lea, Jay, Rose, & Faye

The four of you are my real-life inspiration for my smile every day, and my full head of gray hair ☺'

A special Thank you to my husband Stuart who puts up with me daily! Sorry about all the grey hair I put on your head. Thank you to all of you

CHAPTER 1

Present Day:

You're probably wondering what a short, stout woman—okay, chunky, maybe veering toward the better half of fat, but I'm on the Fast Diet, though I am not losing the weight so fast, no pun intended—where was I? Right. What am I doing crouching behind a police cruiser as someone is shooting at me? I don't want to sound too full of myself, but they are taking pot shots at the two police officers by my side as well, and maybe they are slightly interested in the bright red pocketbook that still has its original tags attached, but they can't have that. I paid for it already.

It all started earlier today. It's two weeks before Christmas, and I just got myself to start my shopping. I am not overly fond of Christmas lately. In fact, anything to do with the holiday downright depresses me. So there I was at the Goodwill. I am not cheap, just a bit strapped for money. Widows have to stay on a budget, you know. Okay, so I am a little cheap.

I should have paid attention this time and seen this situation as it came toward me. The hairs on my neck started to rise when I spotted the fire-engine-red, weaved bag with—did I mention, the original store tags were on it? Did I tell you the price? Two dollars! It was a yellow tag day. *Half price!* The original price was forty-nine dollars. Who'd buy it for that? Not that the bag was scary—it was what stood next to it that made me want to run out the door. I tried to ignore her. Still, a two-hundred-plus-pound woman with blood dripping down the right side of her face, wearing a purple knit dress way too small for her bulk—I envied her courage, though—slightly ripped near the neckline, was very hard to ignore. I do have to say her makeup was perfect. Don't you just hate women who can put on liquid eye-liner straight? Her chocolate brown skin was unwrinkled. Man, I would like to know the moisturizer she uses—er—used.

I could see she was as interested as I was in this particular pocketbook. Okay, so I walked away from it—twice—but, as was usually the case with these things, I just had to go back. Each time I did, she was still standing there, waiting, so, finally, I took it off the metal rack—crammed and practically tipping over with the load of all those handbags just waiting for someone to own them.

As I examined it, I could tell the red weave was synthetic and I instantly regretted taking it. I was looking for new stuff, with tags, for my Christmas presents this year, but it was red, and my late husband's family is Greek. If you don't understand, then you are not married into a Greek family.

Did I mention that the woman in purple was dead? I have a habit of forgetting to mention that little detail. Anyhoo, she was standing very close to the bag now in my hand, and I noticed that there was weight to it—the bag, I mean—so I did what any good Goodwill shopper would do: I peeked inside. The lining was red silk and looked wonderful, but it was empty. There was, however, a little pocket on the side that had a zipper. When I put my fingers on it, I noticed it was hard. Yes, my heart did that racing thing that hidden treasure does to a person.

I tried unzipping it, but the zipper was stuck, and, much to my horror, it ripped. The edges of a blue leather wallet seemed to be peeking out. I figured I'd already done the damage, so I went full blast ahead and ripped it out from what was left of the pocket. I am a bit impulsive. In my hand was a navy blue leather folder the size of a wallet. What shocked me most was that it was stamped with my initials on it in gold—TLL—Theresa Lilian Lewis. That's my given name. I opened it a crack and noted a darker blue little booklet contained within. When I further inspected it, I found out it was a passport. Tucked right under the part with her picture was something even more shocking, a birth certificate. To be clear, there was something wrong with this birth certificate. It shimmered a bit. Not the ordinary glow—you know, something decorative that you might see—but the type that is...well, frankly put...downright eerie. I'd even go as far as to say it was a moldy green plasma color. I tucked it back into the slot where I found it, not wanting to contaminate myself with it. I do have to say it did improve the dreary-colored walls of the place, as the color bounced off the light gray cinder blocks. I have a question. Why do most Goodwills insist on looking like a prison ward? Why not yellow with butterflies?

I looked at the voluminous woman dressed in blood, next to me, and then at the picture in the passport. You already guessed they were one and the same, right? I hadn't expected anything different. Terry Laila Lewis, close enough to my own. Already I was feeling a connection to her. The shredded handbag and I went up to the front of the store. I do admit to stopping a few times to eye some potential great buys. I mean, what could I do?

The woman was already dead. What was a few more minutes? If I rushed, what would I be gaining for her? I see the dead; I don't bring them back to life.

So with an Avon makeup kit, slightly used; last year's computer keyboard—with a mouse, I might add; a twisted metal basket; a ripped pocketbook; and a dead woman, I paid at the counter. Then I exited, passport in hand, into the dark parking lot. I don't know how most of you feel about walking into deserted parking lots with dead people following you, but it really doesn't faze me at all.

I suspect it doesn't affect you either since they follow you all the time, and you don't see them. However, for some reason, I was particularly unnerved this evening. Maybe it was the green glow that I noticed emanating from the shopping bag, the heaviness in the air, or just panic that I hadn't gotten any Christmas presents yet. As I held my loot tightly, protecting it from any unseen used-clothing freak, I ventured to my car in the darkest corner of the lot. What? You thought I'd choose a well-lighted spot? This was the nearest one I could get so close to Christmas. Well, I am not that upset, as I have to put in gym time for this diet, and why can't a girl combine exercise with a little fun?

To my great joy, there was a police cruiser just sitting beside my car, along with two officers, who seemed to be waiting for little ole me. The lady who was accompanying me seemed pleased as well. I even sensed she knew them, and we smiled at one another. Maybe my luck was changing. We both headed toward the police car. One of the officers was an older gentleman—his white hair, the nest of wrinkles around his eyes, and his air of confidence defining him as the more experienced of the pair. I chose to approach him first.

I might add there was a little extra attraction. The

cruiser, which to me seemed to be old, was illuminated. I could tell there was no actual light bulb on in there, so suffice it to say, they had a couple of passengers that seemed to have not quite passed into the light yet, but that would be a whole other story. Like I said, I see dead people, and they see me.

The older officer looked up just as I approached the window on his side. The other, much younger, police officer—alive, I might add—who sat in the passenger seat seemed engrossed in his cell phone. I proceeded to introduce myself to the driver.

"I found this pocketbook with original vendor's tags on it."

He eyed me as if I had leprosy, his water-logged blue eyes boring right through my skull.

"In it was a passport booklet." I produced the little blue item and held it out to him.

He peered at it as if it was a spoiled tuna fish sandwich, dripping juices.

"Aren't you going to look at it?" I asked.

Maybe it was leaking something, but I didn't think he could see it, or maybe he did see the spectral mold.

"Where did you find it?" he finally asked, his voice just barely audible so I had to lean in to hear him.

I pointed to the large brick building. "In the store."

"Uh huh."

Still making no physical contact with the item, the other police officer finally looked up, looked at me, and then I caught him glancing past my shoulder. I briefly looked behind me, but the only person there was the deceased. He saw her. I knew the expression that crossed someone's face when they saw a dead person, especially if they were one of those who denied their ability. The look on his face said he had distinctly spotted her and her wounds. Then he turned to stare at me.

The younger man clenched his teeth at the older officer. "Let's go, Ned."

"Wait a second—this is a lost passport. Her birth certificate is in here too." I pulled it out and tried to shove it at them.

Ned shifted his whole body away from it, ramming into the younger man beside him. Strangely, the green glow dripped onto the seat near where he was sitting. We both stared at it.

"What is that stuff?" I said, a bit too loud.

He stared at it too and paled. To be perfectly frank, it did kind of blend in with the polyester seat cover. I think old Ned turned the same color. He looked grimly at it. "It's Death."

"Ned, call it in and let's scram. You can't handle this tonight." The younger man then growled at him and pushed him back toward me, on top of the goop.

Ned held onto the wheel and lifted his rump up, making the most pained face I had ever seen on a living person.

As I looked at him, I realized he wasn't even seeing me. I tried another tack—let's say, I had a hunch. "They're in the back, you know," I whispered to him.

Ned looked at me then at the seat behind him where two Hispanic teenagers, a boy and a girl, were sitting. All most people would see was black seat belts, hanging loose, and empty maroon leather seats. By the way, these looked nothing like the front ones, which had coverings and almost seemed festive in comparison.

"Those young kids don't look like they are going anywhere very fast, sir."

Okay, so it wasn't nice, and I had no idea if they were or were not going anywhere fast, but, hey, I had a stolen passport in my hand to return. Well, not quite return, but he could at least look at it. The front door of the cab opened. He took the passport from me, still not cracking it open to take a peek.

"Show me where." Ned led the way. Fast!

On the back of his pants was a florescent green stain. He was speedy, and it seemed he was more interested in distancing himself from the car than in investigating what was being tightly gripped in his hand.

I heard the other police officer call after him. "Don't touch it!"

Then the car door slammed hard. Too late. Ned had it in his grip.

"Where did you f—find it, m—miss?" he stuttered, trying to sound calm, but not succeeding.

I pointed to the closed doors of the Goodwill. "On a rack in there where the handbags are."

"Maybe the lady who gave it to Goodwill will realize it's gone and will come back for it," he said, not really believing it himself.

I looked behind me. She already had returned and had come back for it.

"Perhaps you should put it back?"

Was that a very hopeful note in his voice, like let's put it back and go for coffee…doughnuts, anyone?

Was this guy serious? Was he even a real cop? What exactly did the stain on the back of his pants mean? Why was I even looking there?

I sighed. "It expired in 2010, and the bag I found it in still had the tags from the original store. Besides, she's dead—you know—like your passengers?"

He looked at me as if I was speaking Latin. I shook my head, exasperated, so I tried another tactic. "Look, no self-respecting woman is going to stuff her handbag with a passport plus birth certificate and then do a night on the town *with the tags sticking out*."

He had stopped at the doors of the store, pretending

to inspect them, when understanding hit him, and he smiled. He finally cracked the passport open. The smile disappeared, and his long face turned gray. In fact, he looked stricken. "Terry?"

"Mmmmmm."

They knew each other!

"Do you know if the Goodwill catalogs their items?" he asked me. His whole attitude had changed. He was all cop now.

"No, sir."

"Did you tell the employees about it?"

Which part? The dead woman or the lost passport? I only said no. I really didn't know who was working there, and I was worried that it might get into the wrong hands—identity theft and all that. Yes, that is another little quirk I have. I can kind of read places too. It's not that I'm biased against Goodwill workers or anything, but I had a distinctly fishy feeling about this particular store. Maybe it was because the tattooed kid manning the register had the words *Life sucks and sew do U* inked on his face. Would you trust a guy who'd let someone who can't spell mark him for life?

The deceased lady behind me hadn't done much to improve my outlook on the place either, but, then again, she couldn't help her situation. When I mentioned my hesitation about the employees, he glanced at the boy and nodded.

We paraded into the store: me, a uniformed cop, a dead lady, and a red handbag. We came to the purse rack, and I instantly saw a DKNY black bag I had somehow missed in all the excitement of the bloody murder victim. I was seriously considering taking it off the rack and checking it out when I realized he was talking to me again.

"...this is where it was?"

He pointed to the very pocketbook I wanted. Was this a tease, or what?

He scratched his scalp. I nodded. He peered at the silver rack, laden with purses of different varieties, as if it was going to tell him everything he needed to know. When he came to the conclusion that nothing was forthcoming from this piece of equipment, he turned and headed toward the aisle.

I noticed that he was awful careful not to touch anything. Goodwill got mostly donated items, and not all of it was given because the owner wanted to part with their stuff. I assumed some was there because people were moving, some because of divorce, some because of other life changes, and a good deal because of death. A few items might be stolen too. How they got in there was anyone's guess, but Ned, the police officer, didn't want to find out—or so it seemed. He was avoiding anything that might even remotely be heading his way, but as luck would have it, probably a little of my own bad luck, something that he couldn't avoid slammed into him.

Two cheery, bright-eyed little kids had rammed a cart laden with different items that a homely, overwhelmed, redheaded mother—I didn't actually see her face, but thought I noticed facial hair under her kerchief. Really, that's why the Lord created the epi, lady—had carefully collected. It turned over and tipped right onto the now prostrate cop, covering him from head to toe with an odd assortment of merchandise. His face turned several shades of pink. He began gasping for air and hyperventilating, trying to swim out from under it.

I reached down to give him my hand, but he scooted away from that too. He popped his head up just as his partner came over to him and yanked him roughly out of the pile.

"One day—that is all you had!" Ned's partner stormed at him.

The first thing that struck me about this guy was that he was very tall. Of course, since I was only slightly over five feet, most people looked tall.

"Come on, let's get this over with." The partner turned toward me, looking ready to eat me. "Give me the passport and the birth certificate."

At first, I wasn't sure I understood. Was he yelling at me? Wasn't it my civic duty to turn in lost items to the police? Especially a passport? His hand was sticking out, impatiently waiting. I looked at my hands. To my shock, the birth certificate was missing. Ned was looking for the passport he had taken from me and couldn't now find. The mother and the two little critters who had knocked over poor Ned were gone.

"I don't have it anymore. It must have dropped into the pile." I pointed down at the massive hill of junk at our feet. Then I looked at the end of the aisle and saw our dead friend pointing at the closing doors. "Or it is now in the parking lot with that lady and her two—"

He was off after them. Ned looked at me and shot upright as if he were on steroids. He charged after the other police officer. "Andy, no!"

Ned was running full force. In the heat of the moment, I followed him, not really knowing why. We all ended up in the parking lot. The officer named Andy was by the patrol car with the radio mike in hand. I presumed—from probably way too many police TV shows—that he was calling for backup. Just as he finished and tossed the black microphone back in the car, a large green sedan came from nowhere, slammed into the police cruiser, pushing it backward, and caused Andy to fall. As the massive thing was pulling out, Ned got out his gun and began shooting at it. It instantly skidded and gunned back out to make another attempt at the cruiser. The older policeman quickly got himself to his partner's side, helping him up. The younger man now had a cut on his head.

I was an expert on skinned knees, split lips, and vomiting. Gashes on the head weren't really my specialty, since I was the single parent of a twelve-year-old girl who never climbed trees, but I reached into my own beat-up purse and took out a wad of tissues, quickly applying pressure to the gushing wound. He looked at me and smiled weakly.

I tried my best nurse voice. "I am just applying pressure."

He relaxed his hunky body in my arms. He sure was good looking up close. "Thanks, Mom."

Great—here was this stud muffin in my grip and he thought I was his mother. Just my luck.

"Are you hurt anywhere else?" I asked, trying to assure my hurt ego that even Florence Nightingale got called "Mom" at times.

"Did you count how many were in there, Andy? Are the kids in there, too?" Ned's voice was filled with anxiety. Every so often, he scratched his legs and his arms as if they were covered in hives. Andy looked at him and then seemed to realize he was lying prostrate in my arms. He sat up and took my hand with him.

"No, it was dark, but if they have kids, it is safe to assume they aren't too bright—"

Several shots seem to punctuate his words. Both men cowered.

"You." Andy pointed his finger at me like a weapon. "Don't move from here," he growled at me, pulling out his own gun and inching his way toward his partner.

They looked at each other as another round came our way.

"If there are kids in there..." Ned trailed off and stared down at his own gun.

"Ned, just aim for the tires, will you? No kids are gonna get it today." Andy looked around and, for a moment, peered into the cruiser's window where the teens looked back at him. They nodded, and the girl waved at him shyly.

I followed his line of sight and noticed that the teenagers were probably much younger than I thought at first, maybe twelve or thirteen. Wide-eyed, the girl pressed her face flat against the window. The boy, who was squeezing next to her, looked straight at me. His dark brown eyes were imploring me to help them. I turned away. There was nothing I could do right now—or any time. My talent was returning things, not crossing the dead over. That's right. I found something and returned it, not usually something belonging to a murder victim, but, hey, my life wasn't exactly normal, and there was always a first time, right?

Another shot hit the car. Ned's body jerked backward and slammed onto the black, tarred lot. The "thunk" I heard was sickening, but loud and clear. I watched in horror as blood spurted from his body and pooled on the already darkened concrete. I went to him, against orders, and put my hand on his wounds. My hand was already covered in Andy's blood, and I sure hoped he didn't have AIDS because I was definitely mixing it with Ned's now.

In the next moment, I saw it didn't matter what I did. Ned's essence exited his body. I lifted my reddened hand and stared at him. A bright light shone down, and the newly dead policeman looked at it for a moment and then back at the cruiser. The faces of the teens in the back were aglow, looking longingly at the beam, but they didn't come out and join him. He shook his head and withdrew from the light as the arching tentacles reached toward him. The stream vanished. Ned just stood there and sighed. There was a gaping wound in the middle of his chest.

"Put your hand back on it!" A commanding voice, along with a rough push, shoved my hands to where they were before, on the warm, open wound. His partner looked desperate.

"You see him—he's gone. Let him go."

Andy didn't want to hear it. "Now!" He put his gun down and put his own hands there. "Put them on here, will you?"

Tears were streaming down his face and, simply out of compassion for him, I complied.

Ned sat on the ground next to me. He didn't say anything, but we both watched as Andy yelled for an ambulance in the radio mike. "Officer down" was something I had heard on television many times, but had never expected to hear in person. Another gunshot split the air. Andy edged toward the end of the car, but then he came back to me. He was now sobbing as he crawled over to me and picked up Ned's head. He held him, rocking back and forth, the gun inactive at his feet.

"One more day. One lousy day—that's all you had to hold out, Ned."

I didn't understand this, but I watched and held my position on his wound halfheartedly, until two strong able hands removed them and took over.

I hadn't even heard the ambulance approach and reluctantly withdrew from my duty. I was pushed aside by another medic and realized this wasn't the regular paramedics unit, but a Jewish unit called Hatzalah. I looked curiously at the medic in his skullcap. The bearded man smiled at me and asked if I had any injuries.

"We were the closest unit available, so the dispatcher called us first." His soft voice consoled me. He looked back at his partner, who was attending to Ned. Each one worked in silence, only calling in the injuries to an unseen ear device, I supposed, was connected to a hospital. Another had the stretcher ready, and a fourth one that had just screeched into the lot jumped out of the black Landover he was driving. I wasn't sure it even stopped.

He was tall and had the sideburns the Hassidim wear. His yellow vest with his unit's number on it was fluorescent. He went to help load Ned's body. There was a sense of urgency in all their movements as if they knew they had to move fast, but I knew it was useless. Ned looked at his body as it was getting ready to go.

"He is dead, you know," I said numbly.

The rosy-cheeked, round-faced man looked at me with what I realized was compassion.

"It is up to the one up above and not man to decide that. He will intervene if he chooses to," he said with utter belief.

"No, there is no hope. He is dead." I looked at him with great sadness, just beginning to realize that it probably wasn't my own emotions I was feeling. I had the ability to feel the emotions of others on occasion. Even worse, I could feel events that had already happened and the feelings of those involved—or no longer involved, if you know what I mean. No, I wasn't a psychic, exactly. I was just kind of talented that way. But maybe this time it was because I was going into shock.

"There is always hope," he said gently, but I didn't argue with him as darkness had begun to engulf me.

CHAPTER 2

My family was not exactly your conventional family. Actually, neither was my late husband's family. My husband Paulo was killed in action in Afghanistan two years ago. I live with his brother and his family, not to mention my in-laws. I was their unofficial nanny, taking care of their three kids, as well as my one and only daughter, my beautiful, unusual Sophie. I moved in the day the two soldiers came to my door to inform me of Paulo's death. At first, when Sophie called me to the window, she told me there was a parade outside. When I saw all the Arestes in the lineup, I knew what was coming. I was taken, but not forcibly, and, yes I admit it, I never wanted to return home—too much of Paulo everywhere.

As my eyes opened, I was surrounded by big hair and looks of intense concern. Or maybe it was intense hair and big worries, but either way, it would have been a bit disconcerting to a stranger, although not to me. I had grown up as an only child, and I loved being in such hubbub all the time.

A chorus of "How are you feeling?" was flung my way with a cacophony of other comments I couldn't sift through in my drug-induced haze. I noticed one thing that was a bit upsetting. I had an intense pain in my shoulder, and it was becoming more painful with each question.

"Enough." A controlled voice rose above the others, though it wasn't any louder than a whisper. Rydia, my mother-in-law, stood her four-foot-eleven inches and waited until all obeyed her directive.

She was just like her name, which means "Rose petals on still water." Calm, collected and sweet. What most noticed about her were the dark brown eyes matching the color of her soft, loose, curly hair. Her face was smooth for her advanced age. It often seemed to me she was ageless. Behind her, as always, stood Paulo Senior. His intense look at his family probably also helped quiet them down. He looked old. Life had definitely taken a toll on him. His hair was white, and his face was wrinkled. I supposed he had really started looking ancient when my Paulo, his oldest son, had died. Not far behind them was my mother. She always deferred to Paulo's family. I could see her tight ringlets of dyed black curls slightly above my in-laws' poofs. Peripherally, I could make out other forms, but I knew the others didn't see them.

"How are you feeling?" Rydia asked quietly.

"Where am I?" Yeah, I was on drugs, because anyone else would have guessed that sterile white walls, tubes connected to the body, and rails on the bed meant hospital.

"You are in the hospital," my mother-in-law answered patiently in her heavy Greek-accented English.

"Was I shot?"

Rydia's gaze shifted to my daughter. My child's big brown eyes were staring at me with such concern. She always looked so pale to me. I tried to reach my hand out to her, but realized it was attached to something—a board to keep my shoulder immobilized. "Hi, baby."

She didn't push through the crowd to get to me, she never did. Her cousins overwhelmed her, perhaps because she was so thin, and they thought she couldn't possibly barrel through crowds successfully—or maybe she favored my mother in this regard. She wasn't aggressive at all. It sometimes made me very sad. You had to push to get what you wanted in this world. I still hoped that her Greek relations could influence her somehow, give her a little of their confidence.

The other kids came immediately to her aid. It was her little cousin Velma, three years her junior, who dragged her near me. Velma was always her big cousin's protector.

"Come on, Sophs," Velma's gravelly voice coaxed.

The stout little body attached to the pretty, dark-haired girl bulldozed on. Her vibrant smile flashed at the shy person she held onto. Sophie came, but not willingly, her slim body stiff. She looked at the floor and waited for me to talk to her.

"Hi, honey."

She looked up with tear-laden eyes, and my heart broke. I instantly swore off Goodwill forever!

"I am okay, sweetie, really I am."

I tried, I really did, but sometimes we just didn't connect. She was quiet, stable, steady, and I was, to be frank, off the wall. We were just two very different people who somehow were mother and daughter. Her long red hair stuck to her tear-lined face. I was able to reach over with my free hand and gently push the hair back. Touching her made my heart thump. If you had a daughter—or a son—already half an orphan—well, you either knew what I meant, or you don't. Though she was twelve years old, she looked so much younger. It upset her when I made an effort to explain that she would appreciate this later in life. Ever practical, she just calmly told me she was happy with her height and that it was just fine. I was the one who worried about people seeing her as vulnerable and taking advantage of her. I had some history there—vulnerable children, I mean.

"Are you really okay?" my pretty little girl said just above a whisper, her breath smelling of mints because she feared having bad breath so badly.

Greeks use a lot of garlic. What can I say?

"Sure she is, Sophs." Her cousin smiled at her. "She is talking, isn't she?"

Well, to a nine-year-old, that was logical.

Sophie seemed to consider that, and then she gave a half smile. I hadn't seen a real one since just before her father died, so I guess this one would have to do as an acknowledgment that I was in passable shape. "You aren't going to die, are you?" she gasped in my ear and then I began to cry, because I knew that was what she was thinking, and I was determined, no matter what was wrong with me, not to die. "You promised," she added, her moist eyes practically screaming at me.

"Go get ice cream!" my sister-in-law Alysia suddenly commanded.

She was a lawyer and couldn't deal with painful emotions. Somehow that button had been canceled in her brain years before. Velma, always the one in charge, took Sophie's hand and pulled her away from me. My oldest niece, Phoebe, a tall, strikingly pretty girl with long dark locks, grabbed each girl's hand dutifully and began heading toward the door when I took a mental count of the children.

"There's one missing," I said as I scanned the room for my nephew, Alexi. I looked at the ceiling. I tried to look at the floor too. My mother-in-law looked under the bed. His mother opened the cabinets…

Why were we looking in the most obscure places?

you wonder. I would wonder, too, if I hadn't known Alexi all his life. He was almost seven years old, and an only boy in a Greek family, I might add. That means he practically walks on water. What can I tell you?

"Alexi!"

The last cabinet opened and out tumbled the rosy-cheeked little boy. He had a handful of syringes and had already unwrapped three of them. I did have to admit he was a talented little dickens. In pin-pricks, there was the most amazing likeness of a convertible on the back of his hand. It was even red.

"Salu, Aunty, how ya doin?" He was missing the front two teeth and was simply adorable. He had freckles, most unusual on a Greek child.

"Fine, Alexi, nice car."

"Gonna be mine one day." He grinned even wider, wiping the blood on his pants and hopping out of the cabinet.

I didn't doubt it either. Alexi was much the image of his namesake, Alexander the Great. In spite of his Greek parents' Mediterranean coloring, he had blond locks, light skin, and big blue eyes with long, movie-star lashes. He was going to be a lady-killer when he grew older. I do feel bad for my sister-in-law. Phoebe, my sweet, green-eyed, fifteen-year-old niece, calmly, with no drama, walked over to him and scooped him up in her gentle arms. She looked at her mother and warmly smiled. My sister-in-law's face relaxed. All was well in the world of the Aristaes. The tall Greek beauty swept them all out of the room in record time.

Alysia looked intensely at me and shook her head. Dark brown eyes stared at me as if I was lying here just to spite her. She was short, with black hair and dark olive skin. Her red nails were circled around the hospital bed rail. I was slightly envious of her—three children and she hardly looked as if she had birthed anything. I, on the other hand, looked as if I had given life to Moby Dick. Though Sophie, of course, looked more like a gazelle than a whale.

"What were you thinking?" I looked at Alysia and knew she was in full lawyer mode now. "What happened?" I asked again, trying to figure out why she was so upset at me.

"You were shot. That is what. Now the police say you were interfering in a crime scene as it was happening." She put her face right next to mine, so close I could smell all her products. Her perfume was a killer, the lipstick kind of nice. "Not too good, honeybun."

"I bought a red purse, that's all. The whole thing turned out to be a terrible idea," I said.

She frowned even more, and her eyes started to bulge. I knew she hated it when I started out like that. Her brother-in-law did, too. Paulo used to look at me, shake his head, and say in exasperation, "*What*?"

I could almost hear his raspy, slightly-accented voice in my head and it made me smile, but that upset Alysia even more.

"What? Will you please make some sense? They have Internal Affairs outside! A police officer died, you know. They think you had something to do with it, so please just tell me what happened, slowly *and* clearly, and I'll represent you."

"Ned? They think I killed Ned? He was shot by the people in the green sedan. I didn't kill him."

"Officer Cooperman. No, you didn't shoot him, but they think you being there somehow interfered with his ability to perform his duties, and that is what got him killed." She had pulled back her face now, letting me breathe.

"Oh, great." I told her all that had happened and my

impulse to follow him toward his cruiser. "I was trying to evade the bullets. Is that a crime or something?"

She eyed my immobile arm angrily. "You didn't quite do that either."

My fault again.

My sister-in-law listened to what I told her and then gave a wave of her hand. She looked toward the door. The expression of a hungry shark crossed her face. She flipped her dark hair and removed her red-polished talons from my now slightly bent bed rail. She marched right toward the door as her husband, who was a full head taller than she but was always dwarfed by his little wife, moved quickly out of her way.

"Watch out, Mr. Policeman." He began to hum the *Jaws* theme music.

She glared at him, and I swear the man shrank even more.

Then he roared with laughter. He was the man of the house—the very Greek man of the house. "Don't worry, Adelphi, she will take care of it."

My name is Theresa, but he calls me Adelphi, which means "sister" in Greek. The kids shortened it to Delfi. I liked it much better than my real name, which has always reminded me of the fat old woman I am sure to one day become.

"I hope so," I sincerely put in.

My mother then came over to me. She looked so thin and sickly. I always worried about her. I knew she must be worried about me too, but there was no way to comfort her. She looked at me with her teary blue eyes and sighed heavily. She then bent in real close to kiss my head and whispered in my ear, "Was it because of a dead person?"

I knew what she meant. She hated my ability. I did, too, especially when it led me into situations like this. Well, not exactly situations like this, because this was the first time I'd ever been shot, but I had been in other very precarious situations before.

You see, I tended to see people who were either trying to return items to loved ones or, let's say, return things slightly borrowed in life to their original owners. It was a tricky thing either way, but I usually could tell the difference because, when the "borrowers" came to me, they had the distinct aroma of sulfur hanging around them. However, the lady I saw standing in the corner near Ned didn't have that aroma. This was a new finding gig, and I was sure it was something I didn't want to be involved with. It was this that my mother was always afraid of.

I tried to look benign when she asked me this. "Mom, don't worry about me. I am fine."

Her face scrunched up, and she pursed her lips. "I knew it!"

She wrung her veined hands and shook her head in a despairing way. Rydia put her plump hands on her shoulders and started to give her a massage—a sticky situation, since my mother was so thin and hated being touched. I thought it was a sensory thing.

She wasn't cold, but she rarely kissed or hugged me. I couldn't remember her hugging me at all as a child. It was later, when I went to college, that I initiated the affection. I saw other girls with their mothers and decided I wanted that kind of mom. It didn't really work, but it made me feel better. Empowered, as they say. I was still the one to initiate—although not that often, I am ashamed to say. I tried especially hard to be very affectionate with Sophie, but I realized this sensory problem was genetic, and Sophie wasn't comfortable being touched either. I didn't care. I just squeezed her anyway—at least when she was little. My mom just stood there and cringed, but only I saw it.

If Rydia noticed it, she wasn't saying anything.

"Mom, it's not like that," I said.

Her oval face looked at the floor, and I could swear her deep-set eyes were misting up. Then she just walked away from both me and my mother-in-law.

"She'll calm down. " Rydia's voice was a soothing musical instrument, and I instantly felt better. "Alysia will handle the police," she continued. "Your mother loves you very much."

I wondered sometimes. I looked over in the corner. Ned shrugged at me. He looked sorry about the situation. He was standing next to my mother who was sitting under a dark cloud in the corner. She looked to her side, where he was standing, but said nothing. I knew she saw them too, though she denied it. I realized she already knew I had seen the dead because of these spirits in the room with me. My family wasn't really conventional, you see. Not that anyone's was, but mine was a little more offbeat than most. My father was involved in the evacuation of Vietnam veterans right after the war. He had gone with a man named Melvin and, in the course of some very trying situations, the two men became very close.

Right before his last mission into the jungles of Vietnam, my mother met him on an island. This was the last time they saw each other. On his last mission, things got very hairy, and my dad's helicopter went down in the underbrush. While waiting for rescue, my father told his best friend, Melvin, he was sure that my mother was pregnant.

"How do you know?" his friend asked.

My father just shrugged. "My mom mentioned it to me in a dream."

Most people would think a man who had lost so much blood was delirious, but not Melvin. He was a fledgling warlock at the time, and he took premonitions very seriously. Eventually, the two were rescued, but my father didn't make it.

My mother was pregnant then a war widow. Melvin stepped in. My stepfather is a great guy, but heavy into the occult. It was the seventies when I was born, and he was all for love, peace, and a little magic, so he started a commune in upstate New York. My mother, always so prim and proper, then became rebellious, or so she told me. This was hard to imagine. She looked like a Theresa, a Sister Theresa, that is. She, apparently, was also very good with the crystal ball at that time. I vaguely remembered one incident with her and some teenagers. I supposed it was the first time she realized I could see more than what was in this realm. We both saw John Lennon getting robbed, but she saw them come in the door, and I saw them outside on the balcony floating and yelling at the thieves to leave.

Melvin's commune was attracting more followers. Not all of them were totally wholesome. Even as a little girl, I could tell that. Melvin had started a school of Wicca and herbalist medicine, even following up with a university located on the premises. What sort of job any of the graduates could possibly get, I had no idea, but it was accredited. Melvin, my stepfather, was changing too. He even changed his name from Melvin to Circe. Then something bad happened—don't ask me what, but it was bad, so bad my mother grabbed me in the middle of the night and took me to a church in the mountains, where we stayed for months. I was four years old. That was the end of carefree Caroline and the beginning of the mother I had now.

Sometimes, when I was in a dream state, I could still smell the dampness of the room we stayed in. I even heard the chanting of the nuns outside our door. But what haunted me more than anything was the sound of the dogs wailing and crying the whole time we were there. The nuns had been kind at first, but as the days passed, they started looking at us suspiciously. I felt frightened, without knowing why. My mother withered down to nothing, pacing and wringing her hands. She became a gaunt shadow of herself, and the more I tried to get her attention, the less she seemed to see me. Oh, she made sure I was fed, clothed, went to sleep—all of that—but her thoughts were somewhere else. It was a desperate feeling. It took all my natural resilience to get through it.

My mother never quite returned to me. The woman who had been happy-go-lucky, free-thinking, magical, and fun disappeared. My mother and Melvin got divorced, and my mother and I returned to Philadelphia, where she and my biological father's family hailed from. That was less scary than the church, but I remembered my time at the commune as a kind of paradise.

Whenever I asked what was wrong with my mother, I was just told she was sick. It was my father's mother, my mommom, who would eventually clear up the mystery for me.

My biological father was one of nine children and had challenged every rule and regulation ever presented to him. On impulse, he'd joined the army. He married a nice Catholic girl, my mom, and had impregnated her too. It was never explained to me which one came first, but I suspected it was the egg and not the chicken in this case. When he died, I was introduced to his family.

My mommom said the first time she laid eyes on me, she fell in love with me. My mom, who was devastated by her husband's death, let her be part of our life. Once in, she just never left. It was Mommom who talked Mom into coming back to Philadelphia. It was also Mommom who taught me the golden rule: "Love is not a faucet—you can't just turn it off and on when you please." She also informed me about the reality of witchcraft as I described my mother on her knees in front of the Madonna, praying with the rosaries day and night.

Witchcraft, Mommom told me, was real and actually in the Bible. Even when people wanted to use it for good, which was how most started, it always had very bad repercussions. She told me that, in my mother's case, someone had opened the wrong doorway and let something very bad in. She didn't go into detail, except to say that I was safe and that it could never touch me. I just had to keep my faith. However, she never told me which faith to practice. She had blocked the evil from my path with a kabbalistic ritual as soon as we had returned. When I asked about my mother—could it touch her?—Mommom looked sad and very old.

"I am sorry, sweetie, your mother and stepfather need to close the door themselves."

She wouldn't explain any further. She died before Sophie was born, but I named my little girl for her so she would always be around me, and she often was.

My stepfather didn't stop seeing me, though. My mother strictly forbade me from going to the commune, so he made the five-hour trip from Dodgersville, New York, once a month. I loved those weekends with him, but my mother hated them. She would call six or seven times a day and check to see if I were okay. I was fine. He would rent the finest room in the hotel where we'd use the pool and workout room. We'd hit the Franklin Institute and run the Philadelphia Art Museum steps just like Rocky. We ate in the most wonderful restaurants. I could still taste the pastries that he bought as we walked—in fact, I was sure I was still wearing some on my hips—and we'd talk. He was affectionate, in a strictly fatherly way, and I hungered for his warmth and love. He'd tell me stories of my dad, and I actually felt like I knew him. When Melvin would leave, I'd cry, but not in front of either of my parents. I could tell they were both hurting. In fact, I felt things far beyond my ability to understand. Like many children did, I tried to make things better by being good. We all pretended nothing was wrong.

Not that things weren't a bit odd, even so. My stepfather was, to say the least, eccentric, and the fact that I saw dead people didn't help things. Melvin encouraged this—he was proud of me—and you can imagine my mother's reaction when she found out. After I told my mother about a long conversation I had with a dead sea captain while Melvin stood by, commenting on the fellow's tales, I wasn't allowed to see him for three months. They hammered it out in the courts. How Melvin managed to get any visitation when he wasn't my actual birth father, I didn't know. My mother always suspected it had to do with the fact that Melvin was very wealthy and money seemed to be thicker than blood in the court systems. However, I'd watched my stepfather in action, and I could tell you he didn't need money to get what he wanted.

CHAPTER 3

Darkness enveloped me. I was in the Goodwill again. There was a half-price sale on all hand-bags. This time, the reason for the sale was passports. Women were ripping open all sorts of pocketbooks, looking for them. Now, this wouldn't be so bad, except that all the ladies had on tight purple dresses that were leaking a red liquid, and children were sledding through it. As I looked closer at the faces of the kids, I noticed they all had beards. It was strange, and I peered at them with wonder. They came nearer and nearer to me until I realized they were wearing little red Santa hats. All were laughing, pulling at the women's skirts, and looking under them. What perverted kids these were. Where were their mothers?

It was then that good old officer Ned came in, holding a red mesh pocketbook in one hand and a pistol made of a candy cane in the other. He was pushing a shopping cart full of neat items, when two of the bearded brats smashed headlong into him. Ned went flying, and the bag went flying too. Then it opened, and I saw in slow motion the little leather wallet with passport and birth certificate slide under the pajama racks.

Officer Ned began shooting the candy cane at the bearded kids. Big taffy strands came out and looped around the little guys. Their sweet eyes suddenly turned to red beams aiming right at him. Poor Ned started to disappear, but this old boy was a cop, so he continued to shoot his candy cane. The sugary tethers wrapped themselves around the eyes of these little Cretans. Then he looked back under the large rack of purple elephant nighties and pink bunny PJ pants that some store realized no respectable lady would wear, even to bed. Unless if they bought it for half price—at Goodwill.

All of a sudden, I saw little Alexi. He opened his mouth wide. Ned began pouring taffy into his wide-open orifice. I headed toward them, but Alexi stopped me with his big grin and the word "Yum." All his freckles were covered in little pink candy dots the size of half a pea. I sure hoped they didn't stain!

He reached out his now-very-sticky hand, took mine, and pulled me to the doorway where Paulo stood. Paulo...well, he looked good, real good—from the perspective of a woman who had been alone for almost two years. Alexi went back into the store and, at first, I was going to follow him, but Paulo was there, my husband Paulo, and it was the first time since he died that I had seen him. He had never come to me in dreams or in person, and now here he was.

Then I began to panic. Was this a good thing? I was lying in a hospital bed, and my dead husband suddenly appeared? However, before I could think about it more, he hugged me and whispered, "You look real good too, Eros." This may be way too personal, but that means lover in Greek. I must have blushed. "Blushing, you? You drive me to mania!"

I don't think I need to explain that word, right?

"Move on, babe," he said.

Something strange was happening. The robust man who had just engulfed me in his warm embrace was turning into a series of dots. His muscular body dissipated, and then he disappeared. *That's all? I look real good, but move on?* I felt cheated. All the dead people complicating my life and my husband had no time for me?

I stood in the empty parking lot of the Goodwill, staring at a police cruiser. I recognized this scene and began to cry because there was the cranky cop Andy, who thought I looked like his mother and not "real good" at all. As I watched the scenario that had landed me in the hospital, a warm, sticky, little hand entered my own. There stood Alexi, covered in saltwater taffy. It was on his lips, behind his ears, in his hair.

"Your mother is going to kill me," I said. The smell of peppermint and chocolate wafted into my nose. "You do smell good, though."

He really was adorable.

I woke with a start in a dark room. I must have fallen asleep because I was alone. Well, almost alone. In the corner were my two ghosts, each looking at me with intensity.

"I'm okay." When they still looked doubtful, I added, "Really."

Ned came closer to me.

"Did you send me that dream?" I asked.

Ned nodded, trying to look sheepish, not that I believed it for a moment. I was married to a cop—he knew what he was doing.

"Is the item I gave you where you showed me?"

We all looked around the room as if there were someone else listening. He then nodded again. Yep, crafty.

"Are those nasty little guys also looking for it?"

He once more gave his assent, and a red flush rose

up his cheeks. Not the embarrassed kind of flush, the kind that said, 'I am pissed!' His eyes narrowed a bit.

"That's not good, is it?" I asked.

But it wasn't he who answered. It was my other friend in the bloody dress.

"Oh, boy—"

"How are you feeling?" The door opened and a beam of light glared into my eyes. There stood what at first I would swear was an angel, but it was something better. It was a doctor, and he was gorgeous! Tall, blond, and blue-eyed, with a round, intelligent face. Unconsciously, I reached up to straighten my hair. As I did so, my armpit aroma wafted up to my nose. I realized I needed a bath real bad.

"I'm all right." I tried not to talk in his direction. I hadn't brushed my teeth in days and sure wished for one of Sophie's mints.

"Only all right? You got shot, and I did some pretty extensive surgery on your arm." A smile crossed his face. He had nice, white teeth—that was a plus.

"Gee, Doc, thanx." I made like Gomer Pyle and yucked it up a bit.

He chuckled Gomer back at me. "You do that real well."

He took out his stethoscope. As he leaned in closer, I prayed that if he had any deficiencies, one was an inability to smell. Or maybe a miraculous shower would appear? Oh boy, I must be on some real strong drugs.

"You sound okay. Got a very pretty fine sounding ticker."

Did he say pretty? "How long do I have to stay in this joint, Doc?"

He appraised his handiwork on my shoulder, pulling and tugging a bit. "This looks fine, too." He looked thoughtful for a moment and then looked into my eyes.

Man, were his nice ones. "You got a lot of folks outside."

"They're Greek, I'm sorry. They kind of do their own thing."

"Yeah, well, the head nurse is having a conniption." This was nice. I was talking to a man, and he was having a conversation with me too. He shrugged. "It's okay. Sometimes having a conniption is good for the heart." Then he reconsidered, scrunching his nose a bit. Was it me? "I am not sure she owns one, though." He chuckled at this. "You like Chinese, Italian, or Greek food?" Was he propositioning me? Really—in this condition? The old me would have said something smart and out he'd be, but hadn't Paulo just told me to move on?

"Chinese is good. So how much longer do I have to be here, sir?"

"Sir? Forever, if you are going to be calling me sir." He flashed another grin at me. The man looked good even from where I lay.

"Okay, we can change that." I hoped soon because I really didn't want to remain here much longer.

"Chinese, huh?" He unbuttoned my gown to examine the bandages on my shoulder. "Well, we can see about that." He was just peeling off the wrappings. "You, I'd like to keep you here for a while." Just as the last words were out, the door opened again and in walked a nurse who looked like Michelle Pfeiffer.

"Oh, Doctor—" Her eyes narrowed possessively at him.

Was that jealousy I sensed? Of me, really? Now that was new, I'd never caused such an emotion. Was that what Paulo meant?

Right now, the vision in white had the undivided attention of the man who had just offered me Chinese in bed, and I wasn't too thrilled about it either. Wait a second, did they even wear white these days? She was a ghost! I wondered what a ghost wanted from a living man? Then again, I take that back. Looking at this stunningly gorgeous guy, I knew exactly what she wanted. *Can they even do that?*

"He cheated on his MCATs." I recognized that whisper in my ear. Mommom. "Failed three of his last finals and had someone else take the re-take."

As I looked at the two, the dead woman and the hunk, definitely in a canoodle-type situation, I realized the little voice of reason in my ear was saving me from heartache again. I didn't want him touching me, and I certainly hoped he hadn't operated too much on me. I wiggled my fingers just to make sure I still could.

"Thanks, Mommom." I smiled, relieved. Then I looked again at the doorway. She transformed in an instant from a beauty to a...well, exactly what she was I had no idea, but from the warts and boils that now covered her face, not to mention a set of fangs Dracula would be envious of, I was glad she hadn't stuck around!

He walked out the door with her, leaving the stethoscope. I grabbed it and put it under the covers. Alexi would enjoy this—finders keepers, losers weepers and all that. The exam was only half-finished, and he was gone, even better.

I quickly redressed my arm as best I could and buttoned the front of my gown, noticing how far he had gone in the unbuttoning department. I'd have to pay more attention in the future when I was flirting.

I heard loud shouting from the outer hallway. I recognized all the voices involved and instantly felt sorry for the head nurse.

Not only did she have to deal with the Greek side of the family, but now it seemed she had to deal with the spooky side too.

"She is my daughter too, Caroline!" My stepfather

swished into the room, and the whole place lit up in a blink.

"Melvin!" my mother's voice shrilled, and he cringed.

Melvin stood there dressed in a white jumpsuit the BeeGees would have appreciated. A red cape hung over his shoulder, and his steel-gray hair was tied with a black ribbon in a ponytail that fell past his shoulder blades. His face was tight and very thin. His nose was long. It was the first thing anyone noticed about him, but after one conversation, they seemed to forget it was there at all. His long bony hands were on his hips, and he looked sternly at my mother, who was crouched like a feral cat. They were just about to restart what had been going on in the hall when I interrupted.

"Hmmmm," I said rather loudly.

Melvin turned around and flashed his million-dollar smile. He had a pentagon on his front tooth, in sterling silver, put there long before dental bling was in. For some reason, it looked perfectly natural on him, at least to me.

"Hiya, baby." He bent down and hugged me. This made my mother even more miffed. "What? You weren't happy with the Fourth Diamond Hotel? You wanted to try a new one?" He was joking. The Fourth Diamonds chain was where he always took me and his other family on our weekends. "This place is a dump—didn't you read the reviews before checking in?" He pulled out a phone and made like he was asking Siri.

"Booked and non-refundable, Daddy, so I guess I'll just hang here for a while."

"You need a better booking agent then."

We both laughed at this. My dad was so normal— well, sort of. I mean, we could joke and carry on like this our whole time together if it weren't for my mom and Aunt Vienne.

My aunt walked up behind my mother. Where Mom was dark-haired, Vienne was a natural redhead. Where my mother was gaunt and thin, Vienne was curved in all the right places. My mother was pretty, but Vienne was *gorgeous*. However, there was one little difference. My mom was real and always kept it that way, and Vienne was off the wall. Let's just say drama was an understatement when describing her, but she carried it real well, and, even if she wasn't normal, the male population she played to didn't care.

You see, when Mom moved out, Vienne moved in, literally. I think this was why my mother was so mad at Melvin. She thought that when she needed him most, he should have been there for us. Vienne called him Circe like the rest of his community did. She told me it wasn't respectful to call him "Daddy" and I should stop it. Yeah, right.

"Circe," she intoned in a husky voice. "This place has bad vibes. We should do a cleansing of this room." Her thin, silver-ringed fingers spread out like a rake, red fingernails scratching the air.

"No!" my mother shouted. "Nothing is to be done here." She looked at Vienne fiercely. "No magic!"

Yep, this was not going too good.

"Not necessary, my love," he cooed at her. "Carrot Curls's own karma keeps the cooties away." He smiled at my aunt who looked ready to pounce on my mother.

Did I mention that I was a redhead too? My stepfather had called me Carrot Curls since I was a baby. At that moment, the door of the room opened again and in marched a police officer with an iPad in hand. My sister-in-law was right behind him, body weaving to block any move toward me.

"You can't come in here without a warrant," she yelled in her best lawyerese.

"This is a public area, and I don't need a warrant to question a victim, ma'am." He practically swatted her off. He was tall, and his uniform had powdered sugar all down the front of it. I wondered how come. He had almost reached my bed when Melvin stepped in front of him.

"She can't see you now. She is in a coma." He waved his hand in front of the man's eyes, and I heard a crackling sound in the air. I was sure no one else had, by the way they just stared at him. Well, except my unearthly friends, Ned and the passport lady. They quickly stepped backward.

"Geez, she looks unconscious," the policeman said, staring at me, dull blue eyes looking a bit out of focus.

"She is totally out of it and needs this healing session with her family." Melvin looked at me and winked then waved once more in the police officer's direction.

"Yeah, she looks awful. You guys better pray real hard for her."

He nodded his meaty jowls, and his hat fell forward. He caught it, replacing it back on his thick mane of black hair. Mom looked mortified. I wasn't very happy with his statement either. Just how awful did I look?

"Come back in a month," Melvin said, flicking his bony fingers backward as if swatting an annoying fly.

"Yeah, in a month. I'll be back in a month. Right now, I'll just guard the door." He walked out in a stupor.

My sister-in-law looked approvingly at him. "Boy, could we use your dad with some of the judges I deal with in court."

"Not everyone falls so easily," Melvin said and looked at her curiously. She stared back at him with an expression of go-ahead-and try-to-do-it-to-me-buddy. "I doubt you would, Alysia."

At that, her fierce expression softened a bit, but not all the way.

He turned his attention back to me and asked all the usual fatherly things: how I was and the whole story. I didn't mention spirits or dead people, but we both knew that was the only reason I would have been involved with the gaudy red purse, to begin with. You see, it was my stepfather who taught me how to use my talent and figure out what the dead wanted. He was the first person I called when I had a spiritual situation of any sort. The current one wasn't anything I'd ever experienced before. A lost object was one thing, but murder was something else. He definitely would have steered me clear of this. He leaned down closely, blocking the view from my mother.

"Do we have any visitors?" he whispered so that only I could hear him.

"Over there in the corner." He looked over there. "They moved really far back when you used the force," I said.

He smiled at that. "I did steal the hand motions from Obi Kenobi." He looked pleased with himself. "Did you see anything else?"

"No, but I heard crackling." He looked even more pleased. His glance went to the corner, and then my mother was next to us.

"No. Absolutely not, Melvin. She is hurt, and this is all your fault."

Yep, that's right. Anytime something bad happened—a skinned knee, a failed test, a terrorist attack—she blamed Melvin.

My mother never took to calling him Circe. He accepted that she didn't want to be a part of that world, but it irritated Vienne. Don't get me wrong, I liked Vienne, maybe sometimes loved her even. She was an okay stepmother and all that, but sometimes she way overdid it.

"Circe, Caroline!" Vienne's voice rose a few octaves, and all eyes turned toward her. She had that kind of magnetism. "He is the dean of the university and the master of the commune. Be respectful," she said dramatically.

No one was impressed, as they had already seen this act before—my engagement, my wedding, my whole life...

"You see them too, Caroline," he hissed at her. "Just let your natural abilities take over, and you can once more be a functional part of society." A sarcastic tone entered his voice, and we were off to the races.

"Whose society?" Mom demanded. "Yours out there in Hoodooville?"

I wasn't used to seeing my mother so animated. It was fascinating. I was even more amazed that I was the object of her protection. Then again, Melvin did bring out the worst in her, and they did often argue. But to block him directly, that was new.

"She is my daughter!" His pretty turquoise eyes flashed a bit of anger her way, unusual as he was always so composed.

"Just barely!" she whistled between her teeth.

Ooooh, that was a low blow, Mom.

They were at a standstill when Rydia put a gentle hand on each of their shoulders. For just a moment in time, the room was calm, and then in burst Andy the cop. He seemed oblivious to everyone but me—how flattering that would be if it were anyone else but him.

He looked wild-eyed "I need to talk to her."

My father stepped in front of him and waved his hands.

"She is in a coma, and you can't..." His voice was gentle, smooth, the whole force thing going on there.

The cop looked at me and then at my stepfather.

Andy Sneered at him, teeth clenched. "Is he kidding?"

He was really handsome up close. His face had a couple of pockmarks, picked blackheads probably from his teens, but, on him, they looked nice, you know, in a rugged kind of way. I was never the Fruit of the Loom male model type of girl. More of a Sears and Roebucks bordering on Bob's hardware store type.

Dark brown hair that was short, but not too short, the ends curling up—probably curly when long—eyes that were chocolate brown, but also speckled with green flecks. Yeah, he looked real good.

Those peepers were now staring at me with total intensity, blazing actually. With his olive skin, he looked Hispanic or Italian.

"She is unconscious and will not be able to respond to you," my stepfather tried again.

Ned and the purse lady were now totally flattened against the wall from the magic cracklings going on in here.

"Look, she is not unconscious, and she is not in a coma. If you don't get out of my way, I will arrest you for obstructing justice," Andy said hotly. "Or put you in the loony bin!"

My father appraised him. My mother looked relieved until Andy next spoke to me. "Is he here?"

"Who?" I answered, totally confused.

"Ned? Is Ned here?" He sounded almost desperate.

I was a bit unnerved. "I thought you don't believe in that?"

Before he could answer, the first officer burst in the door. He looked totally alarmed. "What are you doing, Andy? She's almost dead!"

My stepfather started to smile and put his fingers to his lips in a *SHHH* motion to me.

Andy looked dumbfounded at his companion's ignorance. "She isn't dead, and she isn't unconscious. Can't you see she is awake?"

"Andy, look, you need some rest and relaxation. You lost a good partner, buddy, but you need to go home." He put a hand on the man's shoulder and started to pull him away from me. "This isn't your case, okay?"

"She isn't unconscious!" Andy veered around to face the bulkier man, but stopped short of hitting him.

"Come with me now, and I won't report this." The other officer was leaning in, whispering, but I heard him. Andy looked like he would balk, then he breathed deeply and walked out the door with the other man.

"He's like me but is a denier," I told my stepdad, who was back sitting next to me.

"Oh, that explains it. At first, I thought I was losing my touch." He pushed his hair out of his eyes and smiled at me. "He asked if you saw this Ned person." He reached up and grabbed a bright sphere from the air. "He popped it, and it burst into little specks. Imp dust?"

"Don't do that," my mother hissed at him as she ducked some particles.

Alysia looked at them and shrugged, as if to say, "Boy, my brother married into the Weirdo family." Which I might add, we probably seemed like, even to Greeks.

"Did you encounter any imps while you were busy getting yourself shot up?" Melvin asked.

Vienne's ears perked up, and she looked over his shoulder. Her eyes were made up dramatically with lines of green silver and gold. She looked like Lillian Munster had done her makeup.

"Imps?" I thought about it. "Do they have beards and wear little Santa hats with pompoms at the ends?"

He clapped in his excitement. "That's right!"

"Not exactly. I did dream of them just before you

came in. Ned, the one Andy was looking for, gave me a dream with them in it." I said it quietly. "I am not that doped up, okay?"

Melvin leaned in, looking intense. "Where is he now?"

I pointed the non-needled hand to the corner where both of them were huddled. "They are smashed up against the wall. With all that voodoo electricity you were spewing, they seem to be afraid to come any closer."

"Electricity? Really?" He smiled, satisfied with his handiwork. "A little something I conjured. We were having a bit of a poltergeist problem. Sometimes the old adage 'fight fire with fire' is what a little nasty needs. So it is affecting them too, huh? That is unfortunate." He meant it. He didn't have a cruel bone in his body.

"Yes, it is." Then I thought about it. "Can imps look like children?"

"If they shave off their beards, they can."

"Well, kids knocked over the cart then scooted right out the Goodwill's door. Why would imps be interested in a passport and a birth certificate from a human?" I wondered aloud.

He looked thoughtful as he grabbed another sphere from the air, popping it as well. My mother ducked and I swear steam was starting to pour from her ears.

"Oh, and can you give me a hint as to why the birth certificate was covered in a green kind of invisible slime?" I asked.

"They are all over here, which means they have been in here already or are here. This is not good. We'll have to set a guard on you." Melvin looked at Vienne, who looked positively in her glory. "Green slime, huh?" he repeated.

My mother was now next to him, making dagger eyes. "You will not!"

This, I knew, was not going to be good. "Like a moldy glow," I put in as quickly as I could before things really got going.

He shook his head. "You know as well as I do, Caroline, that imps anywhere means trouble—tricky, unsavory, and downright spiteful as they are."

The argument was just getting heated when they finally noticed two sets of very young eyes fixed on them.

"Sophie!" My stepfather was a sucker for his granddaughter, but for some reason, Sophie was afraid of him. Maybe that was why he tried so hard with her. He opened his long thin arms to her, but it was Velma that ran into them, pulling Sophie with her. Both girls entered his embrace, and he wrapped them in a bear hug. As I expected, Sophie stiffened her back. Her cousin was all warmth and love, so Velma embraced him back.

"Sophs, it's your grandpapa," the little girl next to mine squealed in delight, coaxing her cousin to give a halfhearted smile.

"Grandfather," Sophie corrected her. "Hello, how are you?" she said formally.

"I am fine, Carrot, Spaghetti, and Meatballs."

She cringed. I would have too. That was an awful moniker. Yeah, my stepdad wasn't great with nicknames, but nobody's perfect.

"Hi, Licorice Curls," he said to Velma, referring to her dark black locks. "How are you girls today?"

Sophie looked aghast and let him see it, but the problem was, no matter what she threw him, he was just so happy to see her. My mother came up behind Sophie and wrapped a dainty protective arm around her shoulders, and my daughter leaned back into her. For a moment, my father looked hurt, but then sensing this, Sophie reached out and held his hand. He gave a tug and my mother released her, letting Sophie hug him too, this time with some feeling. He held onto her for dear life, and she stiffened again. Still, for him, all was right with the world now.

Then the door opened, and the face of authority popped in.

"Everyone out," she boomed.

I looked around and realized my whole family was there. How all of them had managed to do that was a real surprise to me. Maybe the Greek side did have some magical ability.

"*Out!*" Nurse Kratchet with the hatchet repeated.

My stepfather broke contact with his grandchild and waded through the masses. "We've come such a long way to see our daughter."

The crackling began again along with the hand motions.

The nurse's eyes flew to where the electricity was hanging in the air. "Don't try it, buster. I am trained in jujitsu, karate, and anti-witchcraft."

I swear for a moment I saw fangs, but only for a brief instant. It seemed my stepfather did, too, because he stepped back in surprise.

The nurse gave a smug smile. "Now—everyone, move it."

"It means that the person who formerly had the birth certificate is dead," my stepfather said.

It what?

"The green mold as you eloquently put it." My stepfather bent down and kissed my cheek. "And not altogether a wholesome death either. It was a hit—"

Nurse Kratchet didn't let him finish his statement as the procession passed me.

They all complied and left, but not without the proper goodbyes. This, of course, took a mere extra forty-five minutes, and a threat to end visiting privileges altogether.

It was Mom who brought Sophie back to my side to say a real goodnight to me when everyone was gone.

"Remember, you promised," my little girl reminded me.

I wasn't to die tonight—or, for that matter, any night soon.

Mom leaned down and kissed my cheek. She signaled Sophie should do the same. At that moment, I couldn't have loved my mother more, especially when Sophie gave me a real genuine hug.

"I promise!"

She walked out, hand in hand, with Mom.

I sighed in gratitude. "Thanks, Mom."

"No problem," her voice whispered as she passed the watchful eye of the nurse standing there.

"You also." The fangs now were out.

I looked around to see whom she was talking to.

"You heard me, you in the corner."

My what long nails you have, Grandmother. I chuckled. Yep, it was the meds.

Both of them came forward. They looked at me then at her. The purse lady and Ned passed me. A chill crossed over my body as they left the room.

"And you." She was tapping her foot. "I haven't got all day, you know. She is my patient, and I intend for her to get better!"

Off the wall crawled a shadow, which also passed my bedside. The frost it gave off was deeper and more sinister than the two before it. The shadow was feline and used all four legs to exit. As it passed the nurse, it hissed at her. She gnashed a full set of fangs loudly at it, and off it scuttled with more speed.

"Impressive. What was that?" Another chill passed by, but not a good kind.

"You have a watcher assigned to you, sweetie, and

that is never a good thing. That means the community watch knows you are around, though with your stepfather being who he is, I am not really surprised. Don't worry, the room is clean now. You can go to sleep."

A watcher? I could swear I had heard that term before, but when?

She started to close the door then re-opened it. "Hey, you!" A low growl left her throat.

Much to my surprise, a little man with a pointed beard and a red hat with a white pompom at the end crawled out from under my bed. He was heavy in the middle and wore a little gray suit. He looked at me and I at him. I recognized him as one of the kids from the Goodwill—minus the beard, of course.

I was totally bewildered as to why he was here. "What do you want exactly?"

He stared at me.

"I help people return lost items. Is the passport yours?"

Still the defiance in his eyes or maybe he was a mute. I knew it wasn't because it had a dead woman's picture on it.

"It's not what I want, it's what I need." As he started to walk out, he stopped and said snidely, "You won't be able to help yourself soon, so don't bother offering to help others."

"They like to talk big because they're so little," the nurse said.

I hadn't noticed she was so near me.

"Go to sleep and don't bother with his words, big man that he thinks he is." She sounded like an annoyed great aunt speaking of an errant nephew. "Before you ask, yes, I am old."

"I'm sorry?"

I looked at her face. She looked tired. She had a soft,

doughy face with loose white hair that was escaping from under her nurse's cap.

Her eyes were cloudy blue, and her lips were thin, but still, she was very pretty—minus the fangs, the claws, and the fact that she scared me half to death.

"I am much older than you, much older than any patient in this hospital," she said. "You have a lot of power that surrounds you. This watcher is not a new one, you know."

I didn't, but I had seen it before.

"Not just what you can do and see, but who and what you are. It's your daughter and her cousins who seem to carry the most talent. I want you to know I have seen many things in my long life, and I can spot psychic ability a mile away. They will contact you, rest assured, now that you have ended up on their radar. No doubt your stepfather arranged it somehow that you were hidden until now. The older ones can do that. Maybe he still can—when he wants to, that is." She seemed to disapprove of Melvin for some reason.

"The older whats? Who will contact me?" I was becoming very tired, and then I noticed she had hung a new bag from the pole that had a tube that ended in a needle in my vein.

"SUD. The Deamons, I mean." She said it with the soft "ea" like in the word dead.

"The what?" My eyes were getting very heavy. "Who?"

"SUD, the special units department. They are Deamons, trapped ones."

Darkness was encompassing me.

"They need you. Your talent is the only one that can right things again. Then again, maybe things never will be righted."

Boy, this lady sounded like a downer, or maybe it

was what she was injecting into the tube, and I was the one going down, down, downer…

I slept soundly until dawn. My stepfather, mother, and Vienne's arguing woke me up.

CHAPTER 4

Perhaps a hospital stay was fine for most, but I just wanted to go home. The subject they were arguing about was actually this. Whose home was I to go to? His home? Her home? Their home? Just how did I end up with so many homes? you wonder. Well, that's another story.

When I was eleven, my father visited me, along with his new wife, and we stayed at the hotel we always stayed at, the Fourth Stars. It was five stars of everything from accommodations to amenities to food. But Vienne told me, in front of my dad, that this place sucked. She then said how selfish it was that my mom made them come all the way out to this crummy place all the time when they had a perfectly nice *brand new house* in Dodgersville. It even had a pool twice the size of the hotel's.

Now you have to understand, all the time we had lived in Philadelphia I had never been back to Dodgersville. I really missed it. Not that I remembered much about it since I was less than five when I left, but I knew it was big. I also remembered it being a home. Back then, I lived with my mother in a two-bedroom apartment that belonged to her aunt Idey who, to me, must have been one thousand years old. Aunt Idey traveled a lot, so we mostly had the apartment to ourselves, but whenever she was in town, it sure was crowded. The thought of a real home was quite appealing to me. I turned to my stepfather and asked if I could come to his new house next month instead of him coming here to Philadelphia. My already-pale stepfather blanched even whiter and, somehow, I knew the answer was no.

"Please, Daddy."

"She could stay in the newly painted guest room, Circe." Turning her pretty face to me, goading me even further, Vienne said, "It's painted her favorite color, pink."

He looked at her, surprised, and then at me.

"She can sleep on the queen-size bed I got special for her," she continued, laying it on thick. "Then she can go swimming and sit on the hammock in the backyard."

"Can I please?"

I wanted so badly to go home with them. I instinctively sensed that my mother was sick, and I was craving a normal family—whatever that meant for the rest of the world.

For almost an eternity, he was quiet and then with much reluctance he did what any level-headed parent would do. He distracted me. "Let's go for ice cream."

I ate a large cone of chocolate and sprinkles, and Vienne daintily sucked on lemon sherbet because she didn't want to stain her clothes. I didn't care.

"Well, Daddy?" I looked innocently at him. "Can I stay in my room?"

I have to say he did stop it, though. He leaned in real close and hissed at his wife, "No way. Caroline forbids it!" Then he cast her a warning look that would shut up the devil himself.

Maybe I was so miserable, and that was why he took

me out that night by myself. I was smart enough not to bring it up again or maybe just too scared of rejection. I figured if my mother didn't let me, I wasn't going to be welcome anyway, but I sure wanted to be there.

It was that night that I hatched the stupid plan of coming up the next weekend. I had some money stored in a porcelain piggy bank. What I was thinking exactly as an eleven-year-old, planning this harebrained scheme, I'm not quite sure, but it sure seemed like an adventure.

CHAPTER 5

1987:

It was the time of no cell phones, no Internet, and no Big-Brother cameras all over the place, so sneaking out was easy. My mother being half out of it most of the time it made it even easier. It was off to the races for me. I took the bus to the local Septa train and took that to Thirtieth Street Station in the heart of Philadelphia.

Thirtieth Street Station was huge and to say it was a little overwhelming would be an understatement. I passed several benches with people lying on them. An odor emerged from where they lay, and I wondered when they'd last bathed. I believe I actually envied them. It was then I looked up and saw the big announcement boards with all the destinations to and from places. There was one to Trenton, one to New York, and definitely one to Dodgersville.

I looked at my Minnie Mouse watch—yeah, she was the Hannah Montana of my day—to see the time then back up, and, to my shock, every one of the boards that had just a few moments before held the name of a city now read *Go Home, Little Girl*.

I naturally looked around to see which girl the boards could be talking to, but there was only me, the stench of alcohol, and the bums. Then I glanced back at the boards. They were blank. Not one time, not one destination, just blank black slats. I looked over at the ticket booth. It was so early in the morning—six a.m.—that there were only two people waiting on customers.

Now one might say this was my introduction to the supernatural, because at one booth I saw people with trench coats and leather suitcases. All the women wore Sunday church hats, and the men wore fedoras. But this didn't seem unusual to me. What *did* seem odd was the bright light emanating from nowhere and everywhere and shining right on top of them. It all looked very pretty, so I naturally went to that line.

I took my spot behind a tall man in a long brown trench coat and a pretty lady with chestnut hair in a bob hairstyle holding a cherubic-looking baby. The child had a little red cap on and was sucking happily on a glass bottle of milk. For a moment, the woman looked at me and smiled. Her eyes were very blue—sky blue—and kind. I smiled back at her, and the baby cooed at me.

"You lost, little girl?" Her voice was kind of high and not very cultured. The baby was squirming so she was struggling a bit.

The man looked at me, a bit surprised. In a gruff voice that matched his unshaven visage, he said, "You are in the wrong line," as if he knew where I was going.

"Where ya goin?" the woman said kindly, frowning at him.

"*Going*, Peggy; there is a 'G' in there, you know."

"I know, I know, Frankie, it's just that while we are still here in Philly, I'd like to get my last bad grammar in." She giggled, showing perfect white teeth, but he looked positively annoyed.

"Practice makes perfect, Peg. There aren't any second chances in Hollywood, you know." He moved forward, and we all followed his example.

"We're going to Hollywood. Gotta chance at a big part! Some film called *The Wizard of Oz*." Her pretty round face had dimples when she smiled, and I really took a shine to her.

"Isn't that the one with Judy Garland as Dorothy?" I put in.

"She did? So they gotta girl already? You heard that in The Buzz or you read that in the papers?"

The baby was squirming again, and she was trying to calm him.

"I saw it on TV," I said. *Who didn't know Judy Garland played Dorothy?*

"You hear that, Frankie? This girl says someone's already got my gig! Some Judy person or other she saw it in the TEE VEE." She took out a pretty silver rattle and started to shake it for the baby who was starting to fuss again.

"Judy Who? What paper is the TEE VEE?" They extended the syllables. "I ain't heard none of that," he said stubbornly. "Can't you control that kid?"

"Watch your language, Frankie, we *got to* sound all classy and all that," she teased playfully, really sounding the part. "Maybe they need someone else, you know."

At that moment, the chubby, drooling, little baby, who was holding the rattle, teething on it, began to wail. The rattle fell to the ground and rolled away under the bench nearest us. I saw the mother couldn't go for it, so I scooted under and looked for the silver toy. There was a lot of dust and cobwebs. I noticed these were the non-movable types of chairs, nailed down solidly, meant to last for centuries. The back of the bench ran all the way to the ground and in the farthest corner was the rattle. I reached for it and got a handful of webs and dirt. The little silver toy that was shiny a few seconds before looked solid black when I came out from under the piece of furniture. I stared at it and then at where the long line had been just a moment ago. It was gone.

"Big accident happened." An elderly man came up to me, helping me out from under the bench. "Happened a long time ago. My sister, her husband, and their baby were on the train to Hollywood. She was going to try out for the part of Dorothy."

I looked at him, open-mouthed.

"You know, *The Wizard of Oz?*"

I nodded.

"We were twins," he said. "I knew when she died;.I felt it." He looked sad. "Her name was Peggy."

"Was his name Frankie?" I blurted.

"Yes. How did you know?"

I lifted up the rattle. There was an inscription. *To my Peggy and Frankie on the birth of a boy. Love, Mom and Pop.*

A tear ran down his cheek, and his hand was shaking as I handed it to him.

"Where did you find this?"

I pointed under the bench.

His light pink lips quivered a bit, and his sagging cheeks drooped even lower. "Why did you go under there?"

"The baby dropped it."

Maybe he heard me, maybe he didn't. I was just a kid, and he probably thought I was saying a baby dropped it or something.

"My mother and father gave them this when their son was born." He sat down on one of the benches near where we stood, pushed back his silver hair, and breathed hard. "I wanted a sign from her that heaven existed. A real concrete sign." His milky blue eyes stared at me. Then he got up and walked over to a big memorial billboard. "There was a crash on the Hollywood Express. I used to laugh back then and call it the Fading Star. That was because so many people were going out there and then coming back on it all faded out. Not exactly a sure ticket to stardom, you know?"

There were pictures on the sign. One of them was Peggy. She sure looked the same to me.

His finger touched her cheek. "My sister Peggy would have made it, though. Thanks, kid."

As he walked away, I went closer to it.

I looked at his receding form. "She's dead? It says she's dead?"

"Yeah, kid," he called over his shoulder. "She has been gone a long time. Too long, really, but I'll be there soon enough with all of them." He shook the rattle, and a squeaky metal sound came out of it. "I got my sign, Peg." He shook it again.

I looked at him and saw a wavering light around him. It kind of hung for a while and then disappeared along with him. I know what that light means now, but back then…well, it was really cool!

I suppose that you might say that this was the beginning of my career as a professional finder. Of course, I didn't know or understand it at the time.

"Dodgersville, train to Dodgersville," I heard a hollow voice whisper near my ear.

The scent of fetid breath wafted into my nose, and I coughed. When I turned around to see who had spoken, there was no one there. I looked back at the ticket booth. There was no one there either. A cracked *No Entry* sign hung on the drab door, its green paint chipped and faded.

"Hey, sweetie."

I heard a voice call out to me. It was the other ticket booth's occupant.

"Come on over here. That one's been closed for twenty years. No one's going to sell you any tickets from there. Where you going?"

She was much older than Peggy, and her voice was husky. I smelled cigarettes. I went over to her but was instantly alerted to the fact that, like Peggy's brother, her light was also blinking. It wasn't the same clear blue and red. It was a sickly brownish yellow. She gave a wheezing cough, and I stepped back, not wanting to catch what she had.

"It ain't catchy, sweetie. Doctor says there is a spot on my lung. Nothing to worry about, he says."

However, her expression said she was worried. By the way the light was darkening around her, I was worried too.

"Dodgersville," I said hesitantly, not wanting to upset her.

"Dodgersville? That spooky place?"

Spooky? My daddy lived there, but then again he was kind of odd—at least that was what the hotel staff always said when they thought we weren't listening. "My dad lives there. I'm going to visit him."

She cocked an eyebrow at me. "Round trip or one way?"

I hadn't thought about that one. Well, if I went there, I would be saving my father a trip to Philly so I guessed he would drive me back. "How much is a round trip?"

"Twenty-one dollars and fifty cents with tax."

"How much without tax?"

"No, no, that is the price, dearie. One way is eleven dollars." She croaked out a laugh, but it ended once more in a hacking gag.

I only had twelve dollars after the bus rides, so I got

a one-way ticket. No one had told me about bus transfers, and I was too dumb to ask why everyone was walking around with long yellow slips, though I wanted one too. Ahh, the joys of being eleven years old!

I felt a tap on my shoulder. I turned around to see who was tapping, but there was no one. I turned back to the woman to ask where I should go, but she wasn't there anymore either. A cold chill started up my spine.

"Dodgersville!"

I heard an echo of a voice beyond a hallway off to the side. I took my knapsack and turned toward where I thought it was coming from. As I said, I was naive. I walked, listening hard.

"Dodgersville."

Another hollow echo resonated in the building, this time seeming to come directly toward me.

Just before I entered the dark hallway I'd been drawn to, I heard a sweet voice beside me.

"No, no, kiddo, this way." There stood pretty Peggy and the pram with the baby. "Follow me—don't go with them. They ain't got no good on their minds."

She looked so nice and friendly, even if she was dead, so I followed her. "You gotta be wary of them watchers." She crinkled her nose. "They are nasty sorts…"

Her voice trailed off and off we went.

CHAPTER 6

Present Day:

"Watchers, Peggy said watchers."
I woke to an empty room in the hospital, and it dawned on me I had already encountered a watcher, or rather several watchers. I looked up at the ceiling for any unwelcome shadows, but I only saw darkness. Did these guys just arrive or was this the same one that had been with me in the train station way back when?

I'd have to ask someone about it, but not my father. If I showed any sign of sensing danger near me, he immediately forbade me from having anything to do with the spirit world for months. That meant no more finding and no more helping people. No more adventure away from the blah, blah of real life. I definitely liked my other life and didn't want to give it up. And, yes, I was an adult, but—there was no point in getting him all worked up.

Which brought me back to my dead passport lady. She was back in the room, and so was Ned. I guess Nurse Kratchet's hatchet and charming personality could only bar spirits for so long. I was hoping, though, that she had had more luck with the nastier types, like watchers. I was looking toward them when the nymph appeared again. Well, not exactly him, but his spots. Lots of them. I might add they were really pretty: yellows, greens, and some gold ones too. Okay, so I was still a bit drugged. This was some light show he was giving me, but when was he to going to appear?

I must have dozed, because next, I felt the bed rocking. It started as a pleasant sensation weaving into in my dreams, then it got faster and faster. I was becoming dizzy and disoriented, and my shoulder was starting to hurt too, when Ned, my trusty protector, came over and lifted the little bugger up by his hat from the foot of the bed.

"Hey, put me down, put me down!"

I had never seen a nymph up close before. I didn't really count the Goodwill gig since that was a fleeting glance. This guy was cute, in a Santa's elf kind of way. He now was dressed in red with an adorable little hat. His bells were ringing, and he was kicking his little legs in the air as Ned held him.

"You ain't supposed ta be able ta do this!" the nymph yelped at the spirit.

"Watch your grammar," I said with a giggle, thinking of Frankie and his elocution lessons.

His eyes bulged, and his tongue stuck way out. A big fat wet raspberry came my way.

I reached out and pushed the little guy away. "Bad boy."

And with the utmost gentleness, what I used on my own child, I gave a mock smack on his rear end.

"Hey, watch where you touch, lady! Leave the goods alone. I don't need no bruises—I got dames to impress, you know!"

This little guy has ladies? Really? Who'd want him?

His face was cute, and he did have interesting rosy cheeks, a nice nose too—slightly bulbous, but still…

He resembled one of those elf-on-a-shelf thingies that were so hot these days. Maybe girls did want him, after all.

"Who?" I said before I could control myself. "Girls ages six to twelve?"

The lady in the corner laughed. Not a small giggle either. It was the first time I had heard anything from her. Sometimes they could talk—the dead, I mean—but mostly it was gurgles and grunts. Not the good kind either. The kind they called a death rattle.

"Hey, lady, keep your comments to yourself. I am considered a hot dude in the north. A real catch."

Ned turned the nymph toward himself and then he started to laugh, too.

"Let me down, will you, Cop Spook! You ain't even supposed ta be able ta do this at all!"

Then Ned did let him down. He just opened up his fingers and, boom, I heard a plop and a bunch of bubbles came up.

"Hey, you stop it," the nymph squealed.

I looked over the side of the bed. Ned had his booted leg on the nymph. I twisted to look at him. "What do you want, Mr. Northern Stud? Why are you hanging around here?"

"I need the passport, that's all." The boot rolled him a bit. "Okay, okay, call off your dog, will you?"

"My dog?" I looked at Ned, and he shrugged. *All right, I'll play good cop on this one*, I thought. Ned seemed to hear me and nodded. "What else are you looking for?" I asked.

"Nothing."

Roll, squish, and a knock on the head. I'd hate to meet Ned in a real arrest situation. I'd feel bad for the mugger. The little guy looked uncomfortable, and his little light balls were shivering as they flew up at us. I reached up and grabbed at one like Alexi did when I blew bubbles for him.

"Hey, give that back!"

He popped up from underfoot and, just as he grabbed the ball from me, the passport lady hit him with a red mesh bag then swooped him up in it. A red mesh bag, I might mention, that looked very familiar. Before I could say anything, the nymph was in it. The bag was moving this way and that way, and then it just stopped.

"I take it that isn't any ordinary bag?" I said. The lady shook her head no. "Are you ordinary?" What I meant I had no idea. It just hit me that if she could catch nymphs in bags and Ned could hold and step on them while dead how ordinary could these people—er, spirits—be? "Did you know her before, Ned?" Before death I meant. He nodded yes. "Did you know about nymphs, ghosts, and watchers?" He nodded again. "Is Andy part of this, too?" A vehement no! *Well, that eliminates one source of information, no matter how uncomfortable it would have been to talk to him.* The bag began to move all over again.

I heard a muffled, "Okay, okay. I'll come clean."

She unzipped the top a little bit.

A sweaty little head stuck out. "I need the birth certificate, too. They got a hit on this dame."

I wanted to remind him the dame was already hit, but she shook him, and he started to look real sick, like vomit sick.

"Will you please point him in another direction?"

Too late, he threw up on me. Boy, what a stink.

"What did you eat before you came in here?"

He looked positively pleased with himself. "The missus' special. Reindeer rump roast."

"You have a wife too? Along with girlfriends!"

"Heck, no! I don't got no wife. I ain't interested in no ball and chain. I do a part-time gig with Big Guy up north, just from October to January seventh."

"The Big Guy?"

"Nick, you know. St. Nick and all that."

"Is he talking about Santa?" I looked at the two ghosts, who looked up and then just smirked a bit. Real helpful. Then they just shrugged at me. "Boy, do I have to change my story for Sophie from now on. Heck, I could probably blackmail her into being good all year with this knowledge."

"Yeah, well, the old guy has a ledger, but Sophie ain't on the coal list, I checked, have to case all my leads. She's on the wing list. Now if you want to talk coal, we can discuss your nephew." He blew a long whistle.

At that Nurse Krachet came storming in—with her hatchet, I might add. "You! I was looking all over for you!"

She held it up just as he gave another hurl. Not a good idea because he caught her full frontal. There was brown slimy and green gooey all over her white uniform. It wasn't a good combo with the furious purple in her face, black in her eyes, and the gleam of her wicked fangs. Even the passport lady was scared and tossed the red bag in the air. The nurse made a try for it, but just missed, and it went rolling over to a wall where a previously hidden shadow went crawling over onto it.

I heard the distinct sounds of terror arising from the bag. I didn't know what got into me, but I hopped out of bed—not a pretty sight—ran past the surprised group and over to the dark-shadowed bag. I reached into it and ice enveloped my arm. I had never felt such cold in my life. But I was determined that this little guy not be eaten up by this…whatever it was.

"Watcher," I heard a familiar hollow whisper in my ear.

"Get off of him," I yelled.

I was now face to blurry visage with a ghastly being. The eyes were white, the mouth and nose were empty.

"I said, get off of him!"

And much to everyone's shock, it did. My hand, however, took quite a long time to defrost. It was a big concern—and mystery—to all my doctors as well as to me. However, right then and there, I had another concern. I pulled out the little guy, and he hugged me.

"Oh, man, oh, man, they said it, but I didn't believe it. You just looked like some ordinary chick, but you ain't, no, you ain't!"

Nurse Krachet was back to get him and, before he could expound on how exactly I was this extraordinary chick—I liked the sound of that—the chase was on, swing after swing of her weapon.

Her, I didn't try to save him from. I curled my feet under my butt to avoid getting them chopped off. I was terrified of whatever she was, and there was no way I was getting in her space, not even for a cutie like him.

Cutie? What was I thinking? That reindeer puke must have been affecting my brains, or I was just plain desperate. In fact, I was so out of it, I passed out, but not before I spotted the watcher on the wall. He saluted me.

Now, what was that all about?

CHAPTER 7

1987:

I was determined to get to Dodgersville and see Melvin's new house. I followed Peggy to the tracks and a big train. The outside of the train was silver with a blue and red stripe. The conductor was standing there, looking at me strangely. I must have seemed odd talking to the air. I didn't realize that no one but me could actually see Peggy or the baby.

"Now, you be careful. Don't go off with any more spookies." She caressed my cheek. Her hand was cool and sweet. "Thanks for giving my brother the rattle. He really needed it, you know."

I didn't. "Are you really dead?"

She looked so real. I had seen dead people in the zombie movies Aunt Idey let me watch while my mother slept. The train whistle blew and, for a moment, I turned toward it.

"No, kid, I just wear black for the uniform. Are you going to be coming on the train or not?" the conductor answered me, not Peggy.

I looked for Peggy, but she was gone, so I handed

him a ticket, and I heard him mutter under his breath. "Boy, even the kids from this place are weird!"

I knew he meant Dodgersville, but I didn't care because I was fascinated by what I saw.

The train car was packed: men smoking cigars and ladies in real fancy dresses, some nicer then Peggy's. I didn't realize so many people went to Dodgersville so early in the morning. As I looked for a seat, they nodded at me by way of greeting. Of course, when the conductor came up behind me and asked why I wasn't sitting yet, I said I couldn't find a seat. There were none available.

"The place is empty, kid. Pick anyone you want."

I turned to him then back around, and there was no one there.

"Where did they all go?" I asked him, confused.

He just sighed loudly and was off, screaming one word to the thin air. "Tickets!"

I was the only one there, so I handed him mine. He looked around again and shrugged as if to say, "You're crazy."

"Don't mind him. He is always cranky." A little brown-haired boy of around six was sitting next to me. He wore blue jean overalls; the kind farmers wear, but in miniature. His eyes were dark brown, and his hair came down to his shoulders. He had a hat in his hands. A black and white cap with a square brim: the kind train engineers wear. "My dad's an engineer, but not on this train. I'm kind of lost. Do you think you can help me find him?"

I did feel sorry for the kid, so I instantly got into the help-someone-else mode. I didn't mind the distraction because I was becoming very nervous myself. I was starting to think that being on this train was probably not the smartest thing I had ever done. I took his hand and went in search of the conductor.

"He is not going to help us. I ask him all the time for my daddy, and he just ignores me."

True, the guy wasn't Mr. Friendly, but why wouldn't he help the kid? Now that was just plain mean.

As I stood there, the conductor entered again. He looked at me, and I looked at him. I was about to ask him if he could help us when I realized the boy wasn't near me anymore.

"Why aren't you sitting?" He loomed over me. I sat right down on the first seat I found. I didn't even mention little boys or engineers to him. When he disappeared down the aisle, I heard the boy again.

"See what I was saying? Mean!" He stuck his tongue out at the conductor's back.

"Where did you go?"

"I hid. I was too scared to stay." He looked so sad that all I felt was sad for him. "Don't you think he is scary, too?"

I had to agree the guy was scary. He wasn't the type that said "Come to me for help" either. So there we sat in silence for a while as the train moved on.

"What's your name?" he asked.

My name was complicated because I had several names. Theresa Lilian Louis. Or what my father called me: Terry Lou.

"Terry Lou," I decided since I was going to Dodgersville. New house, new beginning, new name.

"Is that a Bible name?" he asked, looking at me strangely.

"Well, no, it's a nickname. It's what my dad calls me. My right name is Theresa."

"Oh, I like that name better. It sounds normal."

Yay, score one for Mom. She called me by my "right" name all the time. "Okay, call me Theresa. What's your name?"

"Abraham."

Abraham? Who named their kid Abraham anymore? Wasn't that the name of a president?

"No, he is in the Bible. Don't you read the Bible?"

"No." I didn't. My mom did. She read it all the time. I sneaked Judy Blume and Agatha Christie into the house.

"Does your mom whip you for it?"

"For not reading the Bible?" *No, but if I did read it, she would kiss me and love me extra if I did that.*

"I mean for sneaking stuff in the house." He laughed. "Yuck, my mom kisses me too much too." Then he sobered.

It was then that I realized I wasn't talking. He was listening to my thoughts.

Mary had a little lamb, I thought.

"Its fleece was white as snow." He giggled. He sure was sweet, and he read minds too. To me, at ten, this was totally cool! We did a lot of that. He read my mind, and I laughed.

He took off his hat and then put it back on. He squeezed it and opened it. The material was good, I had to admit. It didn't wrinkle in the least.

He looked at me and then at the hat. "My pop had my name sewn in it, see?"

Abraham Jenkins, 1955. It was a white tag, and the name had been sewed into it. If I had been an adult, I would have wondered at the date, but I was a kid.

"Mom sewed it in herself." He smiled proudly. "Come to think of it, I wouldn't mind a kiss from her right now."

He went to hand it to me when the hat fell. We both got up to get it, and I kicked it under the seat farther. I was on my knees looking for it when two legs came to a halt by my seat.

"*Shhhhhhhhh.*" He put his fingers up to his lips.

"He's a bad man. He does bad things to kids."

I stayed put, feeling the hairs on the back of my neck rise. For some reason, I knew this guy was looking for me. It was lucky that I had thought to put my knapsack under the seat. We stayed totally still and quiet. Finally, he walked away.

"How do you know him?"

Abraham looked white as a sheet. "I knew his dad. He was bad too."

His look of pain told me more than I wanted to know. We started to get up, but then I realized I didn't have the hat. As I turned my head upward, I saw it wedged into the seat above us. I reached for it and took it to my seat to give to him. "How did that get there?"

The train then came to a stop, and another conductor came over to me.

"Dodgersville, little girlie." He was an elderly man with a wide smile. "Hi, Abraham. You keeping this girl company, aye?" His teeth were yellowed, and he was a bit crumpled. His white hair stuck out around his beat-up hat. Its wide patent leather rim was dull and scratched.

"Yes, sir," The little boy got up and took my hand. "I'm watching her real good."

"Such a good boy you are. Well, give his pop my regards, will you?" he said, addressing me directly. "Tell him Elmer still rides and is waiting for him to take over my shift. Tell him I'm watching Abe for him."

Warmth hit me. I instantly liked Elmer.

"Abraham, sir. It's from the Bible," the boy said solemnly.

"Yup, it certainly is." He winked at me. "Well, Abe, you be good to the little missy here," he said, obviously paying no mind to Abraham's request.

"Well." Another conductor came down the aisle and headed right toward me. To my utter shock and horror, he walked right through Elmer. The man's face was pale, cheeks puffed out a bit, but it was his nose that caught my eye. It looked like a snout of a pig. I even saw green slime dripping out of it. Gross!

"You better get going, missy, this one is up to no good. Tell your pop he pays by the head for the kids he takes, just like he thought." Then he just evaporated in front of me. "Circe will know what to do with him," I heard his voice whisper near me.

Abraham was gone too. He just disappeared again. I looked at the conductor and then back where Elmer had been. Then I scooted right between his feet and ran. My instinct said: move it. I glanced back and saw the man following me. So was a balding, middle-aged man with a fat face. He reminded me of a mad pig I'd once seen in a county fair. It kept thrashing about and ramming the side of its pen. This man headed, shoulder-first, toward me. He looked almost desperate.

"Come on!" I heard Abraham's frightened voice but didn't see him. "Run! You have to run!"

I did, but I didn't know where I was headed. I ran into another empty car and scrunched down under another seat. I saw their pant legs passing me.

'Come on.' I heard Abe's voice in my head now. *'Follow me.'*

We scooted under several seats until we came to the end of the rows back where we came from. I saw the door that separated the cars and looked longingly at it.

'Wait until it stops. We can jump out when it's just the right time. It's kind of fun.' Abe smiled at me, half in reassurance, half as a dare.

It did sound like fun, and I was too scared of the men to think about it properly, so off to the middle of two rolling train cars we went. The little platform rocked back and forth. I was holding the door as if it was a rail, and the wind was whipping in my face. We waited until the train came to a complete stop. This was where trains halted until it was their turn to roll into the station. Only then did we jump and, just in time, because the two men had caught up to us, but the train had started to roll away again, entering the Dodgersville station. Heart thundering, ears rushing with fright, I turned toward the receding train. It felt great. Oh, I wouldn't tell Sophie about it now, but what a thrill!

There were three forms looking at me from where I had just been. Two I knew, but the third one was worse— it was a hollow black form with empty eyes. I saw the two men wrap their arms around their middles as if a sudden chill had gone through them. The piggish one went on all fours onto the ground, and I could swear he turned into an actual pig. They went back into the train.

"Well, best you kids come to my place up the hill until that one goes on break."

I turned, and there was Elmer again. He had a lunch bag in hand, and suddenly I realized I was hungry. He looked at me and at the way I looked at his lunch bag. "I got a package of cookies there if you kids want it."

We did, and both of us followed him through the tracks. Ethereal trains rolled slowly in and out past the three of us. They seemed to run even where the grass grew in between the tracks, some high, some very low. All the tracks were broken, and many were missing whole chunks, but that didn't deter this rail system. We walked past several abandoned train cars, careful to step over the tracks that held them. They were wooden and cracked, with nails sticking up. As we walked farther and farther, I noticed the weeds were growing over the tracks we passed, but still the ghost trains continued. Here the grass was thicker, unkempt, and wild.

The train cabs looked older and older until we finally

came to a totally neat-looking ancient caboose.

It was just the sweetest thing I'd ever seen, big and old, rusted, and high off the ground on platform blocks. I climbed in and nearly fell backward, losing my grip on the moldy flooring. The old man reached out and grabbed me, pulling me right in after him. Then he shut the door with a bang. An old gas light went on, and there were the cookies on the table. Oreos, yum! He even had two big glasses of milk. Now would probably be the time to mention just how hot it was in this particular car. I didn't care, I was so hungry. A lady's voice sang to us.

Elmer sighed. "Ella Fitzgerald. She sings like an angel, even if she is colored."

She was singing "The First Noel." Colored? Didn't he know they were called Blacks now? I supposed he was old. I had noticed old people tended not to care about doing things properly. They even farted in public! That was like a criminal offense to an eleven-year-old girl.

"Do you have a phone here?" I asked him. They both looked at me and then at the table. That was all that was there—a dusty wooden table, three chairs, and a cot in the corner that didn't look too inviting. "Do you sleep here, Mr. Elmer?"

"Sort of, missy. I kind of live here actually." His kind face looked at Abraham. "Sometimes Abraham stays here too, or we go on the trains, riding, helping kids, and all that." He didn't expound on why the kids needed help.

"I like riding the trains," Abraham put in.

He was eating the Oreos and dipping them in the milk. Each time a drip of milk landed on the table, he wiped it with his already dirty shirtsleeve. The music continued. Carol after carol. Behind the music, I could hear something else, voices whispering like memories. There was a female voice arguing, and somebody calling her a name my mother said I wasn't ever to say. All the while, it never occurred to me that there was no refrigeration here and the milk was ice cold. To me, it just tasted real good in the heat. I kept looking for the radio or TV where the music and voices were coming from.

"Delicious, thank you. This is so good—almost like eating a piece of heaven." I sipped the liquid down greedily.

They looked at each other and smiled.

"Where is the music coming from?" I asked.

"Oreos were created in heaven as you guessed already, missy. Sometimes they can be provided, you know, for special people, that is." Then Elmer looked thoughtful. "That is a good question about the music. I think it is just a memory. She used to perform in this very car." He looked around the big cab. "They couldn't ride in the front, you know."

"I'm not special." I proceeded to tell them why I was there, how I snuck off without telling anyone. They said confession was good for the soul. I always wondered who the "they" was, though.

"Does your mom know you are here?" Elmer asked.

I shook my head, and he looked at Abraham.

"I bet she's real scared for you. I know my mom cried a lot when I wasn't home."

I hadn't thought of that. I just wanted to get here to my stepfather's house—my house—and see all the things that Vienne had talked about. It never occurred to my eleven-year-old mind how my mother would feel.

Elmer's sad eyes looked at Abraham. "If you ask me, this stepmother of yours ain't no real mother if you had to sneak out on your first mother."

Vienne was a good person. She was just Vienne, not a maternal bone in her lovely body, but I couldn't explain that to him.

Abraham swallowed. "It was only for a minute. I left

the spot where my pop told me to sit and not move. It was right behind him—well, it was close. So boring!" He looked so sad. "I moved off the seat to try to help the man find his puppy. He said he lost it on the train."

"The pig man?" How I guessed that, I didn't know.

"No, his dad." Abraham sighed deeply. "Only for a minute. We got off the train where you and me jumped, and then it moved. He said he'd bring me home…"

The last word was swallowed in a sob. Elmer put his hand on the child's shoulder.

"It hurt," Abraham was wringing his hands. "It hurt. Only for a minute. I just left for one minute."

It was then I remembered the hat in my knapsack. I pulled it out and was about to hand it to him, when a loud bang sounded outside the closed door.

The gas lamp went out, and darkness encompassed the room.

Chapter 8

Present Day:

H o, ho, ho."
I opened my eyes, and there he was, the Big Guy himself. No, he wasn't wearing a red suit, or anything like that. The smell of sugar cookies and pine emanated from somewhere. He was holding a red mesh bag with a big tear in the side of it. I recognized that bag. It was right now the bane of my existence. For a moment, I thought I was hallucinating, or perhaps I wished this were a hallucination.

"I see my little helper gave you a bit of trouble." His voice was exactly the sound I remembered in all the clay animated movies I had seen. "He'll be receiving a lump of coal this year, I can assure you of that, miss." Still, there was no hostility in his voice at all.

"Don't be too hard on him." I finally got it out, once I stopped gasping.

"Yes, well, he is a pretty decent worker. Good help is hard to find these days up north. These youngsters are a bit spoiled, you know."

I know, I know. I am a nanny for my nieces and nephew and see what my sister and brother-in-law heap on them. I told him so.

"I don't usually use nymphs. He's been with me for two hundred years, and he has never ever had an incident. Can't say that for most of them. They tend to be a bit mischievous. Not at all as reliable as the snow elves I used to employ." He stood and looked out the darkened window and then turned toward me.

"Used to?"

"Reindeer flu. Kind of like your bird flu, but only deadly to elves. Most moved away from the pole to Florida. Can't blame them. They were of retirement age, and I can't keep them forever, I suppose." He sat again. His white beard and bald head gave off a little shine.

"Why did he kill her?"

His blue eyes looked into mine. "Kill her? Who?"

"The lady over there."

She came forward, and Santa looked at her. "Hello, Terry. You don't look so good. Why didn't you go into the light?" He looked at me then back at her. "Well, I suppose you have your reasons." He made a tsking sound. "Barney is an opportunist. Nymphs don't kill. They can't kill. They can lead others to mischief, but actual murder—no. Loci kill. Be careful of them."

I wondered what a Loci was.

Santa shook his head. "No, Barney saw an opportunity to make some extra charms and he took it. Wanted the passport of my friend over there and birth certificate to show the big R she was dead and take the reward in magic."

"Big R?"

"Redburn, head of The Big Organization. Kind of the spirit mafia—not a good group to associate with." Then he realized I needed an explanation and continued. "There are good guys and bad guys, here and there." He pointed up and down. "Usually, they stay separate from one another. However, lately, there has a been a bit of a clash between the two worlds. A door was opened, and those who want to rule both worlds crept out. SUD has had its hands full for quite a while."

"SUD?"

"Special Units Department. They probably have contacted you or will do soon enough." He paused for a moment. "No? SUD is kind of a police force that monitors the two worlds. Terry, over there, is one of their top agents—was, I mean. I do some recon work myself for them." He winked. "I've got a list."

I was a bit confused. He must have taken it as a "please explain further" type of look.

"The naughty and nice list. It's not real accurate, because some of the naughtiness kids do is age-appropriate. Those we got to let go, but I got another list. A watch list for future trouble. I've rarely been wrong with the names on that one."

We sat quietly as the monitor connected to me whirred.

"Alexi is age-appropriate for a boy, by the way. A Greek boy at least." He ho, ho, ho'ed, and I smiled at him. "So how can Barney make up the trouble he caused you?" he asked.

That kind of took me by surprise. I blinked at him and realized that the bag was moving as he picked it up. Looked like Barney was all zipped up again.

"Can he breathe?"

"They don't breathe, miss. They're nymphs. He's fine, I assure you. What can he do to make it up?"

I didn't know. I was dizzy and wasn't sure this wasn't some sort of dream.

"He needs to pay back all this trouble he caused you and your family," Santa insisted. A look of pity crossed his face. "I don't think you need more than you already have."

I wasn't poor…well maybe I was. I guess I could have asked Melvin for cash anytime, if I didn't have that little thing called pride. I lived with my husband's family because I wasn't quite able to raise Sophie alone, at least that was what they thought. Or maybe I didn't want her to be by herself in an apartment since she had already lost her father. Although I wasn't sure I was the mother of the year, no matter how I did it. A head popped out, and there was poor Barney. His cute little hat was askew, and his black curly hair was sticking out at strange angles. His nose was running, and he really did look adorable.

"Well, the kids were begging for an Elf-on-the-Shelf this year." It just popped out of my mouth. "My sister-in-law is really busy, and I was saving for it, but I think they'd love Barney—"

"No!" His eyes got real wide, and he struggled in the bag, something fierce.

"Perfect." The round, jolly man smiled wide. "I couldn't think of a better way to have him serve his time."

He opened the zipper and gently picked the nymph out of it. Barney was about two foot four, if that. However, the big man reached into his pocket and pulled out what looked like snow, but a lot brighter. He sprinkled it on Barney, and he shrunk to the size of an adult hand.

"I hate kids!" he whined, his voice getting tinier as he got littler.

"Learn to love them, or I'll be forced to call Redburn myself." It wasn't said harshly, just sadly.

I wondered who this Redburn was, because Barney turned six shades of white at the mention of the guy's name.

The little nymph hit his head with an elongated moan. "Oh, boy."

Santa had him sitting on the palm of his meaty hand. "Look, it's the perfect place to hide, Barney. He'd never look in a house full of kids. Not for a nymph at least."

Barney seemed to agree with him, or at least he looked resigned to it.

I now wasn't sure I wanted him anymore. "Why is this Redburn after Barney?"

"Barney stole some of his charms."

"I took an advance, that's all. I didn't steal them." Barney looked sincere, but the old man looked at him even more sternly. "I knew the dame was dead already. I just had to find the goods. Then this broad—" The hand closed and the saintly old man wrapped his fingers around the nymph. Not tight, but enough that he had him in a good grip. He gave him a gentle shake. "Okay, okay, I did kinda borrow them." Shake, shake. "Okayyyyy, I stole them. Jeez, he's got so much of it just lying around, I didn't think he'd notice the goods was gone, you know?"

The fingers unwrapped, and Barney lay down, looking sick.

I thought I'd better warn Santa about the vomit situation, but just as I was about to say it the Christmas man gave him a stern warning. "Don't even think about it." He was about to close his hand again.

"Nooooooo. I won't puke!"

"'Naturals' only have natural defenses: spit, puke, vomit—all in the realm of nature. Charms—" Santa glared at the little man again. "—are unnatural and don't go over too well. They weren't given to these guys for a reason." He didn't go into the reasons, but it sounded like they both understood.

"Can he harm the children?" I didn't want him if he was going to cause trouble.

"Oh, he won't do that if he ever wants to work at the

Pole again. In fact, I think he should be set up as their personal watchdog."

"Oh, Nick, you wouldn't. I am your best worker." The old guy still frowned. Barney tried again. "I need the job. I won't bother the kids at all." No change of expression from above him. "I swear it." A crack of lightning flashed outside my window. "I'll protect them. I will, I will!" Then he squeezed a little hand out and made the Boy Scout scouts honor with his little fingers.

"Better be careful with those swears, nymph. There're more powerful bosses than me, you know."

"I ain't swearing falsely, please."

I believed Barney, even though Terry was staring at him in total disbelief, rolling her chocolate-colored eyes at both of them. I wondered if I could do that.

"What you looking at?" Barney demanded.

"Don't bother, Terry. This is the best we are going to get from him. You have to admit a house full of kids is good for reforming any imp, nymph, or Loci."

She nodded and then actually smiled.

Santa rubbed his finger and thumb together and, out of nowhere, appeared a box that was striped silver and blue. He unceremoniously dumped the little guy in it. He put it on the rolling table then put the lid on with a big silver bow. He pulled a ribbon out and tied it around the package. Then a card appeared, and he wrote *Feel better soon, love, Barney.* "That should do."

He smiled and attached it then got up and looked out the window. "Looks like my ride is here, young miss. You're in good hands now with Terry, Ned, and even Barney." He started to head to the window then stopped and looked thoughtfully at me. "Tell Sophie I am working on her order." He continued and was almost out of the room when he returned a second time. "Tell her these exact words, Theresa. Tell her Santa said 'these things take time.' Those are the words I want you to tell her exactly, okay?"

I wasn't sure if this was real or not so I agreed wholeheartedly. It was confusing because Sophie usually gave me her letters to send to Santa, and I don't remember any letters this year. He reached into his pocket and, when his hand came out again, little white fluorescent sprinkle dust was on his fingers. He sprinkled it on me, and I fell into a deep sleep.

CHAPTER 9

1987:

There was total silence in the train car, and I was terrified. The banging on the door was the kind that sounded like, "Let me in or I will huff and puff and break the door in!"

I went to the wall on the side of the door, where the sounds were coming from, and pressed my back against it. Outside, the invaders were making headway on the entrance. It was only a few moments later when the door came crashing open. To all of our surprise, the room was empty. No chairs, no tables, no glasses, and no cookies! There was just me.

They climbed in, and I took the opportunity to jump out the door as they did so. The gravel below made a noise. Too late, they saw me. I ran as fast as I could, with the pig man right behind and Mr. Train Guy after him. They were bigger and faster, but I was small, and I ducked under the abandoned cars. Each time I thought I was out of reach, somehow they appeared right behind me.

"Come on."

I heard Abraham in front of me now. He made no crunching sounds on the gravel as I did—something I noticed but didn't think about. We ran until we were at the edge of the forest that surrounded the train yard. The problem was the men were catching up to us. Fast!

A little hand grabbed mine, and we sprinted under the trees. However, we were backtracking and not going forward.

As we ran, I spotted where he was taking me: the side entrance of the train station. It was down a few steps, just barely visible.

The boy was pulling me toward it. It looked old, as if it hadn't been used for a long time. I had a choice: go down the steps or scoot around the building to hide in the bushes. Something told me not to go in there. It might have been the big black shadow covering the doorway.

Abraham yanked hard. "A watcher. Run, run, Theresa!"

We veered away from it just as the door opened on its own. The two men saw it and ran toward it, thinking we'd ducked in there. As they passed through the door, it slammed shut.

"That sure was close." He was out of breath.

The two of us sat together, shaking.

"What happened to the Oreos?" No chairs, table, or bed—I could live with that—but take away my milk and cookies, it was time to put in a formal complaint to the big boss upstairs.

"Elmer hid them. He didn't want those guys to eat them."

I agreed with that. Still, I was hungry from all the running. It looked like Abe read my mind again because he pulled out a lint-encrusted cookie and split it with me. Yes, it still tasted good.

"I've been through that door. That's where they got

me." He looked sadly at the place we had just evaded then longingly out of the bushes. "I miss my mom and pop. I wish I could see them again."

"Got you? Who got you?"

"They did. They did bad things to me."

He was very upset, and I was upset for him, so I put my arm around his shoulder.

"Why don't you just go home to your parents? I am sure they miss you too."

"I can't find my house." He looked truly pitiful.

"I am sure my father can help you. He lives here, and he probably knows everyone." I believed it too. I knew my stepfather was superhuman, and he would help Abraham. "I just have to call him to pick me up, and we'll both be safe from those guys." The door was still closed, so we crept out of the shrubs. "I am sure the station has phones inside."

We were careful going in. I looked for the bad men everywhere I stepped, hoping never to see them again, but not so positive I wouldn't. The Dodgersville train station was big for a little town. It was made of tan concrete blocks that had the look of solidly built. The inside was teeming with all sorts of people.

"Boy, they sure dress fancy around here." I saw women in hoop skirts and kids in black knickers, like on the train. There were men in top hats as well as girls in frilly dresses. They all looked at me, and I looked at them too. I was feeling uncomfortable—as if pins and needles were going through my whole body. It was like holding hands with Abraham times ten. A girl, with long dark black hair curled from the bottom up, was hula-hooping near us.

"Hi, ya, you want to try?" she asked, stopping for just a moment.

I did, I really did, but I also was worried the bad

guys were going to come up to us at any moment. I wanted to get to a phone. "No, thank you. Where are the phones?"

She was still turning in the hoop, and it was kind of making me dizzy.

"The whats?"

A hand came down and took hers. "Mary, don't talk to strangers."

A white-gloved hand took her away, but I didn't see anyone attached to the appendage.

"Abraham?" He was gone again. I started to walk through the crowd of people. "Excuse me, do you know where the phones are?" I was looking for pay phones.

In those days, eleven-years-olds didn't carry cell phones.

Still, this crowd didn't seem to understand me at all. I was wading through bodies when I nearly got run over by a horse and buggy that came barreling through the lobby, striking a couple of kids, including Mary, the hula-hoop girl.

I looked on in horror. Her mother's hand was next to her, and I could hear her crying. The hoop went rolling in front of me. I watched it as it just rolled right by.

"Little girl? Little girl? Are you lost?" Standing next to me was a pretty lady dressed in a blue uniform that read *Amtrak*. I looked at her then back at the scene of chaos. There was nothing but a couple of benches and a few weary travelers milling around.

"Where are the horses?"

"It happened a long time ago." She shrugged at me, smiling. She smelled of flowers, which made me feel safe.

"But Mary got hurt. She was on the floor." I pointed to her wayward hula hoop.

"You know Mary?" she asked with an upturned

plucked eyebrow. "Try and help one day, okay?" She was kneeling next to me and took my hand in her nice manicured one.

Red. One day I wanted to wear that color too.

"She asked me if I wanted to try her hula hoop and her mom told her not to talk to strangers and pulled her away, at least her hand did. I didn't see her body." Then I looked in the corner where the hoop had rolled, but there was nothing now.

"One day, Mary will get someone to use her hoop, and then she can finally step out of the way of the horses and go to heaven, to her mom. I guess today just wasn't her day. All of us will one day catch that train, you know." She looked so nice. Her face was young, and she had bright red lipstick on.

"What train?"

"To heaven, sweetie."

A big bright light started to shine, and there was an old-fashioned caboose with its big chutes spewing white mist. It zoomed in and passed us by.

The engineer stuck out his head, a grizzled beard surrounding his smile, and called to her. "Any today, Sheila?"

She shook her head then turned her pretty, heart-shaped face back to me.

The train continued on its way right through the station. None of the other travelers seemed to notice it. "Passes by twice a day. You were here just in time to catch a glimpse of it. Most don't even see it..." Then she peered hard at me. "Where are you off to?"

"I need a phone to call my dad. He is..." What should I have said? The truth? No, I just lied. "...supposed to pick me up."

"This is not a safe place for a pretty little girl like you to be on your own. Maybe Mary's mom was right.

Don't talk to strangers, okay?" she said firmly, but not in a cruel way. She pointed to where a sign hung. *Restrooms, Phones, and Sitting Area.* "That's where you can call your father. Don't be overly judgmental of him. Sometimes people mean well, but they don't have all the answers." She paused and smiled at me again. "He is just doing his best. He is a very good man, and he does lots of good for people on this side."

I looked at the sign again and then back at her, and she was gone too. "Boy, people sure do come and go in a hurry around here!"

I went over to the pay phone and picked it up—for those of you who don't know what a pay phone is, I will explain. It's a booth mounted on the wall with a telephone soldered to it. There's a slot that money can be put into to operate it. The money slips into a big black box on the bottom—I pulled out a dime—yes, calls only cost a dime back then—and called my father.

"Hi, Daddy."

"Carrot Curls, is that you?"

"Hi. I'm in Dodgersville. Can you pick me up from the—"

"You are *where*?" His tone changed from warm and welcoming to harsh and maybe a little frightened.

"I'm in Dodgersville. I wanted to come to my new house," I said boldly. Wasn't I his daughter, too? It was my house too.

"In Philadelphia?" he asked, confused. "Your mother bought a house?"

"No, the house you built for us here." Boy, was he being silly.

"I didn't build a house for you here. You need to go back home, Theresa Lilian Lewis!" Now I knew he was mad when he used my full name. "This is not your home."

He was so abrasive that I just hung up the phone while he was still talking. I heard him ask exactly where I was, but I was so hurt that I couldn't tell him. I just stood there and cried.

CHAPTER 10

Present Day:

I woke up crying. Sophie was in the room with her cousins, and they were all holding the box and asking who Barney was.

"Your mom's crying."

I heard Velma's gravelly voice. She was so pretty Alexi Senior would have to have a bat for the boys that would be on his front stoop one day.

"Probably about my dad again," I heard Sophie answer her younger cousin. "She cries a lot."

Did I? Maybe I did do my fair share of crying. Paulo had been taken away from me in a war that had entered these shores through the back door. The news didn't like to even mention the "war on terror" as it was termed. It seemed to me this was the war everyone wanted to forget—except those of us who had lost someone in Iraq or Afghanistan. We seemed to remember just fine. People didn't like to talk about it. At all. But Sophie—I made it my business to only cry in the room after she was asleep or when I was alone in the car. I didn't want her thinking about the war. How did she know I cried?

"She's always real sad," Sophie added matter-of-factly.

Me? Miss Chirpy? Miss Happy as a Lark? Well, maybe not all the time, but certainly mostly, right?

"Who's Barney? " A little blondie popped up. Alexi, Barney's penance, was holding tightly to the package. He gave a good shake, and I heard rattling. "What's in here?"

I reached out to grab it to no avail. "Don't do that, baby."

"I am not a baby," he insisted.

"No, you are not," I corrected myself, not being in the mood to argue with his six-year-old logic or Santa's sleeping dust aftereffects.

"Can we open it, Auntie Delfi?"

Old offenses were erased when a shiny box was in view.

Not surprisingly, it was Phoebe who plucked it out of his hands, her capable fingers holding it just out of reach of the lethal tiger who wanted to tear through it so badly.

"Yes." I was resigned to having it opened sometime, even though I was sure it had all been a dream. It had to be a dream, right? Santa, really?

She opened it and gave a gasp of delight.

"Oh look, it's an Elf-on-the-Shelf, and he is so adorable!" She carefully unruffled him, pulling him out and straightening his cap at the same time. She turned gracefully to her siblings and cousin and presented him to them.

"Meeeeee tooooooo," Alexi whined. "I want to hold him." His little nose reddened a bit, and his big sister gave his head a playful swat.

"Okay, but you need to be gentle, Alexi. This is not a toy. He is magic," she intoned seriously, and all the children gathered to see what was so magic about him.

"What's his name?'

"Barney."

"What kind of elf name is that?" Velma got close to Barney. Then with her ever-observant eyes, she noticed it. "Hey, he doesn't look like an elf." She turned him this way and that. For a moment, Barney looked at me in desperation. I gave him my best Santa warning eyes. "He is really funny-looking, not elf-like at all." She had her hands on his middle and way up close. "I'll look him up."

On what? I wondered. Was there a catalog of fairy folk that I didn't know about? "He's a replacement for Santa." She stared at me in disbelief. I shrugged. "Most of the elves got reindeer flu and moved to Florida, so Santa asked some nymphs to help."

"Velma." Sophie gently took the little man from her hands. "Remember, we looked in *National Geographic* and saw all those shriveled up men on the beach?" Her little cousin nodded sagely. *National Geographic?* "Well, they looked more like elves to me than people," Sophie told her.

Her cousin seemed to be satisfied with that answer.

"Hi, Barney." Sophie's pretty face looked into his funny one. She gave the nymph a gentle kiss on his cap. "I think he's adorable," she proclaimed.

Barney smiled wide with his cheeks reddening to a rosy hue. All the children were astounded he could even do that.

"He is magic," Velma repeated solemnly to everyone.

"Yes, magic." It was Melvin. He looked suspiciously at Barney, who seemed to shrink visibly under his glare. "Best he not cause any mischief with it either," he hissed quietly in my ear. "Or to my granddaughter."

Did I detect a hint of warning in there? "Santa gave him to me," I whispered back.

"The Big Guy himself?" He seemed impressed.

"You must have been a very good girl this year."

"No, I bet he just has a special on widows and orphans, especially these couple of years."

He kissed my cheek and looked on as Sophie continued to marvel at the nymph. "Your mother and I came to an agreement of sorts. You will go home with her."

Not surprising, really. Even though they argued like cats and dogs, my mother always won. I thought she goaded him into it. They stared at one another in an uneasy truce.

I didn't want to home with either of them. I wanted to go to my home. At that moment, Rydia walked in and took one look at my face, one look at my parents glaring, and calmly told them both that I needed twenty-four-hour care, and she was the only one equipped to give it. She said it so firmly that both of my parents acquiesced. I thought my mother looked relieved, but my father just looked resigned. For a man used to being in charge, this entire girl-power thing was a bit much.

CHAPTER 11

I was so hurt I could have just stood there crying all day.

A tiny hand slipped itself into mine. It was Abraham. "Are you all right?"

"No. My father said I can't come home." Tears let loose from my eyes, and that was all I could manage.

"Well, how about if we live together from now on? Most people don't talk to me, and I am kind of lonely."

He did look sad, and I sort of did feel sorry for him, but more sorry for myself. How was I to get home to Philadelphia?

"I spent all of my money, so I suppose I *will* need a place to stay for a while. Do you live with Elmer?" I thought of that little train car the old conductor seemed to inhabit. My stomach had started to rumble, and I remembered Elmer's Oreos, too.

"I start out there, but I always end up where they went. The dark room." He shuddered.

"Why?"

"I don't know. Every time I close my eyes, I wake up

there." We both sat in silence. He looked real serious. "I am stuck in a wall, and I have to find my way out all over again! It's really scary and—" He looked down at the floor.

"And what?"

"Next to me is a skeleton just like on Halloween. I think this one is real, though." He nodded at me with his big eyes. "I have to dig my way out each time. They keep closing up the hole in the wall!" He made scratching motions. "I get so thirsty and hungry. As soon as I get out, I go straight to Elmer who always has cookies and milk. I try never to fall asleep."

I nodded. "I wouldn't either if I kept waking up down there." His eyes widened in fear. I patted his arm. "Do you remember at all how to get home, Abraham?" I looked in my pockets and realized that I didn't have any more change to call my mother.

Then he smiled at me. "No, but I remember what was near it. We can try and find it together."

I considered that for a while, and he seemed kind of excited by my thinking about it. I looked up at him and then just beyond him. "Don't turn around," I whispered.

Coming into the station was the conductor, who now looked all official. The hairs on my neck started to rise, and I became frightened. Abraham dissipated right in front of me. I was so shocked that I forgot all about the man—until a hand clamped down on my shoulder.

"There you are, sweetie. Daddy was looking for you." It was pig face.

I tried to shake him off. "You are not my daddy! Let me go."

"You have been a naughty girl." His vise-like hand was on my arm, and the other man's hand had reached out to take my other one.

For a moment, I was resigned, but then something

that scared me even more started to come my way. A watcher.

I began to struggle in earnest. The few people around were looking at me, but he kept talking like a parent with an errant child. The watcher was coming closer. I could see and feel its blackness as it approached us. The mouth gaped, and the hollow eyes looked straight through me. In total desperation, I kicked the shins of the pig man and then bit the other on his wrist. At that moment, the watcher rose up and headed right for us. Its mouth widened and…well, there was nothing because I beat it right out of there, escaping his grip just in time. I did hear them screaming behind me, but I didn't pull a Lot's wife and look back. I just skedaddled right out of there.

It was then I noticed Abraham running alongside me. I went into the girl's restroom, and so did he. We hid in a stall. I was shaking in my boots—or I would have been if I'd had any boots on.

"You can't be in here," I said.

He just looked at me.

"You're a boy."

"Then they won't look for me here, right?"

That was logical. We just sat there in silence.

I must have fallen asleep. When I woke up, Abraham was resting his little brown-haired head on my arm. His eyes were drooping. I thought that was good—he needed a nap—then I remembered what he'd said about falling asleep. I was about to shake him, but before I could, he nodded off and disappeared. What I was thinking next I'll never be able to explain to you, but I thought he needed rescuing. No, it didn't occur to me that a child who appeared and disappeared might actually be a ghost who was beyond my help. I didn't believe in ghosts or goblins or even nymphs at the time—I did, however, believe in Santa, but that's just a side note and not really relevant.

I knew Abraham. He was in trouble in that awful place on the side of the train station, and I was going to make it my business to help him. I ventured from my hiding place.

It was now night. I had no business being there. The whole station seemed to be shut. There were no lights on. I carefully and quietly went to where I thought the front door of the station might be. It was locked, so when I put my hand on it, of course, it didn't budge.

A little girl of about seven came up to me. She was filthy and had a smear of mud on her face. She was wearing a potato sack dress that looked handmade. "What ya doin?"

"I'm looking for an exit. Do you know how to get out of here?"

"Why do you want to leave?" Her little voice sounded frightened.

"I have a friend who is trapped, and I need to help him. Please, do you know the way out?" I looked behind her, and there were suddenly lots of kids wearing all types of clothes, from all different time periods. It looked like a costume party. Well, except the looks on their faces.

All said, "Don't leave."

But Abraham was my friend, and I knew he was in a very scary place with bad people. It didn't matter that I could do very little against the bad guys.

The sea of children parted. There was hula-hoop Mary. She looked at me, and I stared at her bloody dress. Okay it was not polite, but, man, was it cool at that age and stage of my life.

"You okay, Mary?" I asked as the silence of her arrival stretched out.

"Have you seen my mommy?" she asked, staring at me then at the other kids.

Actually, to my surprise, I saw no adults at all. This might have seemed strange to you, but, to a kid, it was kind of a relief.

"No, not since earlier today." I hadn't seen her at all—just her hand. "Do you know how to leave this place? My friend is in trouble, and I need to get to him."

She stared at me curiously.

"Fast," I implored her.

She took my hand, the tingling thing happening again, but the sea of children opened for us. I watched as frightened face after frightened face looked on.

"The pig man is out there." A boy of about my age came over to me. "Don't go out there."

He took my other hand. There was more tingling, and I could see what had been done to him by the same man. I quickly withdrew my hand.

"Listen to me. He's a bad man."

Others came around us, each touching me each and telling me their stories, putting awful pictures in my head.

Mary still held tight to my other hand. I heard a roar from somewhere beyond all the children. To my shock, they turned into orbs of light and scattered to the ends of the room. I was no dummy. I immediately crawled under the bench and hid. The room thundered with footsteps that sounded as if they were crashing into the marble floors. I felt the vibrations as they neared me.

"Little pig, little pig, let me in," the one who had roared commanded.

"Not by the hair of our chinny, chin, chins," the children's voices, united in unison, answered him.

"Then I'll huff, and I'll puff and reel you in," he boomed.

I heard him inhale. It was a great big breath. From several corners of the room, I saw the spheres being sucked near. It was a terrific struggle of lights, like fireworks in the night sky. They struggled away from him, but he eventually got one and, when she materialized, I could see it was poor bloody Mary. She was squealing and calling for help, but all the other lights just flew away and disappeared.

I couldn't help it—I just had to follow them. I already knew what he was going to do, and I wasn't going to let him hurt her even more. After all, she had already been run over by a stagecoach. How much more could a little girl endure?

I crept out of where I was hiding and followed him as Mary struggled under his arm. He was big and had an awful smell, like rotten meat. I had to stop to catch my breath several times and almost lost them. He was moving very fast, but I was a good runner, and I wouldn't let poor Mary be hurt so soon again. We went to a dark hallway. As he entered, he started to give off a very odd red glow. Mary was glowing too—her glow was white light—and this gave me the courage to continue following them. The tunnel was very deep, but I was able to go down it without much trouble. Then I realized we were there. We had gotten out of the train station through a tunnel that led straight into a room—the room where Abraham was.

When the man stopped, he dropped Mary on the floor. The room was very dirty. There was a broken wooden table in the middle of it. Then, picking her up, he tied her to the table using bright orange strings that glowed. Mary screamed in pain as each one was wrapped around her wrists and ankles. She struggled, and he slapped her, stunning her into silence. He left her there and walked right through the wall.

I quickly got up the nerve to go over to her, putting my hand on the table. As I did so, the corner of it crumbled. Her hand remained suspended in midair, still tied, but there was no table under it. Even to the young me, this was really, really strange. I mean, I had seen this in cartoons, but not in real life. Comic strips were fictional, right?

"You are here?" Her terrified voice rose.

"Shhhhhhh." I tried to untie her, but every time I touched the ropes they just went right through my hands. There was no way to undo what he had done. As I struggled to figure out what to do, I heard yelling through the wall. Mary became more agitated. Then I heard his footsteps. He was returning. I looked around and spotted broken kitchen cabinets on the floor. I went and hid in one of them. Peeking through the doors, I saw him put his lips to Mary's cheek. He began inhaling. The bright white light that was in her began to waver. His powerful red glow grew larger and stronger. Poor Mary began to fade. She was disappearing right in front of me. Her sad little face peered at me from over the table as he made disgusting gorging and slurping sounds. I saw a rusty can of beans in the cabinet, and it occurred to me to throw it across the room to distract him. As I picked it up, a bright orange flashed in the room, and the man was shoved aside.

"Mine!" It was the pig-faced man from the train. "You told me I could have one, Daddy!"

His nose was dripping with green snot and his thinning blond hair was stuck to some of it. I realized he had an overripe smell to him as well and almost gagged.

"Get away, you piece of garbage. She is mine! I did the catching! You get your lazy butt up to the station and get your own." He pushed the other away and headed back to his feast.

For a few moments, the younger man sat dejected in the corner. "I'm really hungry, Daddy." It wasn't a man's voice. It was a little boy's voice.

"Shut up, you little piggy, and go away. Daddy's busy!"

I watched as he broke away from Mary and went over to a little blond child that had once been the snotty man. He picked him up and hurled him, with no mercy, right through a closed door.

It seemed, though, that the boy wasn't through with his father yet. As soon as the older man's back was turned, a teenage version of the little boy came barreling through the wall, with a sound like a bowling ball sliding down a lane, and slammed into the older man again. Then they were pushing and shoving each other, knocking into things, crashing all around the room. Things went flying and toppling over. They twice hit Mary's table. Finally, I saw the boy pick up an ethereal can and smash it down on his father's head. He kept banging until there was no shape to the other's cranium, just a mass of red mush. The older man dissipated into an orange mist that hovered over his body. The pig boy, who was still in his teenage form and just as ugly, came over to the table. Covered in his sire's blood, he leaned over, laid his hand over her eyes, and put his lips to her face, continuing where the older man had left off. I once again looked at the can in my own hand and debated what I should do.

As I gave the tin exterior a once-over, I realized that there was a red crust that wasn't rust, at all. It was blood, bone particles, and hair.

I lifted the can and hurled it into the other corner of the room in revulsion, hoping for what, I didn't know. But the noise did distract him, and he went over to where it was. I then picked up another can and hurled it to the other side of the room. He literally flew over to the other side, looking for its source. Then the most remarkable thing happened.

The door opened and in came the conductor from the

train. He was in pajamas and looked very angry.

The pig boy stopped and looked at the other, grinning at him. "So you're awake?" He had stopped gorging on Mary.

The conductor looked at the table, trying to figure out where the voice was coming from, then at the corner where I had thrown the can. The glowing orange man, the same one a can of beans had killed only moments ago, came alive again and went over to his shoulder.

"Let's go hunting," his distorted lips whispered in the sleepy man's ear.

The younger pigged-faced boy looked stricken. I could feel the sadness and jealousy.

"Mice!" The pajama-clad man began to leave the room, and then the other whispered again in his ear again.

"I'm hungry."

It was more of a hiss than a whisper, and chills edged their way down my arms.

Did he see him? I wondered as the red ball of fire smashed into the head of the sleepy conductor. He grabbed his forehead and went to his knees on the floor, tears springing from his eyes. The teenaged pig man came over to him. Was it concern, compassion, or something else? Disgust maybe.

"Leave him alone. He isn't your son, he's my son, and he's a good boy."

I looked at them all, finally figuring out who was who…well, at least I thought I did. The man in pajamas was the pig man's son, and the smashed-faced man was the pig man's dad. Gee, I really hated being at this little family reunion.

"I don't want the dead for the dinner. I want fresh meat!" The pig man's dad ignored his son as his smashed-up head reformed back to the ugly visage it was pre-baked beans.

A roar sounded in the room from all corners. I felt the vibrations go through me again.

"Meat. That's what I want."

I realized something else. The one in PJs wasn't shining. Now, I know that meant he wasn't dead. I watched from my hidey-hole as he looked at the table and then at the corner. He went over and pulled out a folding table. It was white and looked new. He opened it, and, on each corner, were red silk bands that made a rattling sound when he pushed them. I didn't know why. "Fresh young meat. What do you say, Daddy?" He walked over to a gray metal cabinet and unhinged it, pulling out first a shiny-edged ax that glistened in the light. It looked scary to me. Then he pulled out a large glass jar. Within the liquid was a face I recognized. It was the pig man who was following him. This seemed to stop the other for a moment as he peered into the jar.

"Put it away! Put it away!" the porky-faced man screeched, clearly abhorred by what his son held in the jar. He looked at the fully formed smirking face of his own father and cursed.

The pig man's father sneered at the aging boy. "Now, now, sonny, don't take the good Lord's name in vain."

Mary looked at it and started to whimper.

"Shut up!" The pig man punched the edge of the table, making a sonic boom that resonated around the room as well. It made me dizzy, and I put my hands over my ears. However, it did the job of vibrating the older man into invisibility.

The pig man began to make a squealing sound, and then he turned into to an actual pig. He was a great big, pink and white swine, running loose in the room. Several times the animal passed my door. I peered through a little hole that once had held a handle.

His pajama-clad son put the jar back into the cabinets. "Little pig, little pig, let me in. Not by the hair of my chinny, chin, chin. Then I'll huff and I'll puff and I'll let myself in," he chanted as the other squealed around him trying to get his attention.

"Sonnyyyyyyyyyyyyy." The conductor walked out, trying to close the door on the beast, which managed to squeeze its way through, following him.

I waited what seemed a long time to me—probably about five minutes because that was an eternity at that point of my life. Walking over to Mary, I could see she was unconscious. I started to try and untie her again when the walls began to pound. At first, I thought it was one of the pig guys so I went to hide, but then I heard Abraham's voice.

"Abraham?"

"Help, help, I fell asleep and I am stuck here again. Help, help, help!" He was becoming more and more desperate.

"I'm here, Abraham. Just be a little quiet, will you?" I was looking for something to open the wall with. Okay, so it never occurred to me that ghosts can go through walls. You know I wasn't really in my element, right? I spotted the big ax. I picked it up—just barely. It was heavy.

"It's so dark here! Please help me, Theresa. Please!" Then there was silence. "There's a skeleton here still. I am so scared!"

I was so upset by his cries that I lifted up the big ax and swung at the wall. Well, whatever, as Sophie now says way too often. I didn't even make a dent, but I did attract "His" attention. The pig came in and butted me in the leg. I fell down.

He came at me, squealing his success. "Sonnnnnny, meat!"

However, his son didn't show up. It was just me, the ax, and him. Wait a second. I had an ax. I lifted it up and slammed it down on him. He reared back before it made contact. Then he butted me again with his runny snout, and I shoved him away so I could get another swing at him. He jumped on the table, making it rattle more. As he stood there, I took good aim at him and managed to hit the wall where I had heard Abraham's voice. This time, I made a dent. I guess desperation had its advantages. The porker ran out through the wall as I went after it with the sharp instrument. Then I went back to the wall and began to hit it again, slamming the weapon into it where it had begun to chip.

"Abraham, I am breaking the wall. Talk to me." I listened, but there was no voice. I began to worry maybe he was dead in there. Yes, he was dead already—but I didn't know that. "Abraham?"

"I'm here," I heard from behind the wall where I was striking.

"Move back, so I don't hurt you."

He told me he was as back as far as he could get. I raised the ax and slammed it down again, making the hole even bigger. I hit again and again, making real progress. I was so engrossed in what I was doing that I didn't notice the pig was back. As I neared my destination, I could see the edges of Abraham's little engineer hat. I was so close to him.

Then I wasn't. I was on the floor with the pig straddling me. His breath smelled, his snot dripped, and his eyes were red with squishy stuff in the corners. He turned into a man. As his fetid breath entered my nostrils, a black form appeared above us. The pig man screamed and veered backward. I rolled over and picked up the ax. I gave a swing toward the floor where they were fighting, but as the weapon came down it went right through them

both, the man and the dark shape. A shot of cold air hit
me, hard, and I was slammed against the other wall,
across the room. The black thing was off the pig and
headed toward me. However, instead of being dissuaded
and running away, the stupid critter also was headed my
way.

The watcher turned around and enveloped the animal, like a pig in a blanket. The hog began to freeze. I
turned to the wall again as Abraham started calling for
me in a frenzied fashion.

"Theresa, help! Please let me out. I can almost see
light coming in here."

I swung the big-headed blade on the little space and
continued to hack away as Abraham kept calling. The
animal, which was half covered in frost, was inching toward me. More and more of Abraham was showing. I
wondered just how he had gotten in there, to begin with.
There was hardly any room for a person.

His voice was getting louder and stronger now. I was
really going at it when the pig was there again. I caught a
glimpse of it in the metal ax blade and swung the blade
around, aiming right at its head. What happened next I'll
never forget. The animal shattered into a million pieces of
black and red light, making a sound like breaking glass.
The splinters were on the ground at first, and then they
picked themselves up, aiming their jagged ends at me.
The black shadow also was up off the ground as I held
my ax high. Then a little hand came out of the wall once
again, reminding me that I had to get him out of there.

I reached into the innards of the wall with my free
hand and grabbed at what I thought might be him. The
soft crumbling plaster broke apart in my grip. I yanked
and was shocked to discover that what I held was no flesh
and blood hand.

Oh, an arm had come out—but it was skeletal. I

threw it on the ground and reached for the peak of his hat, pulling hard, but what followed was a child's skull encrusted with years of dust. I jumped back, not realizing that in doing so I had just missed being rammed by the shards of pig glass that were aimed at me. Behind those came a familiar dark shadow.

"Get down!" It was Abraham; he was under the table. "We need to get out of here."

He had tears in his eyes and was shaking very badly.

I pointed upward. "Not without her, but I can't get the ropes off. They just slip through my fingers." I went over to them, avoiding the shadow by a hair.

He climbed out from under and looked at the table. Gently he touched the red straps that were cutting into her flesh. They fell to the ground, and slowly she rose up, jumping off the table. The three of us began to creep past the epic battle taking place. It was a strange play going on. The black shadow thing was now glowing—no, it was pulsating and gyrating—and sharp frozen orange daggers were aimed its way. They gathered together and came toward it just as the door opened. There stood the conductor. Holding his hand was a very scared little boy.

"What the—" His eyes drifted to the wall, to the bones on the floor, and then to me. I still had the ax near me, and I could see he wasn't very happy with my find.

He dropped the kid and headed toward me. "They said one of you would be coming!"

One of who would be coming? My heart was racing, and I felt pure fear. The taste was acrid as the sweat dripped into my mouth.

At that moment, lights collided with the watcher, pushing it into the wall at the exact spot I had opened and extracted Abraham. The hole began to extend even more to reveal twelve child-sized skeletons encased within. Each had their hands reaching for the lights that were again assembling to re-attack the dark form. The whole parameters of the wall then fell away like a window opening. The view was of red molten lava, burping flames spitting upward, and flying creatures above it all. Just that: orange-red lava and crimson red sky, smoky, bleak, and utterly terrifying. I was too scared to move. I saw dragons emerging from the river of hot liquid, their snouts and shining scales dripping fire, their eyes huge as saucers. I wanted to see more, even though I was petrified. Then the watcher moved, so its back was to the scene, covering the depiction of hell almost entirely with its darkness.

The pig lights were still aimed at the dark form. Gathering into one, they formed a spear with a sharp tip and flew at it. It hit with a sound like nothing—like the absence of all sound—and didn't harm the watcher at all. Rather, the spear went right through and into the waiting jaws of the dragons that were now in place, ready to catch the swine-spirits. I heard a horrible squeal, like that of a stuck pig.

Maybe the man heard it, maybe he didn't, but he also looked that way. His eyes widened at something, or maybe it was just the hole itself that caught his attention. He stopped his approach for just a moment. A dragon with a red-hot face and big teeth popped up out of the floor-boards and winked at me. I raised the weapon, took aim, and almost hacked my stepfather to death. What? you ask. Did I say 'my stepfather'?

Melvin had risen out of the floor and blocked the conductor's attack. The dark shadow came to Daddy's aid and knocked the ax from my hands just in time to save Melvin from permanent damage. I backed up and looked at him in shock. How did he get here? Not that I wasn't glad to see him. In fact, I was almost thrilled to have him there, until I remembered that I was mad at him.

The conductor reared back and ran out of the door away from us. Then the wall closed up with a snap. The last thing I saw was the jagged lights still trying to get away from the flying monsters. Soon there was just a nasty hole in the wall and a partial skeleton hanging out.

"Carrot Curls!" He swept around and hugged me. I stiffened like Sophie so often did and barely acknowledged his embrace. He didn't seem to notice. "Are you all right?"

I nodded solemnly at him.

"Shock, sir. She must be in shock."

I wasn't in shock. I was mad at him. That was when I noticed the other man by his side.

"Geez, there's a mess in here," he said.

I looked where he was staring. "Abraham was in there and a skeleton." I pointed to the errant bones on the floor.

"He's fine now. We have him outside with the paramedics."

I looked to the side and saw him in the corner with Mary. I pointed that way, but the room was filling, and soon the two children just faded away.

My stepfather led me out of there. We walked in silence as an EMS worker came over to me. He lay me down on the floor next to the boy that the man had brought in. The kid looked dazed and had a bad cut on his head. Blood was dripping down the side of his face. My stepfather was talking to me as two official-looking men came over to him.

"Sweetheart," one with a dark mustache started. "Were there any other kids in there with you?"

"Mary, Abraham, me, and him. " I pointed to the boy who was bleeding.

"We didn't see any other kids there. Are they locked up, honey?" the EMT asked as he treated the wounded boy.

"Abraham was in the wall, and I was in the closet. Mary was tied on the wooden table." Then I felt compelled to add, "There are a lot of skeletons in that wall too, but don't chop too far because you will fall into the sea of fire water where the pig lights went."

I think shock was setting in because my teeth began to chatter and the shakes were beginning.

First they looked at me and then they looked at my stepfather. He shrugged, picked me up, and held me like a baby with my feet hanging over his arm.

"SUD ought to look further into this scene," I heard him say to the men there. "The firewater and the dragons sound vaguely familiar to me."

I hadn't said dragons to him, but I was so foggy I didn't pick it up at the time, though I remembered later.

"Got some bodies in the wall here," I heard a voice call out, and all the men looked at my father. "Kids," the voice added.

They all groaned.

"Better get on it right away!" Daddy's last words kept ringing in my ears. "I didn't get a chance to finish what I was saying on the phone to you when you hung up on me."

I didn't react at all. Tears left the corners of my eyes, and my sight was blurry.

"I was going to come right over and get you. The train station is not safe, sweetie. I was coming to take you back to Philadelphia. " He could see I wasn't saying a word. "Your mom is worried sick about you. She called the police."

I knew, at this point, my mother must have been freaking.

"Terry Lou…"

He reached over, and I pulled away. A sudden wave of anger hit me. He pulled me tighter.

"Sure you would take me back to Philadelphia. You didn't want me to spoil—" I had started to yell at him. *"—your new life, your new family, your new house!"* Now I was full out sobbing.

He looked shocked, and even a bit hurt, but I didn't care. I believed I understood where I stood in his life.

"First of all," he started, calmly pulling me away from prying eyes. "You are my family." His voice was low, and he was trying to remain civil. "You are in my life. I just can't have you in this life, I made a promise…" Then he looked at the road as now it had begun to snow. "Terry Lou, Carrot Curls, a house is just a shell."

I wasn't listening. The medication the EMT had given me for shock took effect. I was falling asleep.

CHAPTER 12

Present Day:

I was sitting in a wheelchair by the curb waiting for Lexi Senior to pull up. With me was my entire family: Rydia, Alysia, her three kids, my one kid, Paulo Senior, my mother, my stepfather, and Aunt Vienne. The van couldn't pull up fast enough for me. I swear I thought the entire hospital was out there too, cheering for our departure. They could hardly wait to see us go. No matter how many times my family was told the two-visitor rule, inevitably when Nurse the Hun came in, there were no less than eight people in the room, sometimes before visiting hours even started.

Just as the van was pulling up to me here comes the Grinch who stole Christmas. Andy the cop looked like he hadn't slept in weeks, but I'd only known him a few minutes, so maybe I looked that way, and I just put it on him. Either way, he was fast approaching, and I had nowhere to run.

My sister-in-law, the lawyer, intercepted him. "What do you want?" She stood there in black high heel pumps and a black shark suit to match. Though she was tiny, her stance would have made most sumo wrestlers turn and run.

Yet, he was still trying to go around her to speak to me. "I need to speak to her."

She shadowed his every move. It almost looked like they were dancing.

"She's not up to talking to you right now, Officer…"

She was waiting for his surname. Truth be told, I had no idea what his last name was. I had been questioned all week by many different policemen, and one sort of blended with the other. Still, Andy stood out and not just because he was a hottie…well, maybe a little because of that.

"I am her lawyer, and she isn't speaking to anyone on the street."

"I need to speak to her, miss…" So two could play that game, aye? He smirked at her. "Will you move over, please? This is an official police investigation, Counselor."

Ooowee, he could really play it.

"Officer D'Souza, please come here," a strong voice boomed behind him, and there stood a man in a large coat that sported a fur-topped hood pulled over a massive head. A certain haze hung around him. "Detective, this is not your investigation right now."

Did I smell sulfur? Coming up behind him were news cameras.

"Captain Breenan, sir, I am off duty and just asking the young woman a few questions."

Flattery will get you nowhere. I was on the cusp of thirty-nine and looked every year of it at that moment. Okay, what I wanted to know was just exactly how young did I look to Andy the Grinch. The big man had caught up to him and put a firm hand on the younger man's shoulder. The air crackled around them in sparks. Was I

the only one seeing this? The captain became even fuzzi-
er. I began to wonder just how strong the painkillers
were, exactly.

"Now, come on, son, it's not your case. We are doing the best we can to help you out on this. You are interfering in an official—" Two microphones were taping his
every word. "—investigation, and you're on suspension,
so you don't belong here."

Andy colored and tried to break from his grip. The
man's voice now sounded hollow. How could this be,
when he was so powerful before?

"Sir, is it true that Officer D'Souza is being investi-
gated in the death of his partner, Detective Ned Williams?"

What was I hearing? Why would he be looked at for
the death of his partner? It wasn't this guy's fault, no
matter how cranky and miserable he seemed to be. It was
a car full of nymphs and a guy named Redburn who were
responsible. At least that was what I had gathered from
my talk with Santa the other day. I was about to say so to
the captain when I realized he'd think I was a loony bin
candidate if I did.

So, to my shame, I just kept quiet.

"No, he is not being charged with anything. There's
an investigation into negligence…"

"We were caught in gunfire, sir," I heard Andy mutter under his breath.

"Detective D'Souza is on temporary suspension until
things can be cleared up, that's all." The man was
smooth.

The reporters were now at their usual feeding frenzy
like a bunch of piranhas.

"Officer D'Souza, is it true you jeopardized your
partner's life?"

"No!"

They were closing in on him, and he looked ferociously at them.

"Is it true you didn't call for backup?"

"I called for backup."

He did. I saw him. I made an attempt to say so, but my sister-in-law shushed me.

The big man made a sweep of his hand, knocking over a reporter. "That's enough."

The camera then swung around and hit the man back as another arm slapped the captain. Where that arm came from I didn't know, but another reporter in a black T-shirt and sporting a bright red beard punched the captain. As the big man fell down, a full out brawl erupted. The captain sprang up.

I noticed the black T-shirt whisper something in the big man's ear. Then, to the shock and horror of all of us, the captain punched Andy in the jaw. Andy, to his credit, just stood there. At the captain's signal, police officers ran in, the fight stopped, and Andy was promptly arrested and pulled away. Just then, Lexi pulled in and hauled me away too.

"What just happened?" I asked my stunned family.

My stepfather stood on the curb and looked at the reporter with the red beard, shaking his head at him. The other just smirked. The cameraman and reporter disappeared as police gathered to question witnesses. I mean *disappeared*. Could reporters really do that?

"That guy is going to need a good lawyer." My sister-in-law got on the phone right away. Lexi was snickering next to her. "Be quiet, will you?" she snapped.

"Ruff, ruff," he barked at her playfully, leaning over for a kiss.

To which she complied automatically. It was times like this that I missed my Paulo most.

My Paulo, killed in Afghanistan, the war the news

refused to report on. It was like it didn't exist. I felt like this was worse than what happened during the Vietnam War. While there were protests and riots over our partici- pation in that war—and there were many young people blaming the soldiers—now there was only silence. Sol- diers died, and their widows and widowers started to qui- etly disappear too. A hand touched my arm, and I looked behind me. Sophie was looking worried again. I smiled…well, I gave a half a smile at least. It was the best I could do. Her face mirrored mine, and we were like that until we reached home.

CHAPTER 13

1987:

When I awoke in the hospital in Dodgersville, there was an elderly couple sitting there. They looked ancient, but I thought I recognized the man. He looked like an old Abraham.

"Are you Abraham's grandfather?" Only a child could be so bold, and I was.

"I am his father," the shaky voice answered.

"Is he here too?" I meant Abraham.

His father got up and then looked back at me. He wanted to say something, but he didn't. It was left to the old lady sitting next to him.

"Did you see our Abraham?" She looked intently at me. Her watery topaz eyes, surrounded by crinkles, showed she had seen some hard times.

He rolled his equally wrinkled eyes, ashamed. "Emmy, please—"

"Hush up, William." She wore white gloves and had a pocketbook on her lap that she gripped for dear life, just like her son had done with his hat, closing her hands and opening them. "Did you, sweetheart? The policemen said you were calling for him."

"Yes, ma'am." The old man turned toward me now.

"He wanted to go home," I continued. "Is he home with you now?" I thought since I had broken open the wall he should be out of there. I told them so, but they shook their heads no. We all sat quietly for a while.

"Was he happy?" she finally asked.

"He misses you. He wanted a kiss from you, even though he doesn't really like them that much. Kisses, I mean, not you."

Tears welled up in her eyes and poured over the ridges and crevices of her worn face.

She leaned in close to me. "Was he okay?"

I could see she didn't want his dad to hear her.

"Emmy, enough of this spook stuff! Let's be off." He went to take her hand and she reluctantly stood up to go.

It was then I remembered Elmer. "Sir," I called after him. "Elmer said he still rides the trains."

The man whirled around nearly pulling poor Mrs. Jenkins's arm out of its socket. "What?" His voice rose and he was shaking a bit with the shock of this revelation.

"He said to tell you that, and that he's waiting for you to take over his shift. He also said that he's watching over Abraham. I mean Abe, though Abraham always corrects him. Elmer doesn't listen too well."

They came back to the bed, and I could see that he was crying now.

"Abe. No matter how many of us told Elmer to use the proper name, he always called him Abe." Then the elderly man gave a half grunt. "Nope, listening was not Elmer's strong suit."

"Oh, and that you were right. He gets paid by the head to get him the children."

"I knew it! That boy was evil. Didn't I tell you that pig face was as bad his father?"

She nodded at him.

"Pig man was eaten by the dragons in the wall." So

maybe I did sound crazy, but then my stepfather walked in, and I didn't want to talk anymore.

They asked more questions, but I was so mad at Melvin, I didn't answer anything. Reluctantly they left, but at least they knew that Abraham was safe with Elmer.

I felt hurt that Melvin wasn't taking me to his house and worse that he was sending me home right away, without even letting me see the new house. Oh, I remembered the old one…well, at least the smell of it. There was incense burning all the time, and it smelled like Christmas all year round. Cinnamon and cloves. So much so that, when Thanksgiving came, I never could tell if it was pumpkin pie I was sniffing or Daddy's funny Q-Tips that were so fragrant. There was something else that I had tucked in my mind's eye. It was the light that seemed to surround the home. Not always the people who came into it, but the structure itself was full of this pleasant glow. Okay, so I was also in shock, and maybe I wanted to remember that because sulking was so the rage at eleven years old.

The only good thing was that, as soon as my mom saw me, she hugged me and didn't want to let me out of her embrace. I stayed in it as long as I could, milking it for all the misery it seemed to cause my stepfather.

It might sound strange that I had no nightmares about the skeletons in the wall. I did have a lot of visitors that week. They were all dressed like Mary was. In fact, there were thirteen altogether. I was including Abraham, of course. He said that a nice lady named Sheila had gotten all of them a ticket on a train going to heaven. He was a little nervous because his mom and dad weren't going to be there, but Elmer said he was coming too. I told him I saw his parents, and they loved him. He cried, and so did I. I think it finally dawned on me that Abraham might be a little different. After all, he did walk through walls.

I tried to tell my mother about the kids in my room and the fact they came and went, not needing doors. She kept shushing me and counting the rosaries. The more I repeated my story, the more upset she was. Finally, Aunty Idey, who had come with her, told me that I had to stop. I liked Idey a lot. She listened to me and somehow made everything seem normal. I got the feeling my mom wasn't normal at all. I couldn't tell you why, but my eleven-year-old brain kept screaming it at me. Maybe that was why I tried to conform so much to her ideals.

My stepfather called all that week, but I refused to talk to him. I was still mad at him. It wasn't until Christmas that my mom and he cooked up a plan.

It was Christmas Eve. I didn't want to celebrate this year or even bother to help decorate the tree that my Aunt Idey had brought home. Idey had strung the cranberries herself as well as the popcorn. Half the strings she made were for us, and half were for her boyfriend's family, with whom she'd be spending most of the day. I thought we were bringing her down.

There was a knock on my bedroom door. Thinking it was my mom again making sure I was breathing, I yelled, "Come in."

There stood Melvin in a green silk jumpsuit and a red cape that was trimmed with white fur. He had on a long red hat with a silver and white pompom. He looked like the cat who ate the Christmas fruitcake.

"Well, Carrot Curls, Merry Christmas, and all that." My stepfather didn't celebrate the Christian holidays. He was a Wiccan, so I was surprised to see him in the Santa getup. I burst out laughing. My mother was standing behind him, and she started to laugh too.

"What? I'm in the spirit, aren't I?" We both shook our heads, but it was the perfect icebreaker. "Come on, I have you for Christmas Eve, my dear." He held out his hand to me, and I looked at it like it was a dead fish. "Come on. I have a very special gift for you."

I was eleven, so bribery still worked. I got up out of bed. I went with him past my mother and the naked tree. For a moment, I looked at them both, and I felt bad just leaving. He pulled my hand, led me through the front door, and then closed the door with just a wave of his hand.

We drove mostly in silence. He tried asking how I had been and how I felt. I had been asked a lot of questions by the many police officers that had been coming to my house, so I really didn't want to discuss anything with him. I also was afraid to talk about my other visitors. I wasn't sure he would even believe me. He seemed to sense that and didn't do any more talking for a while. I stared out the window as the neighborhood changed. We were in downtown Philadelphia, better known as Center City.

We headed to a back street and drove down a small cobblestone lane and eventually to the back of a brownstone. He pulled out a small remote, opening a hidden garage. We entered, and he clicked again to shut it. The place was immaculate and unused, no dirt, no lived-in feeling. We walked into a rec room filled with all sorts of pinball machines, video games that included Pacman, my favorite—another obvious bribe. In the middle of the room there was a television bigger then I had ever seen with a VCR attached and all! Okay, so bribery was working.

He saw my expression and was encouraged. We then went into a hallway with a set of stairs. Up we went to the dining room, a kitchen, and then into the living room. The floor was covered with a rose, cream and deep blue oriental carpet over polished wide boards. The couch and chairs upholstered in bright patterns. There was a fireplace, with a marble mantel. I could smell fresh paint on the walls. A fully decorated tree stood in the middle of the room with loads of presents waiting for some lucky child. I looked at him in shock.

"Your mother said you refused to decorate your own, so I had this one decorated just for you. Is it good enough?" His blue eyes lifted up as he smiled slyly.

Good? It was just what I always dreamed of. It was absolutely perfect!

"Come, we'll go upstairs and look at your room." I stared at him in disbelief. He shrugged. "You said you wanted a house, so I bought you one of your own. When I come into town, this is where we will stay, okay?"

He looked positively ecstatic, and I was too. Our own home? A house just for me? My room was pink, full of all the things a girl could want—a vanity with a triple mirror, a dresser, a thick carpet, bookshelves jammed with my favorite books—but all it did was make me think of Aunt Vienne. The bed, with its lacy white covering and lots of pillows, was even a queen bed.

"Where's Aunt Vienne?"

"She's back home."

I winced inside and tried not to think about the fact that I wasn't welcome there.

"It's just you and me this holiday, kiddo. Now, what does one do on Christmas Eve?"

We usually went to Mass, but I was sure that was out of the question for him. Some families also had a big Christmas dinner, but it was always just Mom and I. Then I realized Mom was all alone too.

"This is really nice of you, Daddy, but I think I need to go home."

"What? Why?" His face fell. He looked so disappointed, I thought he was going to cry.

"Mom is all alone for Christmas." He didn't seem to

get it. "I am the only one she has." I paused, looking regretfully around the room. "She celebrates the holiday. You don't, Daddy."

"What about if we all go out to dinner?" A smile crossed his face as the idea hit him.

"Really?"

He nodded and went to the hall where the phone was located.

"Meeloo, it's Circe. How are you?" The other seemed to answer something. "Well, give my best to Heelan, will you. Oh, she is there? Well, that is something special!" He listened for a moment. "Yes, of course, it's Christmas, and you would all be there. Do you have any empty tables?" He nodded a lot and then thanked him warmly. "Come on, kiddo, let's go pick up your mom. We have a dinner reservation at Meeloo's!"

I was so excited and didn't even think that it might not be a great idea to have them in the same restaurant, much less the same table. Still, I was so happy.

"Let's not call. Let's just surprise her."

Okay, I was eleven and didn't catch his hesitation.

It seemed like only took a blink to get home. With Melvin's abilities, it might have actually been a blink. Then again excitement could speed up memories.

We knocked, and Mom was surprised!

"Caroline, come join us for dinner and tomorrow for the first day of the holiday." She considered what he was saying. "Please," he added softly.

"I don't want to intrude on you and the girls."

"Vienne is still in Dodgersville." A wave of sadness crossed his features. I thought he missed her.

"That won't do, Melvin! Call her and have her join us tomorrow. Christmas is a family time. We can certainly let bygones be bygones for the holiday."

We went to dinner—with no incidents, I might add.

Mom and I went to church that night, and I prayed real hard that Christmas Day would be this peaceful too.

Vienne did come up the next day. I shared all my presents with everyone, and I could honestly say it was one of the best holidays that I ever had. That *we* ever had!

Even better than that was the house. That's how I ended up with a home for a Christmas gift that year.

CHAPTER 14

Present Day:

It should have occurred to me that something was amiss when everyone became absolutely silent on our approach to the Arestes' house. The fact that there was an eerie glow in the night sky three blocks before getting there also should have set off alarm bells, but I was still a bit doped up from the painkillers. As the silence thickened, the light grew until we pulled up in front of the once beautiful Tudor house.

Have you ever seen a sleigh with all of Santa's reindeer on a lawn? Or the angels heralding the child? Or a manger, life-sized, with all the characters? Or an assortment of Santas, lights, and flickering icicles? Imagine all of that, as well as trains, sleighs, Disney characters, Dora, Snoopy, and assorted humanoid Santas too. I also noticed a pen outside with a real live donkey.

I looked at my mother-in-law who just took my hand. "You like?" she asked. "We wanted to make it a real Christmas for you."

I just kept nodding, speechless, trying not to choke on my own saliva. "Yeah, it's great." I suppose we had to do our share for global warming.

Barney popped his head up and then went straight down. I heard a muffled cry from the box in Sophie's hands. "Geeesh!"

As we approached the front glass doors, I saw the most spectacular sight. Bright little lights twinkled through the frosted windows. It was just overwhelming, which is probably why I didn't notice the life-size mechanical Santa doing the jig right next to me on the front stoop. That was, until he knocked me with his hip.

I looked at him and jumped backward, bumping into Sophie and knocking poor Barney's box out of her hands, spilling him on the ground. He came tumbling out. Santa, the one next to me, peered for a moment and then smiled evilly. Its front tooth had a red spade bling on it. I had never seen such realistic teeth in a machine before. For that matter, I had never seen a red-haired Santa either. Phoebe quickly rescued Barney, but not before I saw the look pass between the red-bearded Santa and the nymph. This was not good, but I had no say in the whole affair. I was ushered in the door by a Greek mob.

Trains, fir garlands, stockings, and a massive pine tree greeted me. A wall covered in little twinkling bells of all colors that would make any discotheque owner envious gave us a tri-colored hello. It was strange how this glitz outdid the already loud furniture. The place was usually a palace of crushed red velvet chairs, purple carpeting, and green, gold-lined end tables that Alexi had picked up at a demolition site, much to Alicia's horror! The potted plants had been removed and placed probably in the basement to make sure that all the Christmas essentials could fit in.

The kids all piled in, each pointing out the ornaments they had carefully put on the gleaming structure. Every one of them telling me the whole story of why, how, and who picked what. Near Sophie's level, I spotted a green ball that had a picture in it. There were three people displayed within: a mother, a husband in uniform, and a child of about nine years. I thought that when the photo was snapped, I had received the worst possible news in my life.

I had just been told I had endometriosis and couldn't have any more kids. I was lucky to even have given birth to Sophie. I thought that was the most horrible day of my life. But that day wasn't the worst day. I looked at my handsome soldier standing there and made a conscious effort not to cry, knowing that my daughter was carefully watching me. She must have picked the ornament. Nobody else would have put it up, for fear of upsetting her.

Billy Squire's "Christmas Is The Time To Say 'I Love You'" came on the stereo. The kids began to clap and then hold hands and dance around the tree. I joined them. We all smiled and laughed. At that moment, my stepfather and Aunt Vienne arrived, and suddenly our circle was even larger. We really rocked the night away. It was a wonder that no neighbor called the police. Even poor Barney lifted his head up and smiled. Okay, maybe he was laughing at and not with us, but who cares?

We did attract some unwanted attention. I saw the shape of a red-suited man through the window. It was only for a short time, though, as a dark form also appeared and covered the portal, making the red suit quickly disappear.

"A watcher," I mumbled.

"Ignore him, Carrot Curls. It's Christmas, you know." Melvin grabbed my hand, and we went round and round. "Even creepy crawlies are entitled to some holiday fun."

CHAPTER 15

The morning dawned, and the pain in my shoulder was throbbing. I got out of bed to walk it off. I made a point not to take too many painkillers. They constipated me. Yes, I tried prunes, water, and I hated to mention what else. So, stooped over and congested, I went downstairs to try one more remedy. Coffee. No, not just any brew, my mother-in-law's special blend of stomach burner. This was stuff a spoon would melt in.

Standing by the pot was Santa. Not the red-haired guy with the teeth bling, but the real deal.

"Santa, how are you?"

He appraised me then he smiled. No, definitely no red spade.

"I heard I had an imposter outside."

Barney was sitting on the edge of the table. He shrugged.

"It isn't all bad," Santa said. "I also was informed a watcher is here, too." His white eyebrow rose, and he looked at me curiously.

"What is a watcher exactly?"

"A guardian of the doors."

I was confused. "What doors?"

"The division between here and there," he said.

"The Spirit World and the Earth?"

"Heavens, no. The Boss has other guardians up there."

He must have meant God and not Bruce Springsteen, but with the pain I was in, I had to think about that.

"He has other ones that are supposed to keep watch over the lower levels."

"There are levels?"

"Oh, yes, there are several levels. The one below this one is where the elves, imps, and Loci live."

Barney kicked his legs as he sat on the edge of the table. "Don't forget nymphs."

"And nymphs. The one below *that* is just noise, although it's rarely heard as these little guys make a lot of noise themselves."

"We like to party. It's not a crime."

Santa ho-ho-ho'ed, and I smiled at Barney. He was such a cutie.

"The third level down is kind of like Dante's description of the Inferno, but really it is just the mirror image of this world except with deamons." Again that word, the "ea" like in "spread."

"I heard that term from Nurse Kratchet in the hospital."

"More like Nurse the Hatchet," Barney grumbled.

Santa swatted his head, and the hat fell over his eyes. "Yes, she is one of the oldest of the lost ones. You should be more respectful of her, mister!" He looked sternly at the nymph, and the shrunken man looked even smaller now. "She probably was here in the time of Moses. She was kidnapped from her land and placed in a human child."

"Moses?"

"This is how it worked. Some hotshot who thought he was better than everybody else would use witchcraft to summon a Loci who was not exactly on the up and up. Then they would get in touch with a Redburn type, and a deal would be negotiated. In those days a goat could have sufficed as payment. A child was then found, and its neck was slit. The lifeblood would pour out and when the body was officially dead, but not yet cold, the Other, a deamon, would be pulled in and then incanted into the newly deceased body. They tried hard to get a young one, but sometimes they couldn't."

"Young what?"

"Young deamon. For some reason, they thought they could manipulate them better. The idea was to have the deamon do their bidding, so that they would not get punished for it. You know, if the deamon did it—whatever the bad deed was—then the mortal couldn't be prosecuted in whatever heavenly court they believed in. Their thinking was skewed because while sabotage, larceny, and murder are bad in general, the biggie is kidnapping. Kidnapping is considered murder, so just the act of taking the child from the other realm was enough to damn them. Of course, those types usually don't think before they do—they just do, and then they wonder why they are punished for their sins. " He scratched his white mane and smiled at me.

"She said my dad is one of them. An old one, I think she called him."

"Circe, yes, he is an old one. Don't look at me that way, Barney. I am not that old. I think he was pulled in in Roman times. Maybe a little before that. I was born actually a century after that, young man." He laughed again, and it was easy to smile with him. "Back to watchers, though. They are one kind of guardian of the below, but they aren't infallible. Sometimes the door opens up, and chaos just walks itself out." He looked thoughtfully at Barney. "About the time I got my current position, a door opened, and about five thousand elves just walked out. To say the human population wasn't all that welcoming of the little folk would have been an understatement. I, on the other hand, couldn't stomach the burnings and be-headings. I saw an opportunity, and I grabbed it. The problem was where to hide out with them. That was how I and my merry band of elves ended up at the ends of the Earth."

"Who are the other guardians?" I asked, trying to sort this all out.

Santa stroked his beard thoughtfully. "Nuns. Usually, they're in charge of the doors."

"Nuns?"

"You ever go to Catholic school?"

"Did I ever. Until I was fifteen years old."

"You remember the nuns?"

Yes, I did, and now that I thought about it, I under-stood why they were picked to guard the gates of hell. I thought of all the bad guys in the universe. "That could be dangerous, couldn't it?"

He shrugged. "They have AK-Forty-Sevens."

I wasn't surprised. I was sure Mother Antoinette, my fifth-grade math teacher, hid one under her desk.

"You ever hear that idea that Muslim jihad terrorists are rewarded forty virgins?"

I made the connection and laughed. "I'll bet those are not quite the virgins they envisioned!"

Santa chuckled.

"So a watcher isn't a bad guy?"

"No, but not really a good guy either. To define them in mortal terms is really not accurate."

"I have one watching me."

He cocked an eye at me.

"Nurse Kratchet chased him out of my room, but I think I picked him up when I was a kid. I remember him from something that happened long ago."

"Yes, you have one attached to you. That's true." It was said matter-of-factly, like everyone in the world had creepy attached to them.

We just stood there.

My stepfather sidled in. He was stick-thin and wearing a long white silk nightshirt. His long hair was loosely tied in a ponytail that flowed over his shoulders. Stray hairs covering parts of his tired visage made his face look even thinner. Wee Willie Winkie flashed through my mind, and I couldn't help smiling.

"Hi, Nick."

"Hello, Circe. You look like hell, pardon the pun."

He yucked it up, and my stepfather smiled at him. "I didn't sleep well and had a dickens of a time getting that police officer released without actually being associated with the incident." He turned to me and kissed my head like I was a child again. Well, I was his child and always would be. "Hello, Carrot Curls." He took a slurp of the black stuff my Greek half of the family actually dared to call coffee. "Oh, I forgot how Rydia likes this stuff." He cringed. Then he gulped another slug of it. He breathed in, coughed, and looked at us. "I was listening to Nick's explanation before I came in. I hope you understand that this information isn't for public consumption."

Santa wasn't fazed. He just shrugged at my stepfather. "You should have told her long ago, Circe. She's in a lot of trouble now," he said, calmly but firmly reproaching him.

I got the feeling they had discussed this before.

"Maybe, but she is not in much danger. Vienne spelled the door, and the watcher took care of Redburn.

He wouldn't even be here if it hadn't been for this sneaky little thief."

"Who you calling a thief?" Barney stood on the table and tried to stare him down. "I just borrowed a couple of things, that's all."

My stepdad, on the other hand, got this very scary look in his eyes. I thought I saw him double blink at him. Barney sat right down.

Santa shook his head. "Now, boys, it's Christmas—good will, peace on Earth, and all that great stuff. Barney is repenting and serving his time in this purgatory."

"Big time! I had to sleep with that little farting brat! He grabbed me right out of Phoebe's arms. Her, I could spend a lifetime with."

He'd have to fight with a lot of children and future boyfriends for that coveted spot.

Melvin put down the cup and went to the sink and got a cup of water. "Nick, do you think having the mouse in here with the cat roaming just outside is a good idea?"

"I put some snow charms out there for good measure. Redburn hates the cold, you know. He will think twice about crossing a guarded line. Vienne's incantations, my stuff, and a watcher—it's all good in here, I think." He got up looked out the window. "My ride is here." He looked back at me. "Please tell Sophie I am working real hard on her letter. You must stress that these things take time. Okay?" His eyes widened, and I realized I hadn't said a word to Sophie for fear of sounding stupid or just plain out of my mind.

I agreed. Santa touched the glass of the frosted window and then just disappeared. I blinked, but the other two seemed unfazed by it. Was I the only one seeing things?

"Have a seat, Carrot Curls." My stepfather pulled out a chair for me, and I sat. Then he scooped out a bit of

Rydia's concoction into my cup, and I took a gulp. It was awful, but I was desperate. I hadn't gone since I was shot!

"What are you, Daddy?"

"I am a deamon, sweetheart."

Yes, that I knew.

"I was pulled in many years ago by a powerful warlock. Unlike most of my counterparts, I was not a child. I was a young adult and what you would term a police officer. I was working on a kidnapping ring just like the one that got me. I was abducted, in order to prevent me from getting too close to catching the perpetrator." He looked at his water cup and drank. "I had a wife and a child. A little girl."

I felt instantly bad for him. No wonder he was so attached to me.

"Couldn't you just go back?"

"It wasn't so easy. They put me in the body of a baby under the age of six months. The mortality rate was high in those days, so this was a virtual death sentence, but the Boss had other ideas for me." He peered out of the same pane that Santa had just gone through. "My human mother was a good woman from a poor but wonderful family. I didn't remember anything from my previous life. Not the ceremony, the people, the pain. I was clueless for a long time about who or what I was. However, I had these dreams. I kept seeing this fiery land, dragons flying, and two little ones pulling at me. The voices were very high, another frequency, and another..." His voice got low. "My wife. I believe she had been calling for me the first few years. If it wasn't for her, I wouldn't know where I belonged at all."

"After all these years would she still be alive?" Barney was as moved as I was.

"No. One day an elderly female deamon came to me

in a dream. She was as beautiful as the day I met her. I was in my human form and she in her own form. She was fading, and I knew she was dying. I longed to hold her, but with the constraints of my current form, it was impossible." He sighed heavily. "She took my hands as if trying to tell me something. Then I turned into a deamon too. I held her for quite a while, and then she passed into the Light. When I woke, I was in my true form!"

"Are you a dragon, like I saw at the train station?"

"Something like that." He looked from side to side, and then he closed the kitchen door. In front of us, he morphed into an eight-foot, two-legged reptile, head like a serpent, two, small claw-like arms, and feet with jagged nails. His teeth were elongated, and his eyes a green gold, with two sets of lids. Barney jumped off the side of the table and onto the fridge, but I stood there. I had seen this before.

"Daddy, you are something to look at!" I marveled at his true form.

He then turned back into my stepfather in night clothes. Hardly impressive to those who didn't know him, but I did know him. He came to me and wrapped his arms around me. "And my mother? Is she one of you?"

"Now, that is a bit complicated, my love. You see at the ceremony there are always witches, warlocks, and innocents. Your mother was an innocent. She participated in the ceremony when she was just seven years old, so she had no knowledge of, or free choice about, what she was doing."

"That would make her real old, right?" Barney was back on the table again, kicking his little feet. "Practically ancient."

"I wouldn't say that in front of her if you like your current form as a nymph. You might find yourself in a pond slurping on bugs and croaking for a living. I dare

say, you wouldn't cause any more trouble for anyone."
He leaned in, and the nymph disappeared.

"Where is he?" I was concerned Dad had made him
vanish.

"Don't worry about nymphs. He's somewhere in the
house or in a cabinet listening in on us."

A door above us closed real fast, and I had to laugh,
even though my shoulder wasn't ready for it yet.

"Why is it important she was an innocent?"

"The only way for one of us to be returned is to find
all the people who brought us over. The Vatican helps
with this, as they consider the worlds mixing as an abom-
ination. In the Vatican basement is a dungeon where no
one is allowed. Languishing there are some of the most
powerful witches and warlocks. These people are all
waiting for their counterparts to be brought in, in order
for the poor victim to be able to go home. However, all
the participants in the ceremony must be found."

"It must be hard to find all the innocents if they were
as young as Mom was."

"Not really. They're the ones that we usually find
first because they can't understand why they have lived
so long. In a way, the nymph is correct. Your mom is
very old. She's waiting for me to find the rest of them so
we can return."

"And Aunt Vienne?"

"Also an innocent at my ceremony. They are really
cousins, both kidnapped. Their parents were murdered to
get them. Virgin status was highly prized in those days."

It's prized in these days.

"I've known your mother forever. We just didn't hit
it off. I kept tabs on her and Vienne. Our lives are a bit
complicated, you see. In order to flush out those who
committed the crime, we have had to infiltrate many covens. Both ladies are very adept in the arts."

"Any success?" *My mother adept in the arts? The arts of what?*

"We found about ninety percent of those who brought me over. About half of them were kidnapped children like your aunt and mother. Some others are down below in Rome." He closed his eyes for a moment. "Some really nasty folk, I might add, so getting information short of torture is nearly impossible. The priests do have their hands full!"

"Why?" *Priests have a secret dungeon under the Vatican? What do they tell their new candidates? 'Oh, by the way, you can't go downstairs, because there are villains that will turn you into mice, demons are real, and we are waiting for the rest of the baddies in order to send them back to hell together?'* Yeah, I wanted to become a priest now.

"Because of the evil magic that these folks do. Whatever incantations are put up to keep them in captivity, they will break eventually. If only they would put all that effort and brains into something constructive—well, 'what a world this could be.'"

He sang the last words, and I realized once again what a nice voice he had.

Paulo used to say the same thing: if the smart criminals would put even half as much effort into doing something positive instead of negative, we'd see master security systems all over the world instead of high-security prisons.

I was learning a lot about my stepfather today, not the least of which was that he was, at a rough estimate, about two thousand years old. "Was my dad also a deamon?"

"No, Carrot Curls, he was just plain folk. A really nice guy whom I was accidentally assigned to watch. It was a mix-up, but I have found there are no accidents in the world." He looked fondly at me and smiled. "He could see dead people too."

"Grandfather?" The kitchen door opened. There stood Sophie in her Minnie Mouse nightgown. "Hi, Mom."

He went over to her and gave her a big hug.

"No, the Boss makes no mistakes."

He let her go, and she looked at him as any pre-teen would after having been crushed in an old guy's embrace. "Have you seen my Barney?"

I pointed to the cabinet. She went there and reached in to get him.

"Except nymphs. I don't know what he was thinking when he created them!"

I did. He was thinking of my Sophie, who held him like a baby and smiled widely at him. Barney stuck his tongue out at my stepfather and Sophie giggled. "Isn't he adorable!" She was gone.

"Adorable?" my stepfather practically spat back at Barney.

CHAPTER 16

Breakfast went as usual in the Arestes house: complete chaos. Cereal, toast, coffee, eggs, and noise. It could make any non-Greek deaf, but my mom and dad didn't seem to mind at all. Vienne always cut out on this tradition, but she was not missed. Her siren effects seem to have no effect on the Arestes men. I liked that about this family. Both Paulos and Alicia's Lexi were completely unaffected by it. Even little Alexi paid her no mind. Vienne often reached out to hold him, but he blatantly ignored her. I think it hurt her feelings a bit, and I usually grabbed him and put him on her lap. This would only last about five minutes, but, hey, she was my step-mother, and I felt bad for her.

I understood her feeling about not fitting in. I was a geek as a girl. Long curly red hair, freckles, big thick glasses, and good grades. What a deadly combo, but add teacher's favorite to the list and, man, it was murder. So when Mom took me out of Catholic school and put me in public school, and the high school jock and quarterback needed extra tutoring in order to barely pass his finals, Mr. Lang assigned him to me.

My heart was pounding. I was sweating and having

an anxiety attack the day he came to my apartment to learn. My mother hovered over us, so I wasn't able to be alone with him.

I found out quite a bit about Ashton McGregor, the blond hunk with the light scar on his upper eyebrow and the black Camaro with a lightning rod on the side. He did a lot of talking about himself, his family's money, his talents, and so on. I thought he was the coolest guy ever. He didn't even seem to fall head over heels in love with Aunt Vienne when he met her the first time. That was usually what happened if I was talking to a guy and she sauntered up. Bye, bye, birdie.

When he asked me to the prom, I was flabbergasted. I didn't catch his smirk or the casual way he said he'd meet me here at the apartment so just buy a dress and be ready at five p.m. Oh and keep it hush-hush. I had been on very few dates and was clueless as to what proper protocol was. The fact that he canceled the last three study sessions with me didn't seem out of the ordinary. Nor did the fact, that I didn't hear from him after he asked me, faze me. My stepdad ordered a chauffeur and a limo to take us, and I even had tickets to an amusement park for that evening as was the custom in those days.

My stepfather had come in with Aunt Vienne. She and Mom worked together on me like a science project. I was standing there in a purple taffeta dress, a hairband to match it, and purple pumps. I was sweating and shaking so badly that I couldn't stand still. My mother looked worried for me, and my dad was positively beaming, Vienne offered a calming spell, but was quickly vetoed. She, in lieu of a magical whammy, had given me all sorts of pointers on how to knee a guy in strategic points if he got too frisky.

At five p.m., there was no Aston. At five-thirty, a police car pulled up with two police officers. One was the hunky dark-haired, dark-eyed Paulo, the other was a ball of vapor. At the time, I wondered why I could barely make him out. This was his partner. I didn't know that, at the moment, my already ruined day was getting worse. They asked us to move the limo from the no-standing zone. My stepfather explained that it was prom night.

"Yes, sir, we know that. It seems like all the city's teens are out, and most of them are driving." The other policeman finally materialized into a very tall and extremely skinny man, with thinning, wispy blond hair. There was still a strange white haze around him that made his form slightly fuzzy. Not in a bad way. In fact, the haze looked quite natural on him, if that was possible.

The darker, stouter, younger, and very handsome police officer came out with a book that looked suspiciously like one of those that you write tickets from. My stepfather was by his side and trying hard to explain how this would totally ruin my big day. Not to mention that the fact it was six p.m. and my date hadn't shown up yet.

"Fact is we just ticketed old man McGregor's kid." the light-haired one continued, seeming not to notice my sudden attention. "His hot rod was going fifty on a thirty-mile-per-hour street. Probably saved the hot mama he was with, but, man, was he angry. Spitting lightning and lava at us."

Hot mama?

"Pointing to the bolts on the side of his rod and all. Don't we know who he is? Uh, yeah!" The other one looked at his partner and shook his head. "Man, was she pretty, long red hair, long legs, a real siren if I ever saw one." Then he breathed in deeply and muttered dreamily, "Michelle."

"M—Michelle! My name isn't Michelle!" I stuttered.

"Yep, that was her name. Man, she was the cat's pajamas!"

What is that expression about anyway? Do cats really wear pajamas? Did I really care at that moment?

"Well, honey, if she ever dumps him, give her my number, will ya?"

Was he serious?

His partner called him over in a heated voice. "Allen, finish this, will you?" his rich voice commanded, and the cloud-covered man floated over to him. He handed him the black leather book with all the scary white papers in it.

Somebody else was out with my prom date. I felt so stupid. I just turned on my heel and walked into the building. Where I was going, I had no idea, but into its bowels, I plodded. I hit the aromatic smells of yesterday's meals and years' worth of rot as I entered the disposal area in all its glory: cement walls painted battleship gray, dirty cans, stacks of newspaper tied in bundles. There was an old green leather office chair with a ripped seat. I sat down and had myself a good cry.

"I'm sorry, miss."

I looked up through smudged makeup and runny eyeliner at him. His dark smooth skin and deep brown, sympathetic eyes bored into me as he handed me a tissue to wipe the snot running down my lips. It was Ronny, the garbage man. He was a nice old man that sort of lived down here. I was kind of on the lone wolf side, and I tended to hang out in odd places. I didn't mind the smell. He looked me over. "You look real pretty. You going somewhere?"

"I was supposed to go to the prom, but somebody snagged the guy," I groused to him.

"Why she do that?" he asked innocently as I let the tears fall freely down my cheeks.

"She's probably smarter, classier, richer, and much, much prettier than me, that's why!"

"No, not prettier," a quiet voice behind me said. "Not at all."

It was the other police officer. I whirled around to him. Now I was mortified. "You!"

"Who are you talking to?"

Oh, did I mention that Ronny was also kind of dead? He had died in a trash compactor accident in the forties, but he didn't want to give up his position to some upstart. Never mind that the upstart was now dead and in heaven himself! "Myself, as usual."

I heard Ronny laughing behind me. "Liar, liar, pants on fire."

The police officer looked over my shoulder and smiled. "I think I can handle it from here, sir."

He saw him? It was the first time I'd met anyone who could see Ronny besides me.

"Don't look so surprised. I have a little talent. Gives me an edge over the other guys."

"I suppose it would," I mumbled, relieved I didn't sound like a total raving lunatic. "I suppose you can interview the victim first thing then."

"Not really. Most murder victims are in the light already, and the others are in too much shock to answer questions or else are in plain denial. Those are the worst. They can get a little scary at times. I went back into traffic because the strain of the newly dead was getting to me."

Oh, so that's how he ended up with the fuzzball for a partner.

We heard a commotion coming from behind him. I knew that voice. It was Vienne's. I picked myself up and started to go deeper into the trash room.

"My, what a racket she's making."

It was Ronny again. I guess he figured since the policeman could see him he'd just come along for the ride!

We kept walking, and I still heard her. She could do that—make her voice carry. It was strange, because that voice always made men run back and drop at her feet, but the cop just kept following me.

"Look, you can't run away from your problems." The policeman stopped and me with him.

True.

I looked at Ronnie, and he nodded. Vienne stormed into the room. She was dressed in a long green dress that accentuated all her highlights. Her slim, curvy body was like something out of a movie magazine. Her high heels were gold with little bells that rang as she came in the room. She looked so beautiful, I burst out crying. Why couldn't I even look a little like that?

What was I thinking when I believed that the high school quarterback, the town's golden boy, would want to take me to the prom?

"We'll turn him into a toad!"

Her eyes were intense. I swear steam was coming out of her ears. I actually began to feel bad for Aston.

The wispy cop was floating right behind her. He was just behind her, because when she stopped, he slammed into her.

Once I stopped crying, I realized his cloudy tentacles were literally spun around my stepmother.

Paulo looked at it too. He turned to me and shrugged. We were so entrenched in our wonder that I hardly realized she was talking to me.

She was standing next to me now, and the scent of Bath & Body Works burnt vanilla made me cough. She put her arms around me. "He is a creep! I don't know, Terry Lou. We would be doing the world a real service in changing him into an amphibian!"

Was she being funny? Vienne?

"She is telling the truth," he whispered in my ear.

Boy, his breath smelled great. In fact, he looked good, too. "Hey, why don't I take you to the prom?"

Was this dark and handsome policeman propositioning me, on duty yet? I was shocked. Was this guy serious?

"Allen, will you take over my shift?"

I guess he was.

We turned again toward Allen, but he wasn't paying attention at all. His cloudy tentacles had encased my stepmother entirely now.

"Look at me, you!" Melvin commanded in a voice of authority. "You must control your mists. You are choking us all, will 'o the wisp. Cut it out, will you? And get your grubby vapors off my wife!"

We all began to choke, coughing and gasping for air. His partner looked at us all with confusion. My mother walked in and touched the cloudy strands. All of them dissipated. We all breathed a little easier.

Mom's eyes were watering, and I got the distinct impression she had been crying. "What are you doing here, and where is your swamp?"

"Okay, what?" Vienne said in surprise.

Was she totally clueless that she had just been wrangled? All eyes were on her. I thought she was rather enjoying the attention. Figured—my big drama spoiled by her.

Of course, I wanted to go with the cop who had introduced himself as Paulo. Yeah, he had my heart from the beginning. He took my hand, and I felt the tingles. You know—those shivers that were reserved only for the precious few.

"Are you actually allowed to go with me?" I asked him as surprised looks wished us well.

"Of course. It's my civic duty." He winked a sexy, long-lashed brown eye at me and gave me a toothy grin.

"You know, to serve and protect and all that."

"Oh, really?" I lifted up my face and saw his was shining.

"Definitely. Besides, it would be a waste to just leave that limo unattended."

He had a point. I went to the prom with him, and I never looked back. That was, until the day he was sent home from Afghanistan in a box. Then the party was really over.

CHAPTER 17

I was thinking about that when the door suddenly began to shake. We all just stared at it. No one moved. The banging stopped. Then started. Then stopped.

"I know you are in there!" Andy, the cop. "Come on! Open up, will you?" Bang! Bang!

"Shall we? Carrot Curls? You have to face him sometime," my stepfather encouraged me.

I stood up and walked toward the reverberating portal. It screamed at me to make him stop hurting it, pulled me near it for relief, and left me terrified to even touch it. Next to the door appeared my friend Terry, the murdered lady, as well as Ned. They both beckoned me to open it. Another pound, and I became concerned the door would splinter. Terry shrugged and stuck out her tongue in a silent raspberry. Yeah, I agreed, but it wasn't my door.

I pulled it open, and there stood Andy in yesterday's outfit and a unique smell all his own. His hair was sticking up at odd angles. He sort of resembled Barney after Santa had shaken him. Maybe that was why I felt bad for him. The room quickly emptied out. Maybe Body Works should bottle it, calling something like Repulse Aude Andy. My eyes had started watering, but I was stuck in the room with him and, at that moment, I resented my family horribly for being able to leave.

He looked wildly around the room. "Do you see him?"

"Thank you, I feel much better." He just grimaced at me. "And how are you, Police Officer Andy?"

"Good? I think."

Did I surprise him? Not the immovable Andrew D'Souza?

"How are you?" he mumbled, looking at his shoes.

"Fine."

Civility. So there was a human being in there.

"Well, yes or no? Is Ned here? I need to talk to him."

Somewhere deep down, I supposed. "Yes, he's here."

He started to pace. "I knew it! I knew you wouldn't desert me, buddy. So tell me, where are they?"

He seemed desperate, so I turned to Ned who just shrugged.

"He's shrugging. Does that mean something to you?"

He looked expectantly at me. "No."

"Now he is shaking, er, vibrating, spinning around."

He was agitated.

Then it hit me. "Look, you need to give him some time. Paulo told me the newly dead, especially the murdered, are not able to communicate right away. They're a little anxious."

"Great. Just great. I just got suspended, I'm accused of hindering an investigation, as well as being partly the cause of his death, and Ned's got an anxiety issue. Well, let me tell you, Ned old boy, I am anxious too!" He was shouting at the wall.

Barney had appeared and was kicking his little feet, watching him—quite entertained, I might add.

I looked at the lady in the ruined dress. She seemed

only too willing to spill the beans. "We can try to ask Terry."

He looked at me blankly. "Terry? Who's Terry?"

"The dead lady whose passport and birth certificate I found."

"Oh, her—the one that got my partner killed, aye! Is she here too?"

Terry looked at him and made a distinctly negative sound like '*Hmph*' or something like that. Then she disappeared. Ned shook his head sadly and disappeared too.

"You really should watch your temper. Both of your sources of information just left the room. Oh, and you better apologize to Terry." Frankly, I wanted to leave too. "Remember, you can't see them, but they can see you."

He put his hands on his hips and crinkled his nose at me. Like he had a right to do that. Then shook his head, a distinct *no way*.

At that moment, Vienne walked in the room. Her long legs were encased in black silk pants, she wore heels I'd fall on my tooty patooty if I wore and an emerald green sweater that clung to her perfect body. She zeroed in on Andy. She didn't seem affected by his aroma. Amazing. Maybe she had an automatic air freshener in her perfect nose.

"Vienne, my um…" Well, as much I liked her and all her wackiness, I was always stumped as to what to call her. "Aunt Vienne, Andy, aka Officer D'Souza."

I was resigned to my fate.

"She's your *aunt*?"

Why did they say it like that? Really? We both had red hair! Yeah, so nothing else even resembled each other—is that such a big deal!

"Hi." She smiled brightly at him, and I moseyed out of the room, defeated.

I was attracted to the guy, even stinky as he was, and

the truth was he was totally hot. And he did inquire about my health, sort of. Okay, right now maybe I needed fresh air too. Besides, I was invisible when Vienne was around.

I went into the kitchen, which was quiet, the aroma of Rydia's coffee still permeating the air. I watched the sun stream into the room. For a moment, I just looked at the rays and the dust that was floating in the light.

"Excuse me?"

I smelled him before I saw him.

"Don't ever leave me in a room alone with her!" he commanded. He looked particularly out of sorts.

"Why? Are you afraid of her?" I was amused at this thought.

"Yeah. She's like one of those sirens in the sea that bewitch a man and then drown him in the deep for fun."

He did look scared. This was funny.

"She is one, in fact. But she's married to my stepfather, and she didn't kill him," I told him defensively.

"Oh, lucky man to have gotten out before the deed was done. I met your stepdad, and he is kind of scary too, you know." Then he breathed in the scent of coffee too. "In a weird kind of way."

"He married her because he loves her." Why was I defending her? I wondered. Maybe just to annoy Andy.

"Why?" His voice was incredulous. Andy must have seen the look in my eye and changed gears. "What does your husband do?"

"He was a policeman," I said it as if he was alive and doing something else.

"What's he do now? Security?" This he said just a bit disdainfully.

"No, he went to Afghanistan." *Back at you.* I looked away from him. Maybe he'd leave. I couldn't help him, and he really needed a shower.

"How long ago did he die?"

I actually heard compassion. This was new. I was shocked. I hadn't said he was dead. Just a moment before Andy had been sure he was alive. "Almost two years ago."

One miserable day in January, his body was shipped back. There were no crowds at the airport. There was an honor guard, the formality. The solemnness that a fallen hero should bring was there, and, really, that was enough. Oh, and us wet and cold family members who had prayed so hard for his safe return. He did return, and the plane hadn't crashed. However, my life had. "He was killed in a Christmas raid."

I hadn't told Sophie this. She still thought he died in January. Why ruin Christmas for the kid?

"My dad died around Easter. I've never celebrated it again with a full heart." I turned toward him. He sighed. "He was a vet too. The Gulf War, but it wasn't the war. It was a car accident years later."

Were we communicating civilly?

"That war was talked about," I said fiercely. He eyed me strangely. I shook my head, "The media keeps mum about this one. It's as if there is no war at all. I guess if they don't publicize it, it doesn't exist?"

"What do you mean?"

"That Americans aren't dying. That thousands aren't being left disabled, without limbs, with PTSD." He stared at me blankly. "Post-traumatic syndrome, suicidal," I continued. "And what about us widows—are we invisible to them too?"

My heart was beating fast. I would never get over the disregard most people had for veterans. Yeah, sure, they said, "I support our troops," but it was all talk. Mostly.

He looked thoughtful. "Yeah, well, the media has a lot of power, so there must be someone really big putting the kibosh on advertising there's a war going on."

I heard all sorts of things. I had heard that the media didn't mind keeping it in the news when George Bush was in office because it looked bad for him to have a war going on. I had also heard that they distinctly didn't want it advertised during the Obama administration because it looked better if there wasn't any war at all. Now with the war between Fox News and the Obama administration, maybe there would be a sudden interest in the war on terrorism. Perhaps.

"Do you want to go out with me one night?"

In my reverie, I wasn't sure I heard him clearly, so I just stared at him.

"Tomorrow night, maybe?"

Did he just ask me on a date? This was a first. Well, except for Paulo. I looked at this hot guy who desperately needed to shower, have a personality implant, and human out a bit.

"How about tomorrow at six p.m.?"

Tomorrow? Did he say "tomorrow"? I heard the words, and all I did was nod. What was I thinking? He got up, and he and his scent started to walk away.

"Can I ask you a favor, please?"

He turned back toward me.

"Can you please take a shower before tomorrow night?"

Okay, so I wasn't totally out of my mind.

CHAPTER 18

The chair turned and voila! The person facing me wasn't me. As I looked in the mirror, I realized it had been a mistake to let three Greek women work their beauty arts on me. My hair was teased to such a point that an alien might recognize me as a kinswoman. Alysia had put on the bright red lipstick—making my mouth significantly bigger than it actually was—Rydia had added ferocious streaks of scarlet rouge on my cheeks and Sophie had decorated my eyes with splashes of sparkly blue and green. I looked like the stickers the kids got on their papers: big happy clown faces stuck on a balloon. It was grotesque, but all I could say was, "Great job!" Positive reinforcement, right?

The doorbell rang. All four of us looked at me then at the stairwell below us. I got up and bravely kissed all of them, holding onto my composure with difficulty. Sophie looked at me with apprehension, but I smiled as she gave her half grin back at me. I then hugged her closer. She stiffened—what else was new?

I went down the stairs, wobbling all the way, and there in the doorway stood Andy. He was wearing a T-shirt with a picture of Mick Jagger on it and a pair of

jeans. His feet were adorned with sneakers. Somehow I
didn't think this matched my family's expectations. They
all stared at him with daggers in their eyes. Stabbing at
him hard. Then they looked at me with pity.

I was wearing a blue silk dress, high heels, and
stockings. I hated stockings! I already resented this guy.
It wasn't fair that he would be much more comfortable
than me. Whine, whine, whine. Yeah, well, a good kvetch
is therapeutic sometimes. Still, it did seem he looked
good in everything he wore. I hobbled over to him as he
looked oddly at me. We proceeded out of the house with
all eyes on us. We were heading to a beat-up Chevy
pickup.

Now, I don't know if you can understand this or not,
but I was in heels, a dress, and did I mention stockings?
Also, I am only five feet tall. So this was going to be a
real challenge. We got to the end of the drive, and he
went right to the driver's side and got in. Then, to my
horror, he started to rev the engine. I looked at the street
and then up to the step. First, I lifted a leg and heard a
slight…well, rip. Then I grabbed the seat and pulled myself—belly up—and slid straight into his leg. He looked
down at me and then at his newly decorated pants. Okay,
the makeup was not pant-leg proof.

Red lipstick, the new "in." Red looked good with
blue, really. I smiled weakly as he straightened me out.
My dress slid up my thighs and headed to territories not
yet ready to be explored. I quickly picked my butt up and
promptly hit my poofed red hair on the top of the cab. I
should mention that the roof fabric of this particular vehicle was ripped and had white fluff sticking out of it. I am
not sure if you are aware of this, but Greeks use a lot of
hairspray, and I, the little white implant, was subject to
all their rules and regulations. I was afraid to move the
entire time and barely talked because I was busy praying

to any god who would listen that none of the fluffy white stuff was going to stick to my hair. It did, of course. I hadn't prayed for a long time, and no one was listening.

I didn't have to worry about where we were going. When I exited the truck, my hair adorned with fuzz, my stockings ripped and only half my lipstick on, I fit right into Dannie's Pizza and Grub. The place was a dive. The lights were dim, it smelled like old grease, the tables didn't match, and there wasn't a surface that didn't have a sticky substance glistening on it. Yep, I matched the décor real well.

A large man with a white apron and slick, black greased hair came toward us. I can't explain it, but just looking at this guy, I knew we had a problem. A queasy feeling rose in my stomach. Maybe it was his empty dark eyes or the hairs growing out of his bulbous nose. I asked for the bathroom. He licked his lips and pointed to his right with a half a thumb.

I walked in the direction he indicated, trying not to stare at his missing appendage. A faded silhouette of a woman in an old-fashioned hat with a feather announced the ladies room. I pushed open the door, only to find a more depressing scene than the dining area, and one that smelled worse too. Going over to a paint-streaked mirror above a stained and dirty sink, with liquid soap leaking out of a dispenser and making a yellow scum on the wall, I ventured to look at my reflection. I began to chastise myself out loud. Don't tell me you haven't ever done this. I know every woman on a bad date has.

"Look at you, all dressed up," I said, picking out white pieces of cotton from my hair. "Stupid, that's what you are. Did you think that if you dressed up, you wouldn't look like yourself?" A rogue tear started down my cheek. "No, you don't!" I looked fiercely at myself and then realized that with this Bozo face, I didn't even resemble me. It took me almost fifteen minutes to wash off the outer layer the Arestes women had painted on. As I scrubbed, I was surprised to see a thin elderly lady with white hair standing off to one side, smiling at me.

"It took so long to really be myself after my husband died," she said. "I mean, I was so used to Harold that it didn't occur to me that other men were different, but, of course, they are."

She began to wring her hands, and I felt sad for her, but I totally understood what she was saying.

"My husband died two years ago, and this is my first date since then," I said. "I'm not sure I really know how it is to date at all." *I only went out because my husband had said, 'Move on.'*

"Your first date and he brought you here?" She gave a pleasant giggle. It made me smile too. "Don't worry, dearie, you'll be able to move on soon enough. Eventually, we all have to do it."

Then she looked at the wall behind me, and I saw it. I don't mean just that the tiles were different from the others on the wall. There was a spot that looked big enough to hide a body in. I say this because, as she walked toward it, I saw the back of her head was smashed in, and her brains were spilling out. There were rust-red stains on the back of her dress. I went to the first stall and puked what little I had eaten that day.

Afterward, I exited and headed toward the table where the little old lady was now standing. She was talking to Andy—rather, talking at him. He was pretending he didn't see her. As I approached, I heard her saying she needed help: her son was missing, and she couldn't find him.

"She needs your help," I told him, as if he didn't know this already.

"We're leaving." He stood up. "Now."

He took my hand and started to lead me to the door. The big man came out of the kitchen and watched our hasty exit with a sneer.

"She needs to just talk to you."

What was the big deal? This one was telling him who did it.

"I'm not staying here, and we're not helping anyone! I'm off duty."

I looked back and saw how she shrank at the sight of the greasy fellow. I could plainly see the terror on her face.

"He did it," I said through my gritted teeth.

We were rapidly approaching the truck.

"Don't care." He went around to the other side and left me standing there in the fumes as he started the truck. I climbed in a little more gracefully, trying hard to not bang my head on him again. He hauled out of there fast. We didn't talk for a few minutes until he pulled into the nearest spot, which turned out to be an all-night pharmacy parking lot. Then he turned toward me and just stared. "Did you do something in the bathroom to make yourself different?"

"I took off all the excess makeup. It kind of made me look like a clown," I said self-consciously.

"You sure did!" he said, laughing at me. "You look a whole lot better now."

"Take me home." I know, I know I said it about myself, but the last thing you wanted to hear on your first date in years was that you looked like a clown to him too. Couldn't the guy have just lied to me?

He looked at me and then at the steering wheel and sighed. Maybe he knew what he said was not the line of the century. Then, looking at his confusion, I thought maybe he hadn't figured it out. Maybe he was a little *slow*. I just wanted to go home.

We drove in a very uncomfortable silence to the house, which was ruining what was left of the ozone layer with its pumped-up lights. He pretended to be focused on the road. I had found a distraction of my own on the floor of the truck, and I pretended the splash of what resembled egg whites located on the side of my door, near my—oh just great—ripped pantyhose, as if this remotely interested me. Come to think of it, it did interest me. I was reminded of a Rorschach test I took as a kid and wondered what material this was made of, but as I followed the splash downward and saw lumps in it, I thought maybe I didn't want to know. Okay, great, someone had hurled all their cookies in here and hadn't bothered to clean it up yet. My luck was getting better and better. When we pulled up to the house, I was not only sad, but also nauseous again. I was so desperate to exit the vomitmobile, that I opened the door before he stopped moving.

"Will you wait until the vehicle comes to a complete stop?" my truck operator yelled at me.

Actually, I really couldn't. I already felt the tears rolling down my cheeks, and I needed to leave. This I definitely didn't want him to see. It was like the humiliation I felt when my date wanted to take someone else to the prom. I knew there wasn't any Prince Charming waiting for me in that house. The pretty structure that belonged to my husband's family only contained high expectations of this lousy evening.

As we parked, I gripped the partially open door. The handle came off in my hand, and I tumbled to the grass outside. I lay on the ground face down in the mud. One hand held the door handle, and another barely covered my rear end that was now sticking out of the hiked-up skirt. I tried with all my might to pull myself up, but as luck would have it, he came around to the other side to help me up. For a moment, we stared at each other. I could see the beginnings of a smile on his face. That was all I needed to propel myself the rest of the way on my own. I tossed the errant door handle at him. Sadly, he ducked. It missed. Then I ran for it.

I could hear his voice behind me. "I don't like dead people."

So, he sounded pathetic—what could I do? I wasn't in the mood to commiserate. "Leave me alone, will you?" I started to go around the back, hoping no one would be in the kitchen to see me in this state. "I am not dead, and I don't like you, Andy, the cop!"

I had made it almost to the door, when he put his hand on it and pushed it open for me.

To our surprise, there stood Sophie. She looked at me—muddy, ripped dress, missing a shoe. First with grave concern and then with Greek fire in those peepers, aimed not at me, at him. Oh boy, I didn't want to be around an angry Arestes woman.

I almost felt sorry for him, but I still went past her, up the back stairs to my small room, and had myself an old-fashioned cry.

CHAPTER 19

It might have been an hour, maybe more, but I had showered and scrubbed off the rest of the makeup. I was sitting with my hair wet, scraggly and clean, when a quiet knock came at the door. When I opened it, there stood a very concerned Sophie. A tear-stained face greeted her as she came over to the looking glass next to me. We stared at one another in the mirror and, for a moment that I will remember forever, she wrapped her thin arms around my tired body and hugged me.

Laying her head on my shoulder, she whispered in my ear, "Papa said you looked real *fine* tonight. Emphasis on the *fine*."

Paulo's and my joke from the day I came down in a slinky dress just for him, asked how I looked, and he made the mistake of saying I looked fine. I went back upstairs, defeated. He asked all his friends what he had said wrong. They all asked the same thing: "How exactly did you say the 'fine'? Was it like a not-paying-attention fine or a macho with emphasis and rhythm *fine*?" Since then, whenever I asked how I looked, he said with real pizzazz, "*Fine*." And that was just how Sophie had said it.

"Do you mean Grandpapa?" I was hoping that it was

my Paulo but, then again, I wasn't sure Sophie saw the dead too. It wasn't surprising, but this was the first I'd heard of it.

"No, Paulo Papa. He especially liked when you rolled out of the truck with the door handle in your hand, and your dress went up." She giggled. "Did it really go up, Mama?"

Could she see from the window? Then it occurred to me I had thrown the handle at him. Did she see that too? Then I saw she was smiling. A real smile—not the half ones she so often wore. I looked at her and admired her pretty face.

"He also said you should help the lady in the restaurant. She really needs you."

Now, that, she couldn't have seen, and I was sure Andy would not have said anything about it to anyone. She actually saw and heard Paulo.

"Do you see Papa a lot, baby?"

This was serious, and she knew it, so the smile was wiped away. I was sorry I had asked her that now.

She came round and sat on my lap. "Well, yes and no."

I saw and felt what a big girl she really was and just how skinny too. Both rear end bones were poking into my padded thighs.

"I prayed for him."

I peeked over her shoulder, and she looked very thoughtful.

"I kept praying, and I prayed hardest when we went to the cemetery." She pushed her hair out of her eyes. "Then he came to me. He comes mostly when I'm sad."

I couldn't believe it. I was sad too. He had been coming to her for a year, and me it took getting shot for him to finally pop up—and that that just to tell me, "Move on, baby."

"Do you see a lot of...ummmm..." This was new territory for me. I mean, most moms just have to have a few normal talks with their girls...you know what I mean...the period talk, the sex talk, and the where-to-kick-a-boy-when-he-gets-frisky talk. Okay, so Aunt Idey handled the kicking discussion. I was a bit too squeamish about those things. I was now embarking on the 'do you see spookies talk' and frankly finding it harder than any other I had encountered. "...ghosts, honey?"

"Yes, Mama, I see a lot of them. Papa says not to worry about them too much. Just tell them that, when I grow up, I will help them." She looked at me with her pretty, round face. Her widow's peak made her look all the more exotic. "I tell them to go into the light too. You know, like the little lady in the movie *Poltergeist*."

Oh, boy, I had forgotten I let her watch that campy movie!

"Do they?" Was that her talent?

"Some do. The Light is real pretty."

A dreamy look crossed her face, and I remembered the first time I encountered the Light. It was in a dream. My mommom lay dying in a hospital room. She had just been taken off a respirator and was so, so tired. I was at her feet when the Light came for her. I remember the most wonderful sensation coming over me. A chill that was not at all scary, but so comforting and loving.

"I love the feeling when it comes. Sometimes, I just want to jump right in there with them."

I got scared, real scared. I didn't want to lose her too. I wrapped my arms around her tight. To my relief, she didn't stiffen this time. I thought of Paulo, on the other side, waiting. "Don't go in it!" I'd die if she did. "You have your whole life ahead of you, and they are done with theirs."

She nodded solemnly.

I knew she was too sensible to just jump in there. That would be a more of a me thing to do. "Be careful of the ones that smell." It occurred to me that some of them might not be wholesome.

"You mean the ones that kind of smell like rotten eggs and farts?"

Yeah, that would be an adequate description of the ones to avoid. I nodded at her.

"You don't need to worry about that. Papa told me about them. He said they are on their way to HE-double-hockey-sticks. There was only one, and I didn't even say hello to him."

She looked brave—even a smidge grown-up. Maybe seeing ghosts wasn't as bad for her as my mother would definitely think it was once she found out.

"Besides, Papa came to me and made him go away."

"I wish he would come to me sometimes." A tear threatened to come pouring out.

"He does, Mama, you just don't see him. He stands right next to you, just like he is now."

I looked to my side but saw no Paulo.

"I told him to show himself to you, but he said he's afraid to make you cry so he won't."

And just like that, I started to cry. She cried too, and we sat together for a few minutes.

"You see?" she finally got out between sobs.

I saw. "Thanks, Sophs, for being here. Tonight was a disaster."

She got up and came behind me again. I put my fingers through my wet hair and brushed it just like that, letting it air dry. I sprinkled her with a few leftover shower drops. She laughed again, a good sound.

"I think you should go out with him again." I turned the chair to face her. "I mean, he did say he was sorry." *He did?* "After I yelled at him of course." *She did?*

"You yelled at him?" Silent Sophie spoke to a stranger? No, she said she had yelled at him. "What did you say?"

"I told him he made you cry, and it wasn't nice to make my mother cry." She put her hands on her hips and looked at me. "He said he was sorry. He didn't know what he had said. I told him he called you a clown and gentlemen don't call ladies clowns."

Wow, she was good.

"Papa said Andy is a good person, but a bit of a dud when it comes to dating. He said he was all cop—before today, that is—but was going to change, sort of." Her lips curled a bit. "He called him a work-in-progress, kind of a fixer-upper."

Paulo was a police officer, too, but he was nothing like Andy. I didn't think this was a good enough reason to face the man again. Besides, I wasn't handy with a hammer, and Andy, the cop, looked like he needed a couple of bangs on the head.

"He said he had a bright white light, Mama, whatever that means." She shrugged. "Besides, Papa said he is a nice person, once you get to know him."

Who wanted to get to know him?

"The type to take the shirt off his back if you needed it."

Now that was getting a bit too graphic. Besides, Sophie was way too young to know about super studs taking off shirts. Was it hot in here or was that just me? "Did he now?"

So now Paulo was playing matchmaker from the far beyond. Boy, the man seemed to have a lot of time on his hands. Why wasn't he on the nearest cloud playing the harp or something?

"When he asks you again just say yes, will you?" she said seriously and then looked expectantly at the closed door. "Velma wants me to read her a story."

As the last word left her mouth, the door vibrated with hard knocks. My niece Velma had arrived. She unceremoniously opened the door. Privacy was not a highly valued commodity at the Arestes house.

"You coming, Sophs?" Her big eyes looked at Sophie then at me with concern. Somehow she knew when Sophie was upset and came to her aid.

Sophie got up lightly and almost seemed to float across the floor. She took her little cousin's hand and then flipped her long red hair at me.

"They don't play harps, Mama. Papa says they play cellos." She giggled and she was out of the room.

"Cellos, Paulo? You?" The image of short, stout Paulo with a big bad cello made me laugh. "So you saw my rear end, you fresh ghost."

"I miss you so much." A breath touched my ear and then nothing else.

"I miss you too, Paulo. I miss you too much."

I looked at the bed next to the vanity and climbed into it. Sleep came and with it came nothing else. I was very thankful for that, indeed!

CHAPTER 20

"Mama, get dressed." Sophie was holding a long skirt with a pretty shirt in her hands.

I looked at it and then at her, confused. Why was she holding this nice outfit for me? Then she darted back out the door. I heard Velma giggling out there, too. What were they laughing about? I swung my feet over the edge of the bed and looked at the clothes.

It was a long black gauzy skirt with a black lining. I touched it and it crinkled. The shirt was an off-white and slightly shiny. The stockings were only pulled in a few places; at least they didn't run when I put them on. She popped her head back in and then stuck in a pair of black pumps. I took them. I remembered these. The fake diamond accents on the side. I held them, and they sparkled in the sunlight. My honeymoon shoes. *Stop that—oh, I can't help it.*

After I finished dressing, I looked at myself and saw a different person than last night. I was happy to see her. She looked pretty good! I put my hair up in a bun with a few curls that seemed to not want to behave falling out. The makeup I chose was all neutrals, no Bozo the Clown today. When I opened the bedroom door, two faces looked at me. They giggled again at a private joke.

Surprisingly, I remembered how to walk in two-inch pumps without falling all the way down the stairs. But it's a good thing I was holding on to the railing because I might have slipped looking at the scene before me. There were bunches and bunches of roses: pinks, yellows, oranges, and even blues, but not a red one amongst them. In the middle of them was Andy down on one knee. He was dressed in a dark blue suit and had another bunch of roses in his hands that he promptly lifted up toward me.

Now picture this. There was this stud muffin in the middle of the living room surrounded by my mother-in-law, father-in-law, brother-in-law, sister-in-law, mother, stepfather, aunt, my two nieces, a nephew, and Sophie. Not to mention my grandmother, Ned, and the dead purse lady named Terry. This couldn't have been easy for him, but still, my first instinct was to head back up those stairs and slam the door shut. I must have looked it because my stepfather came forward and took my hand, leading me down the rest of the steps. He kissed me like a man giving away his daughter at her wedding.

"I am sorry about last night." Andy's voice was a bit shaky as he made to stand. Paulo Senior put his hand on his shoulder, and the man went back on one knee. Melvin left my side to add his own hand to the vacant shoulder. "Please go out to breakfast with me." Andy glanced at the two older faces behind him for approval. They both nodded at him. He got up and flashed a lopsided smile at me, shoving the flowers into my chest as he fell forward, off balance. I caught him, and he looked up at me as I held him. "Sorry. These are for you." He was blushing, but it looked nice on him. I set him on his feet and heard the peanut gallery snickering, so I relieved him of them. "And all these too." He waved a hand at the hundreds in the room.

I heard a voice whisper in my ear. "Go ahead, Eros, say yes. He can't help it if he isn't Greek."

I had to stifle a laugh at that. "Well, I suppose, since you went to all this trouble."

He was quick on the uptake. He took the flowers from my hands and tossed them at Sophie. She winked at him and gave him the thumbs up. He pulled me out the door, and I nearly balked until I saw a sleek dark blue Camaro parked outside the door. He brought me all the way up to the vehicle, unlocked it, and then, to my surprise, even opened the door. He waited until I was seated—both feet in the car I might add—to close the door. He came round and sat down. He was starting to breathe easy when the gang began filing out the front door to watch us leave. He put his foot on the gas pedal and pulled away from the curb, fast!

I smelled fear, and it didn't smell that bad on him really, better than the day he asked me out. It kind of smelled like Axe. He was almost on Interstate 95 when he stopped to breathe. He quickly pulled over to the curb right before its entrance. He turned toward me and just sat there, catching his breath.

"You look lovely, my dear."

Now I knew Lexi Senior had given him some lessons. This is what he always said when Alysia was really PO'd at him. Although he said it more smoothly and with a bit more humor than poor Andy, who kept looking behind us to see if the Greek police were following.

I, of course, started to laugh.

"You do! You look great!"

"That's more Andy, I think, than Lexi."

He smiled at this and relaxed a bit. "I'm so sorry about last night. I've got this thing about dead people with bloody heads and all that." Then he banged his head on the steering wheel. When he looked at me again, there was a red mark on his forehead; boy, that must have hurt. "I am not good with women." He blushed. You know, it looked kind of sweet on him. "I live with a permanent affliction of foot-in-mouth syndrome. I kind of don't date much." He stared out the front window. "I like you, and I really would like to get to know you. You seem like an interesting woman."

Interesting? I would have preferred nice, sweet, dear—interesting kind of sounded like a science project he needed to dissect. "Why did you become a police officer exactly?" I thought he must have known he had his ability before the job started.

"My dad was a cop, his dad was a cop, and so on." That seemed to be the playlist of police officers and firemen I knew. Paulo's dad was a cop, Paulo was a cop. Apparently, in Greece, there was a whole host of policemen connected to his family. "I stayed in traffic so I wouldn't have to deal with dead people, and I was successful at it until I met Ned. He was a magnet for dead people."

I had thought poor Ned came along with some dead people and a whole lot of talent too. "Oh, I see."

I didn't, but an uncomfortable silence had come between us now.

"You ever hear of the Moxi? Ned used to talk about it all the time."

I had and had thought it was out of business and up for demolition or something like that. Andy handed me a flier advertising a special on breakfast for police officers, SUD, and nannies. I read it again and saw the same words. To say this was an unusual combination would be an understatement! It was one day only, and the menu did look good. I liked food; what can I say? Poached eggs, pancakes, waffles à la mode, pecan pie...

Did it just say pecan pie? Okay, I was hooked. I loved that gooey concoction.

"SUD?"

"The Spooks and UFO division." For a moment he lifted his hands and wiggled his fingers, whistling *The Twilight Zone* theme.

"You've heard of them, huh? Ned was one of them, you know," I revealed to him.

"He was?" This was news to him.

"So was Terry."

"Terry?"

Why did he always forget her?

"The dead lady whose passport I found?" *Hello, Mr. Policeman*, I wanted to say, but I held my tongue.

"Oh, the broad who started this whole thing!"

Terry knocked his seat from the back. His body shoved forward, and his head hit the wheel lightly, again.

"Hey, cut it out, will you!" At first, he looked at me and then he realized it came from the back of the car. "Any of the kids back there?"

I looked and shook my head no.

"You sure? That little blondie, the one that has trouble written all over his forehead, was inspecting the car. Look on the floor, will you?"

I did, but all I saw were Terry and Ned. I knew who had kicked the seat. She apparently was as powerful as a ghost as she was as a person.

"No, and he isn't going to be trouble. Santa says he's age appropriate, that's all." For a Greek only son, anyway, but that would be a little too much information for Andy right now. "I guess he's on the higher end of normal, but he isn't on the bad list."

"Santa? As in Ho, ho, ho?"

I proceeded to tell him about my encounter with the Big Guy. Hey, my policy was to get it all out in the beginning. At least he would have a clear idea of who I was from the start. Or he might just have me committed, and I'd spend the rest of Christmas vacation in the psych ward.

For a moment I think he was considering calling me in, but then he just shrugged. "That was her, right? She punched my seat or kicked it?"

"Terry?"

"Yeah, whoever." Another shove of the seat. "Hey, I'm driving, lady!"

We were driving now. I was glad there was only light traffic, because we swerved into the other lane for a moment.

"Hmph!" Terry said.

"Okay, lady, I hear you."

Oh, this was the Andy I had grown to tolerate. We stopped suddenly at a looming gray structure in front of us. I say it was sudden because it was. One moment there was just street, and the next there was a building. He slammed on the brakes, and we just missed smashing into the big stone wall. "Geez, lady, you are a distraction!"

The seat flew forward again, and he quickly opened the door, literally flying out.

Ned was cracking up. He couldn't stop laughing. At first, Terry was pissed, but then she also began to smile. I just sat there, smiling at Andy. He misunderstood me, quickly ran over to my side, and opened the door. I was liking this version of Andy. If he'd only stay a while and visit.

The Moxi was a monstrosity of architecture. It could hardly be called a building or a hotel. It just *was.* The odd thing was I saw the hues right away. The pulsating oranges and whites mixed with little black spots as Andy took my hand and led me to the front door. Standing there, all dressed in white tuxedos, were two very large men. They didn't acknowledge us as we walked in. I did note that they didn't have any feet…well, let me amend that. They had two feet, just not two legs. It seemed that the pants were one long tube. In their hands were something you don't see every day, bows. As in bows and arrows. Oh, and bowties, too. Yeah, they were kind of geeky looking.

I was going to say something to Andy, who was walking a mile a minute, but the smells of eggs, bacon, and fresh baked goods wafted up into my nostrils, and I got distracted. So I got easily distracted by food. It wasn't a crime, you know.

In addition, there was this great music playing. It wasn't contemporary, more like Big Band, but what greeted my eyes as we walked in was what really stunned me.

The people were dressed in all sorts of period clothing. Some were wearing twenties flapper outfits and big feather headbands. There were nineteen-thirties beaded beauties, and the classic forties dresses that receptionists still wore today. There were hats with exotic bird feathers. The men wore suits, ties, suspenders, and caps of all shades.

The place was packed, and smoke was hanging in the air. There was something else there too, just a hint—it was an odd sulfur smell that I couldn't quite pin down—but I instantly suspected what it was. Andy looked around in wonder.

A waiter came over to us and smiled. He looked in a black, leather-bound book. "Andrew D'Souza?"

Andy looked curiously at the man. "I didn't make a reservation."

"Well, someone did. You are listed here, and I see the word 'guest.' That must be you, young lady?"

He was suave, that was for sure. I barely resembled a

young lady, especially compared to the ladies that were floating around here.

"Probably Lexi," I said over the music as another patron whispered something in the host's ear.

"Yeah, I did mention the brunch flier." Andy still looked unconvinced.

The man was back to paying us attention. "I see that there is a table open for two in the back. Follow me, please."

His pants had pleats, and he wore black patent leather shoes that clicked as he walked. His long tailcoat swished, and all who saw him nodded hello. I noticed some eyes straying to Andy. As we neared the back, we had to weave in and out of the dancers gyrating all over the room. There was a particularly drunk man who came swaggering toward us. He was wearing a black pinstripe suit and a fedora hat with a red and gray feather. His wide tie stuck out over his big belly.

"Yo, D'Souza! What're you doing here?" His speech was slurred, and his steps were getting faster.

He was barreling through people to get to Andy. He moved so fast that the two guards who had been standing at the door nearly didn't catch him before he arrived in Andy's face.

Andy turned around. "I am sorry, sir. Do I know you?"

The man stopped. As he did so, to my horror, the two men with the bows drew their arrows and aimed them at the drunk.

The tipsy man seemed to be considering Andy's question. He didn't even notice the weapons pointed at him. "No, you ain't him. No, you ain't Andrew D'Souza. You ain't got no scar down your face."

"Indeed, he is not Andrew Lionel D'Souza," a deep voice intoned.

We both turned to see a tall, nice-looking gentleman. He was in his fifties, if not older.

"Go back to your seat and have another drink. It's on me."

"Thanks, Doc. I much appreciate it!" The heavy man turned around and headed toward the bar.

Andy looked confused. "Andrew Lionel. That's my grandfather. Did he know him?"

"Pay no mind to him. He's a drunk. It's a permanent state of affairs with him, I'm afraid..." The soothing voice trailed off as he marched off back into the crowd.

A trumpet was blaring now, playing "The Chattanooga Choo Choo." Three pretty ladies were singing the melodies of yesteryear.

"Shall we?" the host asked us.

But we were enamored by the ladies on the stage, who were dressed in the most exquisite dresses.

"The Andrew sisters," he said. When we just smiled at him, he added, "On loan just for the day. It's Maxwell Sampler's birthday. He always liked them."

"The bootlegger?" Andy asked him.

"The same. His table is near yours." He pointed to a man in his forties sitting with two women who were almost perfect Marilyn Monroe lookalikes, except they weren't her.

"Boy, they like nostalgia around here, don't they?"

We caught up with the man, and he smiled benignly at us, pointing to the table. Andy went around and pulled out the seat for me. Lexi still had his pull, I saw. The man then lit the candle and handed us two plates. He motioned to a table on the other side of the room. Then he asked us what we wanted to drink. The music started, the dancing began again, and Mr. Sampler went over to one of the Marilyns and offered a hand. The other just sucked on her cigarette, and I noted she was older than the first one. It occurred to me that the young girl he was dancing with was his daughter and not just some young hussy. While she resembled her mother, she had the distinct features of her father as well.

"Happy birthday, Mr. Sampler," I offered.

He smiled and looked at me. He had a gap in his front teeth. The young woman looked too and offered a smile. The same gapped grin—yep, his daughter. Her blonde hair was bobbed, and she shook it to the beat of the music. I liked how it got messed up only to straighten itself with a simple touch of her finger. Ahh, the luck of the dead.

"Thank you, young lady." Then he turned to Andy. "Well, D'Souza, I am surprised to see you here. You were always such a straight ace, but you never know, huh?"

He walked off with the girl. Once he was out of sight, the other lady turned around.

"You are Andrew D'Souza's grandchild, right?" Her voice was husky, and she was the same age as the man. "He can't tell the difference. He lives in the yesterday. I remember when your dad was born. Your grandfather was so proud. He had pictures of him hanging up all over his office. I remember because I was so jealous of him."

She smiled a lopsided grin at us. A stroke maybe? I noticed there were three empty martini glasses standing in front of her. An old man in a tux came by and asked her to dance.

She accepted, but before she did, she turned to Andy one more time. "Maxie never hung up Annie's picture. Not until the accident and then the place became a shrine!"

And away she went.

"They really get into their characters, huh?" Andy turned to me. "Kooky. Real weird!"

He didn't get it. I knew already, but he was a denier. He still couldn't see the lights around them. They were all dead. Well, not all dead. The doc was alive, whoever he was. I had a suspicion, though. He had a certain savoir-faire—one that Melvin had as well—and he smelled of age. Oh, and the old man, whoever he was, dancing with Sampler's wife was alive too.

The doc was talking to a lot of the patrons, who were drinking, socializing, and dancing. Wow, could the man move! Andy had picked up his plate and motioned that I should do the same. I was praying the food was real and not just dust. Then again, when we arrived at the buffet, I was hoping it was dust that wouldn't stick to my ribs, especially the BBQ ribs. Oh, and the cakes—I was in deep trouble now! I hoped it was all air that only tasted like food.

Yikes, I was in real trouble here. I was sure I was Julia Child's twin in another life. I loved food. I loved to cook, to taste, and to experiment. I was lucky Paulo was so easygoing. He'd try anything once. I remembered when I was on this one-pot kick. I had bought a used crockpot at a yard sale and began to stew everything together. Even artichokes and chicken. Well, maybe that wasn't such a great idea, as poor Paulo had never eaten an artichoke and when I went into the kitchen, my husband took a leaf of a whole artichoke and proceeded to pop it in his mouth—spike and all. When I came out with a plate of bread, he told me these artichokes sure were chewy. Then he began to choke on it in earnest. I did the Heimlich and saved that handsome Greek, but that was the end of the crockpot, and I never got him to try another artichoke.

There were artichokes here too, fried in olive oil, and soufflés that practically floated off the plates. Well, that might have actually been happening, as they probably were spirits too. The mousse was fluffy. There was every kind of egg dish, thick fluffy pancakes, and buckets of ice cream in a dozen flavors. However, what got me was the pecan pie. Man, it looked like an old Southern grandma made it. Oh, oh, oh, did it look rich with syrup and pecans in every piece!

We filled our plates and tried to go back to our seats, but as we approached, we saw the two guardians breaking up a fight between the old man who had asked Max's wife to dance and Mr. Sampler himself.

"Cut it out, Maxie. All he did was ask me to dance!" the older Marilyn crooned a drunken slurred plea at him.

"You ain't supposed to dance with no one else but me!" He turned to the two guys with the arrows pointed straight at his chest. "Ain't that right, fellas?"

They didn't answer. They looked completely like statues.

"He's my husband, Maxie. I remarried, and I can dance with him if I want to. I am a big girl now." She blew out a stream of smoke from her cigarette holder. The other man seemed just as ready to defend his right to be with his own wife.

"A shoe salesman? Really? Could you find a mope more boring than that? When's the last time he took you dancing?" She didn't answer him. "I thought so. He probably can't afford this joint at all, right? Minimum wage doesn't cover the Moxi Hotel lobby fee, much less the actual meal! Loser! Now beat it, or I'll bust your face off!"

The host was there again, trying to calm things. "Now, now, Mr. Sampler, you know the rules. Birthday or not, there is no fighting here."

"Shut up, Giles. This is my day, and she ain't supposed to dance with no one else but me!"

Maxi got up, and his hand was poised to punch the

interloper when the first arrow was loosed. It was a shock, for sure. The man disappeared.

Well, let me clarify that. He turned into dots, mouth roaring with anger, and, where he once stood, was a scorch mark on the floor. Oh, and the smell of sulfur. Phew, it stunk, but old Giles was there with a spray bottle. It smelled good, whatever he sprayed, almost like heaven. Maybe it was the smell of Eden—the garden, I mean.

Crack! Andy dropped his plate. It broke in a few places, and all his food splattered on the floor. It was a good distraction, and we all looked at it. He, however, seemed unaware that syrup had spilled all over his well-tailored pants cuffs. Giles was very quick on his feet and had out the little sweeper with an enclosed trash bin, and soon all the glass was gone.

Andy began to babble. "He—he—just disappeared!"

I didn't have the heart to tell him the guy was dead anyway. I saw Maxie's daughter and wife looking at the scorch mark. I felt bad, at least for Annie. She looked devastated. Poor kid. She couldn't have been older than nineteen years old. Her mother, though, looked like the cat that ate the canary. I suspected what happened wasn't totally unexpected to her...or accidental. Either way, both ladies were served a glass of amber liquid, which I suspected might have been sherry. The shoe salesman sat down but refused the drink. He was alive and looking fondly at his wife. It was obvious he still was in love with her. She turned toward him and just as fondly touched his hand. She reached out to her daughter who sat ramrod still.

Did I see her flinch when her mother touched her? I thought instantly of Sophie, but I realized she knew what her mother had done. I felt even worse for her. Sophie knew I would never play games like that, I hoped.

"Giles, my good man, please refill Officer D'Souza's plate." It was the doctor again.

Giles went to fulfill his request with a nod.

"Officer, why don't you eat your meal and then adjourn to my table for dessert?" The doc had startling green eyes that resembled cat's eyes. His face was chiseled, and I could have sworn I had seen him before—perhaps in a history book somewhere. He looked at Annie and reached his hand out to her. She slowly reached for his, and they headed to the dance floor together.

Tommy Dorsey began playing the "Boogie Woogie" and, wow, did the two of them dance! He was just grooving and moving, and everyone's eyes were riveted on this amazing couple. \

Annie matched every step he did. They were such an inspiring pair that the whole dance floor opened up. I didn't notice, but Andy was looking at me.

"Do you get the feeling this place is kind of weird?" he said quietly in my ear.

"Don't you get it?" I had to look at him. "They're dead! The two who shot Mr. Sampler were angels—you know, Gabriel and company?"

His face clouded and he looked at the dance floor.

"Oh, except them." I pointed to the old man and then at the doctor. "They're alive."

They were talking together. The dance floor was slowly filling up so, I suspected in resignation, Andy took my hand and led me to onto it.

"I am not sure about the efficient Mr. Giles," I said. "He's not dead, but he isn't alive either. I think he's a Barney of some sort."

"Who do you think he is?"

He pulled me close to him. Now, let me tell you, Andy D'Souza was no slouch on the dance floor either. He swung me around, and I was so glad my stepfather had financed my dance lessons as a child.

Showgirls and pinstripes joined us in the crowded space, making comments like, "I had no idea a copper could dance like that."

They thought he was his grandfather. I was sure of it.

Andy seemed resigned to being there with the dead.

"You seem calmer. Is this okay with you?" I asked him as we danced cheek to cheek.

"My eyes are closed."

Oh, that was nice. I was busy having fantasies about him, and he was showing me the blind eye.

"I can't see the lights if they're closed. I don't even think this is real." He sighed, and the hot breath was nice as it caressed my ear. "I mean, I'll be asked by your brother-in law-how the date went, and what should I answer him? 'I was surrounded by dead people, a mobster celebrating his birthday was turned into ashes, the bouncers are angels who use bows and arrows, and our waiter isn't a waiter, he's a Barney'?" He looked at me with open eyes and a *fine* smile.

"He is a nymph."

He looked at me skeptically.

"The Elf on the Shelf is Santa's gift. He is our temporary Elf on the Shelf."

He rolled his eyes.

"It's his penance for causing me some trouble." And Ned, I thought, but didn't tell him, for fear he would ring poor Barney's neck.

"It's real," the doctor's low musical voice called above the music to him. "Lexi is a rational man, so he won't believe a word you say." Then the doctor danced his pretty partner away.

"Welcome, Andrew." A tall police officer with dark curly hair, olive skin, and a smile that could melt the heart of Genghis Khan arrived on the dance floor. I knew he was a policeman because he was wearing his freshly-pressed uniform. He had no partner and was, shall I say, dancing with himself. Everyone moved away from him as he gyrated and made a spectacle doing it. Annie seemed amused by him. She had stopped dancing with her partner and stood watching, smiling. I suspected she had somewhat of a crush on him.

"Hello, Yaniv, it's nice of you to join us." The doctor stood with his arms crossed as the band was playing "All Of Me."

The policeman's feet were moving, and his face was scrunched up in a strange expression. He kicked up his long appendages and took over the entire floor. It was rather comical, which I was beginning to think was the intention.

"Wow, this guy is nuts!" Andy took my hand as we headed back to our table, which had been cleared. He looked at the white tablecloth and frowned.

"I am sorry. Giles, please, can you refill Officer D'Souza's plate and Mrs. Arestes's plate as well? Bring them over to my table. I think we need to talk." The doctor walked away from us. "Now." And he was swallowed up by the crowd.

Two men, who very much resembled younger versions of Mark Twain and Benjamin Franklin, followed him.

"He's not dead." Andy was looking at the dance floor where the dark police officer was now dancing with Annie to "Chicago."

"No, but—" I saw something that I hadn't realized I'd always known. "They are old. These must be the lost ones Nurse Krachet talked about." It was then I recognized the doctor as one of the Minutemen who had ridden with Paul Revere. "Dr. Samuel Prescott." Or a darn close double of his.

"Why do you say that?"

"I saw him in the history books." Then I realized that wasn't the question he wanted to be answered. "Melvin has that same kind of age to him." Then it hit me Andy hadn't asked what an old one is. "You know about the trapped ones?"

"Every so often we have a call to some basement, and there are at least a dozen dead kids with their throats slit. These kids are usually ones who have never appeared on a milk carton, you know?" He stopped and looked at the empty table. "Ned told me how there are these crazy covens of witches that think they can pull up a demon and stick it in a kid's body and control it to do their will or something." His voice got real low and husky. "These kids, man, it's so pathetic. My first time I saw it was about eighteen years ago when we arrested two of these supposed witches. Total whack jobs, spilled the whole procedure out to us—would you believe one of the kids was their own?" His eyes were sad, and I could see he was truly upset about this. "I can't forget his face."

"Why would they kill their own child?"

"Immortality. They said if it went right, their child would live forever and, worse yet, so would they."

"Did the child live?" I felt a wave of nausea rising in my gut.

"No, he died—a little blue-eyed kid with curly blond hair, looked kind of like that cute little devil in your house. He was still breathing when we got to him, but he died in the hospital. Bled out onto the floor. They had cut an artery or something." He shook his head and turned in the direction the doctor had gone. "I wanted the death penalty, but some slick lawyer for the coven got them into the loony bin instead. They disappeared, somehow, a few weeks later."

"You ever see them again?"

"Yes, we found them—or what was left of them. There was a forest fire that July. It actually burned down very little of the park, which was probably not what the people who killed these two wanted. In the middle of the forest, where the fire was begun, were two very well-done corpses that had been tied to a stake. The police never formally identified them, their teeth were missing, but I knew who they were." He smiled a mean grin.

"How?"

"I saw them standing there staring at their bodies— or what was left. They had no teeth, and the tips of each finger were cut off and bleeding on the ground. To tell you the truth, that was one time I was glad to see the dead!"

Giles was back next to us with two full plates of food. He nodded his head at us and motioned that we should follow him.

He walked fast, his suit pants making a swishing sound as he maneuvered us through the crowd. People moved out of the way as he passed them. They were talking, drinking, and eating. We headed all the way to the back of the room where there was an opening in the wall. A red curtain hung there, held up by a red silk cord. A table covered by a white cloth was surrounded by an assortment of people.

"Andrew, please join us." The doctor motioned to two empty seats. Giles put the plates down and looked expectantly at the man. "That will be all, Giles. Andrew, Theresa, please."

He pointed. We entered.

CHAPTER 21

The table was in the back of the banquet hall. The door, if one could call it that, was really a deep red velvet curtain. It was held back by two thickly-corded ropes with heavy tassels hanging at the ends of each. There was a large wooden table that held an assortment of people, including the police officer named Yaniv, the dancing doctor and a few others. There also, much to my surprise, was Garrett Morgan, the inventor of the gas mask and the traffic light. Sitting to his right was the beautiful spy Nancy Wake, and beside her must have been her beloved husband, Captain Henry, who had been murdered protecting her from the Nazis.

"Do you know who that is?" I asked Andy as he scanned the table.

"Which one?"

"The lady in the small hat and dark suit."

"The one who looks like a stewardess?"

Well, I guess she kind of did look like one although she was hardly a stewardess. She was a famous resistance fighter and spy. She was on the Gestapo's top ten most wanted list. She was also a personal hero of mine. I had done a report on her. Melvin had helped me. Now, knowing what I knew, I guessed the information he provided was probably from personal knowledge. What had inspired me most about her was her sense of morality. In the thirties, she had arrived in Vienna only to witness a horrific scene of the Nazi rise to power. Jews were chained to massive wheels and were being whipped by their Gestapo persecutors. This was one of the reasons she had chosen to join the French resistance.

"Her name is Nancy Wake. She's called 'The White Mouse.' That's her husband, Captain Henry Fiocca."

"White what?"

"She was such a master of disguise in World War II that the Gestapo named her The White Mouse. They hated her and wanted her dead."

The doctor got up and motioned for us to sit next to the tall policeman. Next to him were two empty chairs.

"Ahhh, Andrew, Theresa, welcome. I am Dr. Samuel Prescott, but my friends call me Sam." The doctor extended his hand to Andy.

For a moment, Andy just looked at it.

"Come on, Andy boy, it's not polite to stare."

Ned. I'd lost track of him on our date. He had come with us, but then he disappeared into the crowd. To tell the truth, I was so preoccupied with the interesting happenings around me it never occurred to me to keep track of him or Terry. Andy reluctantly shook Sam's hand.

"Now, that wasn't so bad, was it?" Then his partner almost shoved the other man out of the way to give the younger man a great big hug.

Andrew D'Souza, hard as nails, crumpled in Ned's arms and cried. I knew there was a softer side to my date. I was secretly pleased to find it, but sad it had happened this way. The doctor took my hand and led me to one of the empty seats to let them sort things out. Next to me was Terry. She looked better here. She didn't have her injuries anymore, and she was wearing a blue-sequined dress that came to mid-thigh. The woman was brave. I would never show so much leg, and hers was twice the size of mine.

She saw me looking and smiled broadly at me. "I got it, I show it."

Well, my chair nearly tipped over backward. "You talk?"

"I can in here, honey. They got a special dispensation for us here and, man, the food is good." She dug into all the items at the buffet I had purposely avoided. "One of the benefits of being dead is not one bit of this changes this gorgeous body of mine."

I liked her. I had actually liked her the first time she kicked Andy's seat from the back of the car. I could see she was probably a hit with the men too. "I envy you. I just look at it, and suddenly I am wearing the extra pounds."

"Well, there is your problem. Every time I added a few to my body, I gave myself a free shopping day. I never wore the same dress twice to an event!" She shoved a forkful of pecan pie into her mouth, savoring every chew. "I miss eating the most. For skinny people, it's a survival skill, for me, it's just pure pleasure." She was pretty, and guys passing the open red curtain looked in at her. She picked up her head when a short African American man passed the curtain. "I arrested him two weeks before I died. He must be a new arrival." He waved to her, and she gritted her teeth. Then, with a speed that I would have thought impossible for her girth, she stood up and made a fist at him. He scrammed really fast. "Got to keep them in check, you know." She was back down to her chair and shoveling away. Another man took his place, and she gave him a brief wave. "Them I don't miss, honey. I could live my whole life without another one, but don't take away my chocolate mousse pie."

I really liked her now.

Andy and Ned were taking their seats. I could see the streaks and tear tracks on Andy's face. I felt bad for him. I knew that this wasn't going to be a permanent arrangement between him and Ned.

The doctor stood up. "Well, my friends," he started, "we have new arrivals and new faces to add to our numbers. We all know Ned and Terry from before." Faces turned to them, smiled and nodded. "Theresa over there is Paulo's wife." A few murmurs headed my way. "She has some talent herself."

Well, that was nice. I wasn't sure what he was talking about, but maybe seeing dead people was the "some talent."

"And there is Andrew's grandson, Andy."

The others smiled at Andy. It seemed they already knew us. Andy's eyes darkened a bit, and Ned patted his shoulder.

"Cool it, kid. They're the good guys," he said softly.

"Truth is, Officer D'Souza, we are the good guys. We belong to a unit called SUD, as did your great-grandfather. He was a friend of mine in Bulgaria." The doctor pulled out a black and white picture and passed it down to us.

There was the doctor, looking the same as now. Next to him was a heavier, older and mustached Andy. If this was what he would look like later—well, I could get accustomed to it. Minus the mustache, that was. I had never liked them. When Paulo had one, it tickled too much when I kissed him.

Ned looked amused and patted his extended belly in a tease. "I see you resemble him, Andy!"

"Yeah, well, my nona is a great cook!" Andy laughed, looking at the picture. "Dr. Prescott? That's your name, right? Or at least it is now."

"Yes, that is the name I have had these several years. I do like it a lot. It was my grandfather's, and I am very proud of our heritage."

"One of the Minutemen?" I added, a bit enamored.

"Along with a few other men, including Paul Revere."

"Why are we here, sir? I mean I don't mean to be rude, but how is it we came to be here? Is this like one of them dinner theaters?" Then Andy looked at Ned. "I mean is he—is this a parlor trick?" This idea seemed to worry him.

"No, this is a respite of four hours a week for the people who are beyond the red curtain there." He pointed his silk sleeve at the doorway. "In less than an hour, they will be returned from whence they came."

"And just where is that, sir?"

"Back to the inferno, my boy." When we both just stared at him, he added, "To Purgatory."

"You are kidding, right? They are let out of hell for four hours a week to scarf down food, drink, dance, laugh, and have a good time? I saw Harley the Hatchet in there—he killed fifty-three men."

"Fifty-seven men," Yaniv put in. "Two call girls, three cats, fifteen squirrels, and his mother," his heavily-accented voice added lightly. "Yes, yes, yes," he said in rapid succession.

Andy was incredulous. "Oh, that's even better. People are honest their whole lives, and these guys get to party four hours a week!"

"No, they only get four hours a week as well as Christmas and New Year's." Doc Prescott raised his eyebrows at the younger man, slightly amused. "A friend of mine once said, 'The only way to keep your health is to eat what you don't want, drink what you don't like, and do what you'd rather not.'" He waited a beat for Andy to calm down. "Benjamin Franklin, my boy, you have heard of him, right?" Andy still looked a bit star-struck. "Key? Electricity?" When he got no better response, Sam shrugged and added, "Except in Heaven, my boy. You eat what you never did, drink what you never would, and do what you wished you could, and the best thing is it can't kill you again!"

They all laughed at his wit. I was already enjoying myself here. Then, to our astonishment, in walked Benjamin Franklin himself.

"Oh," Andy said sheepishly. "Why are we here, though?"

"Where should you be?" the doctor asked him. "You no longer work for the police department after that little show you put on the other day for millions of viewers."

"I didn't punch him. I can't understand how it looked like I did." He did look confused.

"Redburn is good at that. He arranged it and had some poor nymphs do the deed. They are pranksters, good for mischief like this."

"Redburn?"

"He is a bad character. Somehow the door opened—" He passed a look over at me. "—and out he came. Ever since, he has been playing around with mankind, doing all sorts of things, not particularly good things either. It's a power play. He wants this world for himself." He said it low, almost in a growl. The others looked at him. "Never mind. The man, if he can be called that, is full of tricks and treachery. It is the way he was created."

"Tricks and Treachery are the practice of fools who don't have brains enough to be honest!" Benjamin Franklin put in. "Although some fools are brighter than others."

I had to agree with the man. I had already met Barney!

"The first order of business is to close the door he came through. Miss Wake, were you able to procure the map?"

She looked at her husband who picked up a leather briefcase and unzipped it. Out came a parchment that looked worn and old. They handed it to Dr. Prescott. He took it a look at it, and a dark expression crossed his face. "This is in the middle of Philadelphia, right here." The paper came down, and he pointed.

"Jeez, that's near the Constitution Center." Andy also peeked at it. "And here's the Mint across the road. What's this guy Redburn got in mind?"

"He wants to take over the world—what else would any self-respecting supervillain want?" The doctor waved a coifed hand at us.

Where was I, in a Marvel comic book or something?

"So the entrance is by the Mint. That just proves money is the root of all evil."

"Well, who killed Ned? Did this Redburn guy do it?"

They looked at Andy and then at Ned.

"In a way. He was a casualty of war, as was Terry. Ned and Terry had been working on this separately. Although I didn't want the ladies to be involved in this. War is no place for women."

"I hate wars, and I hate violence, but they come I don't see why we women should just wave our men a proud goodbye and then knit them balaclavas!" Miss Wake looked at her captain fondly, and he nodded proudly at her. "Besides, it's healthy to kick some butt sometimes."

I liked this lady. So did Terry, I could see. She had folded her arms and given her a resounding Amen!

"Mmmmhmmm!"

"Yes, but for some women, it isn't healthy," Miss Wake added.

We looked at Terry sideways.

"What? I'm not worried. Well, I wasn't worried. I mean now that I'm dead, I've got the best of both worlds. I don't gain any weight, and I can ride in as many taxis as I want, for free. Oh, and I can sleep with every man who turned me down and his woman won't know any better!"

Boy, that was a comforting thought. Dead Terry with some poor guy who thought he just had a draft going in his pants!

"Oh." It looked like Dr. Prescott wasn't all that enthralled with that thought either. "Then let's get to it, shall we. Terry, you had the passport. Do you still have it?"

"I'm dead, honey. I haven't got anything anymore. Last time I saw it was in the Goodwill when little Miss Fire Head ripped my pocketbook. A brand new one too!"

"The zipper jammed and I couldn't pull out the passport. Why is your passport so important anyway? And why were the tags still on the bag?"

"It isn't actually mine—I just put my picture on it. That's why I put the birth certificate in there too. It was a disguise, a cover story to put off them nymphs. You see I was snooping in some of Redburn's papers. In this house he kind of borrowed and when I saw he left the door open, after I stuck a hairpin in it, I kind of went in. That's where I saw the birth certificate."

We all stared as she related how she broke into a supervillain's house.

Cool!

"I saw it was marked. You know, as in I had a hit on me. I thought if I procured it, well, it couldn't actually occur. I guess I was wrong."

Yeah. You are dead, lady!

"They're clever in their tricks, but dumb as my brother Ronnie."

I looked at her, wondering what Ronnie did to make him dumber than poor Barney.

"He decided to rob a store and go down the chimney. Had to be rescued, dummy that he was. He dressed as Santa—pillows, shiny black boots, and a bag of presents. He got wedged into the chimney so tight the fire department had to rescue him."

"What gave him away that he just wasn't trying to give the owners some gifts?" I couldn't help myself.

"It was July. One hundred and four degrees and he was wearing velour. Oh, and his gifts included a rifle, pliers, and a book on how to deprogram alarms!" She rolled her pretty brown eyes.

We both laughed.

"Except when charms are involved. I didn't reckon on that little detail. These little guys will do almost anything for them! It's like a drug."

"The passport, ladies." Dr. Prescott didn't look amused. I wondered if I should tell him about my dream and where I thought it was. "We can't detain or arrest anyone without proof," he added.

Ned didn't volunteer anything either. It seemed he was keeping mum too. When I got a chance, I was going back to the Goodwill to take a peek under some fuzzy bunny PJ bottoms.

Then what? I wondered. *Should I turn it in to these people? Would I sound like a loon? Or was I sitting amongst people who belonged in the loony bin, along with me?*

"Mrs. Arestes?" The tall Greek police officer was staring at me, his chocolate eyes boring through me.

"Yes, sir?"

"Yaniv. I am Yaniv. You are thinking you may know where it is yes, yes, yes?" He was almost drilling a hole in my head. I almost said the words, "had a dream," but then my name wasn't Martin, so I stopped myself.

"I am thinking that it probably is in the van with the kids, er, nymphs," Andy interjected, delightfully unawares.

Well, it might be…

"It's not. Redburn has followed you everywhere. He is standing outside of your family's home. I assume he thinks you know where it is." Dr. Prescott did some boring of his own. "Or maybe you have it."

"I don't even know what it is, except what Barney told me—Barney is a nymph—and he needed it to prove Terry was dead so he could have some charms." *That he stole anyway*. I didn't mention that because these were the fairy police, and I suspected Barney would be in deep doo-doo if I did. They were giving me cop looks.

"Why did you take the purse, to begin with?"

"Because Terry was standing there and, well, I usually find things and return them to the family member. When I realized it was a passport, I knew I had to bring it to the police." I looked at Ned. "They were in the parking lot, right next to my car. I just moseyed over and well…" I trailed off.

It just occurred to me that Ned had been waiting for me. He looked at the table, but it seemed the doctor had the same idea. "Were you waiting for her, Ned?" his smooth voice intoned.

"Yes. I knew I had to be there."

Andy looked at him with a sudden realization. "You knew you were going to die that day. Why did you go there?" he asked his partner hotly.

"When it's your time, it's your time. No matter what, that was my day, Andy," he said softly and compassionately. "My family always knows their death days. None has escaped it yet, no matter how their wife, husband, or partners have tried." He looked earnestly at his partner. "I had to be there, kid. There is a reason for it. We just don't understand it, that's all."

"Andrew, there is a reason you are here too. You need to understand that this situation that the two of you got caught up in involves us all. I am offering you a chance to solve his murder and be reinstated as a police officer." The doc pulled out a contract and handed it to him. "Read it and then, if you wish, sign it."

We all watched intently as Andy began to read it.

"What am I, chopped liver?" Terry put in. "Isn't anyone going to investigate who killed me?"

Poor Terry. Until a few days ago no one even knew she was dead.

"Of course, my dear, that goes without saying," the doctor put in smoothly. "Let's close the door, catch the killer or killers, and then call it a night, shall we? Are you done reading, Andrew?"

I didn't think Andy had even looked at it. He just held it.

The others started asking questions. I wondered what two dead inventors, a dead writer, a deceased spy, and two departed cops could do. In fact, I wondered what my own little padded butt could add to this mix. What was I doing here, exactly? A few faces peered in from the door and were carefully ushered away by Giles, who then stepped in.

"Uh, sirs, it's just about time…"

A certain smell started to permeate the room. It was sulfur—the smell of the gates of hell opening. Giles dramatically pulled the red curtain shut. I noticed that Yaniv had pulled out a white handkerchief and was covering his nose. A crackling noise began, and the earth started to move beneath us.

Instinctively, I thought, Andy put his arm around me. I looked at him, but then the room was shaking, and a whole lot of screaming started. Ned and Terry looked terrified but didn't hold onto anything. It lasted a good five minutes. I noticed no one was near the red curtain, which was drawn shut. Giles was standing inside. Once the room stopped shaking, two large figures entered it. Their distinctive bows hung on their shoulders as they approached the doctor.

"Thank you, Gabriel, thank you, Uriel." The doctor nodded his head solemnly. "Done?"

They nodded back and turned to leave. That's when I saw them. Wings. They had wings!

"Geez, do you see them?" Andy whispered.

"Angels. Gabriel and Uriel are angels, Andy." I was so excited. I had just seen something incredible.

"Or fairy godmothers."

That was funny, and I nearly laughed out loud. Then it occurred to me that—in light of the fact that nymphs, partying dead gangsters, and Santa were real—there probably could be a fairy godmother or two hanging around somewhere, and I didn't want to piss her off. After all, I needed all the help I could get.

"Okay, now that all the children have been safely returned to hell and have been locked within, we need to shut our own little back door." They discussed logistics, Miss Wade and the captain were off to the Mint, looking into the alarm system, and the inventor Garrett Morgan awaited his orders. "Garrett, were you able to make the device to close it?"

The old African American inventor bowed his head. He looked under the table and reached, pulling a package out. It was wrapped in brown paper and string.

"I have it here. If we can reach the doorway and find the passport, I'll be able to place it where it has to go. Then it will detonate, and we can close it once and for all." He slowly opened it. It looked like a clock. It was

shaped in a golden arc, suspended by a wire. He placed it
gently on the table, and the little clock shook back and
forth. We all stared at it. "We need to attach it to the handle. That's why I have it open here." He put his wrinkled
finger in the arc. I could see it would hold a doorknob
between the sides. "It will blow it shut, but we need to
make sure we get all of them back within its beams."

"Well, Andrew?"

Back to Andy. The poor guy hadn't even looked at
the papers in his hand.

"I'm in. I'll help you get this guy Redburn and find
who killed Ned." Then Andy looked at Terry. "And you
too, miss. Then I am retiring." There was a soft murmur.

Yaniv got up and smiled at them. "Good. He will
work with me, yes, yes, yes."

"I work with Ned and Ned alone."

Uh-oh, Andy had an ace up his sleeve. He wasn't officially joining, so I gathered he thought he could call his
own shots.

"And Ned too! I like him well enough." Yaniv was
not one to be hindered.

Andy was about to protest when Ned put a hand on
his lips. "Isn't worth it, kid. He will be coming with us
anyway. He's like a dog who gets a bone and won't share
it unless he can lick it too."

This amused Yaniv and he began to laugh then lick
an imaginary bone. "Fine!" He was back to his pleasant
self.

"Hey, what about chopped liver over here?" Terry
stood up, but her dress didn't follow suit. I swear all the
men's tongues were lying on the table. I wasn't sure if the
show was intentional or not, but she got a lot of offers.
Both Garrett and the Doc, looking like the wolf that ate
Peter Rabbit, got her in the end.

"Now that we have settled into who is with whom

and have our assignments, let's finish our desserts and then head out." The doctor started to poke at his pecan pie then stopped as all eyes seem to settle on me. "She's off limits."

Yaniv looked at me curiously. "Off limits? The orders are from whom?"

"Circe." It was low and almost a growl.

Yaniv sat down. For the first time, he stopped smiling.

To say the mood was dampened by my stepfather's name would be an understatement! I was sort of curious as to how he carried so much weight and, even more so, why there seemed to be so much resentment.

CHAPTER 22

We finished eating and were led out through the red curtain. Now, I don't know how to say this, but there was nothing in the room. No people, no tables, no bands. Everything was gone except a big scorch mark in the middle of the room where Max Sampler had been shot. Annie stood there staring down at it sadly.

"Don't walk right on it, it's still hot," Giles intoned.

"What are you?" Andy demanded, demonstrating his ever-gracious manners.

I guessed he was still annoyed at being railroaded into being with Yaniv positive Polly.

The tall man smiled at him broadly. "I am an elf." He pushed aside his hair that went down to his shoulder blades. There was a pointed ear.

"Oh. You live here, or…"

"I live on the next level, but I also work for SUD when our interests align." He then turned to me. "Please, my lady, will you give my warmest regards to your father, Melvin?"

I nodded as we came to the rim of the big, black, smoldering spot.

"Can we fall through it?" Yes, I have a morbid sense of curiosity.

"You? Oh no, the living can't fall through it, but sometimes the dead can if they are on a reprieve."

"Reprieve?"

"Well, if they are doing community service. SUD utilizes a variety of talents. I worked with your great-grandfather, by the way, Detective D'Souza. He was very talented as well."

"He wasn't on a reprieve!" It was a challenge as everything with Andy was. Giles looked amused.

"No, no, he wasn't. You are so much like him, you know." He put his long fingers together and tapped them gently. "It's very interesting, your genetics. We don't procreate—well, barely. If we do, it's usually as a result of a mixed marriage with a mortal. Or if there are mortals in both partners' heritages."

"Well, that's genetics, isn't it?" I asked him.

He raised an eyebrow at me and nodded. "I suppose it is. Yes, I suppose you are correct."

"Why the waiter's getup?" Andy was all cop.

"It's easier to ease drop in this getup, as the client says." He mimicked a Max Sampler accent. I laughed. He winked at me. "I get lots of scoops this way. Most of it not at all useful, as they have been dead for years, but on occasion…"

I think I started to blush. It'd been a long time since a guy made eyes at me. Okay, so he wasn't a guy, but he was male. I think. Were elves male and female?

Andy put his hand in mine and gave one of those "she's mine" glares and, for the first time, I realized that he perhaps actually felt that way. Then again, it seemed Andy glared a lot at everyone and everything.

"Yes, so much like your grandfather. His taste in women was impeccable too. I was dazzled by your grandmother. She is *très magnifique!*" He kissed the air and moved gracefully away from us. "Goodnight, Andrew."

"I'm Andy, not Andrew. That was his name." A questioning look came his way and another grin. "You hear how he talked about my nona?" Andy took a breath. "In French!"

"It was a compliment, Andy."

"She's my grandmother, and they aren't *trey* anything! They're just…old!" His face was red.

"Is she still alive, Andy?" I realized I knew nothing about him or his family.

"Nona? Yeah, she's still here. I, um, live with her."

We were walking toward the exit, or where he guessed it was.

"Really? You live with your grandmother?"

"Well, she kind of took us in. My parents were killed in the same accident. My sister and I were kids."

"Sister? You have a sister?"

"She still lives at home too."

We got to the door and passed the place we first saw Gabriel, the angel. There was nothing there. We exited, and there was the Camaro parked out in front.

"How did this get here?" He rooted in his pockets. The keys were still there.

We got to the cool, slick auto and the doors were locked. He went over to my side and opened it. His temper may have returned, but his manners seemed still intact.

He went to his side and studied the seat position. "Moved back." He sighed heavily and frowned. "She has Down's syndrome."

"How do you know that?" I mean, the only thing I would gather from a seat having been moved back was that the person was taller than him.

"She was born with it." He gave me a sideways glance. "My sister, Sarah. She's a great kid!"

He flashed a genuine grin and instantly I was attracted to him again. How did he keep doing that? I thought Paulo was right that this guy was definitely that work in progress. "I still don't like the way that Giles said to say hello to Nona. He's so young!"

"Uh, Andy, he's an elf. He is probably is thousands of years old."

"Dirty old man!"

I had a feeling no one was going to be good enough for his grandmother. It was rather charming, actually. Yeah, I was using that hammer big time. I smiled, and he smiled back at me. Maybe there was something there.

"Yeah, I know, she's a grown woman and all, but she is my nona and, well…"

What, old ladies have no feelings? They suddenly become nuns or are clinically dead?

"She needs someone special who will be good to her, not an ease-dropping old guy in a zoot suit."

Yep, no one would be good enough. "How about we stop at the Goodwill?" I asked.

This kind of took him by surprise. He looked behind our car and then switched lanes real fast. He made a right turn and then a left turn, and then he was back on the same stretch of road as before. He then pulled over and once more peered in the rearview mirror. He got out and then came around and opened my door. He put his finger to his lips and took my hand.

"Shall we walk, my lady?"

Very gallant indeed. He reached out his hands to me, and I took them. They were warm. I had to admit I got the tingles again.

Look, I was married for twenty years and had been a widow for two. I had been alone almost the entire nine years of our marriage while Paulo was in the army, so tingles were far and few between. Let me enjoy them, will you? As we passed little white picket fences and kids playing in yards, Andy was silent. I guessed he was lost in his own thoughts.

"What do you make of that bunch?" He stopped and wiped an imaginary speck from his black patent shoes. I supposed he meant the SUD crowd we had left behind at the hotel. "Do you think they're for real?"

"Well, if they aren't, they sure were good at what they did." I thought of the scorched floor and the empty room. I didn't mention that poor Annie was still there. She had been looking at the floor as well.

"My grandmother told me that my grandfather worked for some strange characters. She showed me some pictures—ones she kept in a book under her bed. I had sort of found them." He looked down at the same shoe, a bit embarrassed. "Well, kind of. My grandfather had come to me and showed me the box. Nona was in bad financial shape, and he had an insurance policy the precinct had given him. She didn't speak good English at the time, and forget about-a reading," he said in his best Italian accent. "I read it for her. It was almost expired, and we really needed the cash."

"Were you scared when you saw him?" I remembered seeing my own mommom for the first time. I was so scared.

"No. I thought I was dreaming." He touched his head and pushed a stray hair out of his eyes. "But I woke up with the box in my arms. I saw them, Dr. Prescott and that Yaniv Popov. I even saw Giles." He closed his eyes. "Giles's form was sort of blurred, but I recognized him. Though the doc—he was just the same. There were orbs too, lots of them. My nona told me not to pay attention to them, though, so I didn't."

Nymph bubbles. There must have been one around when the picture was taken.

"Did you see Annie when we left?" I ventured carefully.

"Sampler's kid?"

I nodded.

"Yeah, I saw her. She must have committed suicide. Them I see all the time. Hanging from trees, on murder scenes bleeding out. If I wasn't careful, I would sometimes go to them first, before the victim. I was lucky I had a captain who was talented too. Captain Williams, he was a great man. I only worked under him for two years, but he taught me a lot."

"He didn't refer you to SUD?"

"Nah! He told me to utilize my talents. I was hesitant at first. Nona hated this kind of stuff. Still, I, um..." He looked at me I guess to gauge my reaction to both of these statements. "I speak to the suicides. They're—sorry for the pun—usually just hanging around and see everything."

And here I thought he was a staunch denier. I saw that it wasn't so when it suited his purposes. "I don't usually see suicides. Do you see a lot of them?" I asked.

It was curious what people saw and didn't see.

"All over the place. I always did, even in my nona's house. We had some relative that offed himself. He was my best friend for years. My family thought it was cute I had an imaginary friend named Uncle Charlie. My grandfather, well, he used to ask questions about Uncle Charlie, and then he just stopped asking. I guess he figured he was harmless."

"You still see him?"

"Yeah, but I don't pay him much mind. Sarah is the one that has the most to do with him. I don't stop it because she's kind of lonely." An expression of sadness crossed his features. "I think you'll like her."

Will like her? Did this mean he wanted a second date?

"Goodwill. Why do you want to go there?"

Or maybe not.

"I think I need a pair of fuzzy bunny pants." I smiled. He didn't. "I had a dream. Well, Ned sort of gave me a dream of the place where I guess he thinks it is."

"Oh, okay."

We turned right around and headed back to the car.

"Why did we get out of the car?" It occurred to me that he was looking all over the place, but trying to be discreet about it.

"We're being followed." I looked around. There was no one. "To my left, there is a pick-up truck." I looked again. "Powder blue," he said. "Jeez, would you believe they picked that color to follow someone in?"

I thought it was rather a nice color. With so many cars with assorted logos splattered all over them, it was nice to see a car that was one tone. Granted, it was an effeminate color for a pickup truck, but I was a woman, and Redburn...was he a he or a what?

"We'll have to do some fancy footwork on the pedals, in order to get to Goodwill without being tailed."

I wondered if that meant I was about to lose all my cookies in the process of ditching the people following us. It was such good pecan pie too! We got to the car, and I saw the truck was parked several cars from where we were.

"Redburn," I said as I stared that way.

"You're kidding. Who'd have thought he would have the gall to come after us himself?" Andy had started to head that way when the powder blue's engine turned on. Trying to hurry, it first hit the car behind it, a purple job proclaiming that grape juice was the drink of life—only seventy-five percent sugar added. I wondered which life they were talking about. The redheaded driver then slammed forward, hitting the turbo flusher man's truck. Finally, Redburn got himself out of the spot and on to the sidewalk. Who taught this...whatever he was...to drive anyway? Did they have cars on the lower levels?

Andy was practically in his line of fire. Powder Blue saw his opportunity and gunned it toward him. Andy jumped out of the way. Then, seeing he missed his first quarry, Redburn aimed for me.

I saw the truck coming, but I wasn't as swift on my feet as Andy was. No cop reflexes on this woman. The big blue machine was headed my way, chewed-up grass in its wake. Boy, were the owners of these pretty, picket-fenced houses going to be mad. I started to run, but he was faster. I had no easy escape, as there were fences on both sides of the street. He was just about to run me down when I felt a hand reach up from under the ground and close around my ankle. It literally pulled me into the dirt beneath my feet in the time it takes to say those words. Don't ask me how. I was struggling and coughing and quite frankly crying when I heard the familiar voice.

"Carrot Curls, calm down. It's Daddy."

Melvin? Then just as I thought I would suffocate, we were topside again. Andy had his gun out. He was shooting at the truck, but stopped as soon as he saw us. He ran up to us, grabbed me from my stepfather, hugged me, and then, of all things, kissed my cheek. Of course, he kissed Melvin on both of his cheeks. Male Italians!

"Where did you come from?"

Andy was panting, and I realized I was too—or maybe I was just trying to cough out all of the dirt still in my mouth and nose. Andy stared intensely at Melvin.

"She's my daughter. Of course, I came for her," Melvin answered calmly.

There was no dirt on him. His clothes were impeccable.

Andy was staring at him, open-mouthed. "You are one of them, right? An old one?"

"I am old." He looked at me and kissed my cheek too. "Now, you have a good time and stay out of trouble, my dear."

"Why am I off limits, Daddy? To SUD?"

He stopped in tracks and turned with a flourish. "I promised your mother, and I keep my promises. Even if I think they might not be the best idea. She is well-intentioned," he said, as if I were a school child. He then sank into the ground and disappeared.

We both looked at the earth below us with wonder. *What a useful talent*, I thought. *Why can't I do that?* Of course, if I could, I would have freaked out a lot of people from high school onward.

Andy sat down and counted from ten backward. "I'm taking you home."

That was that. My date was over. From his look, so was the relationship.

"I'm going shopping." Call me impulsive. I reached toward my pocket for my wallet, but being in fancy duds, I had no pocket. "Right after you take me home, and I get my money."

"Where?"

"My brother-in-law's house."

"No, where are you going shopping?"

"Around," I hedged.

"Around where?" His eyes narrowed and caught me in their high beams. Man, were they pretty.

I tried to look away, but my stomach did flip-flops on me. Or maybe that was more dirt. I started to cough up black stuff—and then a worm! A long, black one. I vomited. The delicious pecan pie came out, and all of the brunch did too. How attractive was that? He reached in his pocket and handed me a tissue.

"Thanks. Sorry." I moved away from the puke, and so did he.

"I'll take you there." He dabbed a speck I had missed, wrapped up the wad, and of all things tucked the tissue back in his pocket.

"Where?"

"The Goodwill. I'll take you there, okay?" He half smiled, and I coughed again. He put his hand in mine, and we walked to the car. He opened the door, and I slid in. Then he handed me a plastic WAWA bag. "Vomit in this please." He caressed the seat behind me. "We've been through a lot."

Great—my competition was a car!

We pulled out and off we went. There wasn't a powder blue truck to be seen. Andy dodged into parking lots, gas stations, and corners. I needed the bag for the corners. We did make it to the Goodwill in one piece, though. As we pulled into the lot, he stopped. We both looked where the shootout had been, and he cringed.

I could feel them behind me before they materialized.

CHAPTER 23

"Be careful, Andy, they have the place watched. I am sure of it."

Andy jumped out of the car, on edge, until he realized it was Ned and Terry. Boy that was fast. Maybe the doctor couldn't handle a twenty-first-century woman.

Unfortunately, Andy bumped right into Yaniv!

"You? What are you doing here?"

Andy looked right at him. He was a few inches shorter than the Greek, and the smile that could light a thousand cities wasted its wattage on the Italian who could suck all light from the sun.

"I'm here for the same reason you are."

"Yeah, and what's that?" The taller man stuck his head in the Camaro. "What's that?"

He was cute, too. However, I had the distinct feeling that he was all policeman, which made him all Doberman—handsome, well built, determined, and probably downright mean if things didn't go his way. Or maybe he wasn't. Perhaps he was a bulldog puppy, lots of muscle, but all a mush of love and kisses—

Oh, boy, I must be delirious from losing so much food at once.

Before I could say boo, the door opened. "All right, come on," Andy growled at Yaniv. "I feel like I am being chaperoned at the prom." He bit hard on his lip and pulled me out by my sore shoulder. "Your brother-in-law tells me how to act, your daughter tells me what flowers to get, and Attila over here is escorting me into the Goodwill!" He took a deep breath then added an ominous word. "Greeks." He still had my shoulder firmly in his grip, and pain was beginning to shoot through it. Noticing my grimace, he released me, and it slowly subsided to a gentle throb. "Sorry. I forgot."

We all went into the store. The electric doors opened and closed behind us. It was just as I remembered, but somehow different. First off, there were no people. Yes, it was crowded, but all the humans were missing. Secondly, the racks were all turned over. The place had been, to say the least, ransacked. Also, there was a lot of noise—oh, and did I mention there were nymphs everywhere? Little copies of Barney, with all different colored hats, were literally hanging from the rafters. It actually looked like a lot of fun. Really. If you liked that kind of thing—heights, electricity flowing through your body. My nephew Lexi would have loved this scene.

Andy was speechless, but Terry...well, she was hitting them. Having a good old time, actually, bopping them on the head. She was singing "Little Rabbit Foo Foo" as she did so. "Little rabbit mother son of a foo-foo!" Bop! She slammed the red silk purse on a green hat. "Hopping through the Goodwill." Bop! "Scooping up the nasty nymphs." Bop! "And bopping them on their silly little heads!"

She did several bops for emphasis on one orange-hatted fellow. I almost felt bad for him. Almost. I did sort of empathize with her, though. After all, she was dead because of them.

After she had finished the last lines of the song, there were little bodies everywhere. All the others had fled the store. Yaniv looked impressed as he strode forward.

"So where should we look?" He picked up some ties, scrutinized them closely, then tossed them on the already littered floor. "Not my color."

"Under a rack with little bunny PJ bottoms," I said weakly.

They all stared at the chaos before them.

"You are kidding aren't you, honey?" Terry said and then hooted with laughter.

"No, I am afraid not." I looked helplessly at Ned, who just nodded.

"Well, let's start looking." Yaniv started picking up racks and tossing them to one side or the other. Terry went to the back where the dresses were, managing to somehow step on every prostrate nymph she could find. I went to where I had seen them in my dream, and Andy went behind the counter to release the employees who were hog-tied and petrified.

I suppose I could have stopped and looked at a few things. I hadn't really Christmas shopped at all, and I was beginning to feel guilty. Then again, I had been shot. I did have a valid excuse, but try explaining that to a pre-teen girl who was looking forward to a present, any present.

I was walking toward the walls, trying not to trip over anything, when I heard a distinct, "Psst."

I looked over to the side, and there was a little old lady wearing a dark hat with a flower hanging out of it.

She smiled at me kindly. "Can you help me for a moment, dearie?" Her rosy cheeks glistened. I could tell she had been crying. "My favorite pair of glasses."

Glasses? Really? How was I to find them in this mess?

"They were under a rack of pajama bottoms that were over there before those wretched undisciplined children came in here." She looked absolutely befuddled and pointed to the next row over.

I became hopeful. "Does it have fuzzy bunny pants on it?"

She shook her head in wonder. "Bought yesterday, by a pimpled boy with pink hair. Actually, they matched his hair."

I traipsed over to where she pointed. There was the rack. Empty, but surrounded by helpless PJ halves. I began my voyage to the center of the pile, digging past silk bottoms, cotton pants, and the cutest pair of leggings with Rudolf on them. I looked at them—red tags, yay, half price! Sophie would love them. The old woman was peering at me, and I realized I better move my own rear end. "Sorry, but aren't they adorable?"

She nodded. "Sophie would love them."

She knew my daughter's name. Did I know her? Did she know me? It was in that moment of wonder that a head popped up. Before I could do any more digging, he grabbed for me. The sweet little old lady's face changed to that of a fanged, saliva-dripping monster.

"I wouldn't do that if I were you." she roared in a whole other voice.

For a moment, the yellow-hatted nymph hesitated, but then the wet saliva dripped on him, and he backed away. He promptly dove back into the pile. Red eyes turned my way, and then she morphed back into the sweet lady from before. "I always wanted to do that. Worked on the creature from the coat closet movie and I just about fell in love with it." She giggled. "It was 1952. We had great makeup artists on that set. In fact, I married the creature. Very impulsive on my part. The marriage only lasted about five minutes."

"What are you doing here?" I was really curious now and suspicious too.

"I told you, looking for my glasses." She winked as Yaniv came over to us.

He bowed to her very gallantly, and she curtseyed back at him.

"Ma'am?"

She pointed to the pile where the nymph had gone, and he reached in his long arm and yanked him out. Then he took the screaming creature and flung him on another pile. Yaniv kneeled down and frisked him. He pulled out a white piece of paper. The birth certificate.

"Hey, keep your hands out of my privates, you pervert!" The nymph squirmed as Yaniv reached back in and pulled out a blue booklet—or, rather, half of a blue booklet.

"Where is the other half?"

"I don't got it."

I didn't see exactly what happened, but suddenly his voice got three octaves higher.

"I told you, I ain't got it." His face turned an odd color purple that clashed with his yellow cap. "Redburn has it," he gasped.

"Where is he?" Yaniv still had his body blocking what he was doing. "Where?"

White teeth gritted. Yep, Doberman. I was definitely staying out this guy's way.

"I—don't—know." Each word came out slowly and looked difficult for him to say. "Look, you can make it so I never procreate ever, but I still don't know where he is. He keeps moving." He must have been released because the color came back to this face. "He's afraid of her." He pointed at me. "Witch!"

Before Yaniv could stop him, he dove back into the pile of pajamas. Andy had joined us and started after him.

"No, no, no, don't bother. He has given us all he knows." Yaniv held the half of a passport by the corner. Even when miffed, his face held a smile. An odd one, but a smile all the same.

"Don't tell me he had that where the sun don't shine!" Terry looked a bit out of sorts about this—odd coming from a woman who strode around half naked.

"It's only half. Redburn has the other part." Yaniv handed it to Andy who looked as if he was going to drop it from revulsion. "Put it in the bag." Yaniv pulled out a little baggie and pushed it toward him. Andy grabbed at it, and faster than I can pop a Hershey kiss in my mouth, he put that stinky thing in there. "Good, good, good."

Andy tried to hand it back to him. "What now?"

"No, no, no. You are the lead investigator. I am just helping." Yaniv got up and bowed again to the lady. She smiled coyly at him.

I knew that look. Vienne had it too when flirting with men.

"Oh, look at that." She picked up the glasses on a pretty chain hanging around her neck. "Here are my glasses, after all. See you around, Love Bug."

And she was gone. I noticed that Yaniv looked at the space she left and sighed deeply. "What a woman!" He kissed his fingertips and blew the kiss in the air.

Now I understood what *IT* is. Men flocked to this kind of lady in droves. Vienne had *IT* too—at least on most men.

"I'll meet you both later. You keep that safe." Yaniv got up and, to all our astonishment, sank into the floor and disappeared.

I'd have to ask Melvin about this one day. Maybe it was a skill that could be taught.

"You ready?" Andy got up and motioned toward the front doors. I looked at the Rudolf leggings and walked toward the cash registers. "You are kidding, right?"

"I didn't buy Sophie one Christmas present. In fact, I didn't buy any of the kids anything." Boy, I really was Auntie Scrooge. I started to look around. Within the next hour, I had gifts. Just stocking stuffers, but I had one for every person in the Arestes family. They may or may not need or even want what I got for them, but that wasn't the point, was it?

Andy followed me. All the nymphs had disappeared, leaving us, two ghosts, and the petrified cashiers. I wondered what they would tell their friends. Or would they just discuss the crazy lady who shopped for Christmas presents and talked to air?

When we got to the car, I felt it. The pain in my shoulder had now morphed from a gentle ache to a full-out agitation of nerves and muscle and was crying out for meds. We drove in silence. Andy looked like he was in another world. I already knew that look. It was the "how do I tell her that it was nice knowing you and we should just be friends" look. Or with Andy, it was probably the "I never want to see you again—too many dead people to deal with" look, compounded by the "I have to make this awful speech and be polite, or Lexi will break my leg" look.

We pulled up in front of the house, and suffice it to say, it looked worse in the daylight. The hot air blowups were deflated and lying across the assorted decorations. There wasn't a square inch of grass showing. This would be a great place for nymphs to hide, not to mention Santa, all his elves, and Redburn too. We sat staring at it for a while. Andy started to laugh, and I looked at him. He really was very handsome when he smiled. I wondered if he ever let loose and just let himself be happy.

"My sister would love this place." He finally broke the silence. I was glad because I was wondering if my hearing was working. "She loves lights and shiny things." He turned toward me. "I think she would really like you too. I know I like you."

Oh, my gosh, I wanted to scream He *what*? Did he say he liked me? Really? This wasn't a goodbye? I tried to remain calm. "I am rather fond of you as well."

"How about you and me go out again?"

"Okay." I felt like a teenager again, waiting for him to ask me out. Then we just stared some more. "When?"

"Tomorrow at noon. Let's do lunch."

I agreed. What could I do? It never occurred to me that there would be a slight complication. Actually, there were going to be four complications…

CHAPTER 24

Five, if you counted Barney, and count him, we did. "No way. I ain't going to stay here without anyone home. The guy hates kids. They are my only cover," he kvetched, stamping his booted foot. "Redburn has half the passport—do you know what that means?"

I had no idea what it meant. What was so special about this passport? What did it do and why were so many people after it?

It was ruining my love life. Alysia had a big case. Lexi had a job he had scheduled and put off while I was in the hospital. Rydia and Paulo Senior were on some much-needed R and R after having to take care of the kids, mostly Alexi, which would drain the strength of Hercules. I was assured it wasn't going to be so bad. After all, Phoebe was there. True as that was, I had the other issue. Andy. I realized a bit too late that I didn't have a phone number for this dude. I had a feeling four kids riding shotgun with us would be a serious cramp in his style. Not to mention, I wasn't sure we would all fit in his little car. Still, if I added Barney…

Barney looked at the kids and then back at me. I guess that was my cue to stash him somewhere, but I wasn't sure where, as the house was filled with Christmas and there was no place for any of them to go. Not even poor Barney himself, as his box had been re-gifted. When I tried to explain to Alysia that it was Barney's, she looked at me as I had overdosed again. That might have been true, but still…

"It's a toy!" she said.

Yes. To all the world except me, the kids, and Santa.

I took the kids to the next room and then returned. "Okay, Barney, level with me. Why does Redburn want the passport?"

He sort of did the jig. One foot lifted; the other came down. He looked west, east, north, and then behind me. "Because it will allow him to remain on the human plane."

What? Had I heard right?

"Why does he want to be on the human plane?" I thought living on the magic planes would be much more fun.

"To control you all. You know—rule the world, at least this world. He thinks the big boss is out of control and that he isn't reaping all he could reap, you know?"

No, I didn't know. Supervillains were the stuff of comics and sci-fi movies, not part of the real world, or even my world. Well, maybe some sci-fi or horror occasionally enters my world, but not major drama stuff like deamons and nymphs.

"Is he the Devil?" It hit me like a two-ton elephant on the head.

"No, he ain't him. The Devil don't really exist, you know. He's just some poor schnook that was made up to blame the underworld mischief on." When I didn't comprehend, he added, "Us, the stuff we do. You know the little things that make your world more interesting?"

"Like getting shot in the shoulder or—" I looked at

Terry and Ned in the corner of the room, now fully atten-
tive. "—or ending up dead?"

"Only sometimes. I mean, we don't kill no one, but,
with the passport, he could. Sort of."

"He did already, Barney."

"No, he didn't kill the lady or the cop."

"Who did?"

"I don't know."

I looked at him doubtfully.

"Really. I do know there was a contract out on her
because she had possession of the passport. I mean that's
when I borrowed the charms," he said in a real hushed
tone. "Still, I'm not sure who actually did it. And why did
they ditch the goods?"

That was a good question. Why would they throw
away what they were collecting in the first place? Could
that mean they weren't working for Redburn and they
killed Terry just to kill her? Having spoken to Terry, I
didn't find it hard to believe. Then again, who tipped
them off to the passport in the Goodwill?

"Anyway, I can't stay here alone. He'll torture me
and make me tell him where the passport is."

I looked at him suspiciously. "Which is where?"

He shrugged. "With your boyfriend, Andy."

"He's not my boyfriend." Even if he was *almost* my
boyfriend, after stuffing four kids, a nymph, and myself
in his tiny little car, he wouldn't be anymore. We'd had
one date. Or maybe one and a half, if I counted the disaster that happened the night before, which I didn't. Did. I
heard the honk outside. "Fine, you can come. But no rude
comments from the back," I growled at him.

Andy put Barney in the trunk. It was there or on the
roof. For a few moments, I actually felt bad for poor old
Barney. Then we stuffed into the car, and I realized there
was absolutely no room for him, or even the six humans.

Barney kept up a steady stream of banging from the rear, though, so no one forgot him for long.

"That nymph is going to ruin the interior of my trunk!" Andy slammed on the brakes and got out of the car.

I didn't realize it, the car being so crammed that one person missing was not noticeable, but Phoebe followed him out.

I heard some screaming and then quiet. They both returned. Safely nestled in Phoebe's arms was Barney. He was clinging to her for dear life. I thought it was the first time he had been terrified of anything. Though my niece had that effect on the worst of beasts, she was so composed and put together that I almost forgot she was only fifteen years old.

We arrived at the amusement park. I doubt that was Andy's first choice for our date, but on seeing my tag-alongs, he made a quick decision. Personally, I was glad we were here. The sights and sounds surrounding us brought back childhood memories. The rides were all running, and the smells of cotton candy, funnel cake, and hot dogs made me dizzy with happiness. Of course, I had to keep a tight grip on Alexi who wanted to climb the first Ferris wheel he saw. Phoebe still had Barney. Sophie and Velma traveled arm in arm.

For a moment he looked around and smiled like a kid. He liked this kind of place too. We had something in common, yay. He said that he had finally read SUD's contract, and it was actually not a bad deal. He'd be starting work the next day as a lead investigator.

"They want me to use my talents." He looked up at the roller coaster. "I have never officially done that before."

To me, he seemed reluctant to start. Then again, I hardly knew him. "It's not so bad. I do it all the time."

"I've avoided it my whole life. I tried to block them out, you know?"

I did know. I had been discouraged by my mother, let do my thing by my stepfather, and cautioned by my grandmother. It didn't matter. I was bombarded by spirits of all kinds anyway.

"How could you avoid it?"

"I used to close my eyes. When I opened them, they were gone. Then I met Ned and his backseat hitchhikers, and all sorts of things started to happen again."

"How long were you with Ned?"

"Only about a year, but we were close." A sad look crossed his face. "I didn't know he was part of another unit, but a lot of what he did and said makes sense now." He stopped as we reached the merry-go-round and the four kids and Barney took off for it. "He knew he was going to die that day. He said it was the curse of his family to know those things. I told him it was nonsense, but he just accepted it. Said his family members had tried and failed to avoid the Grim Reaper for hundreds of years. I was going to help him to do it." He kicked an empty coke bottle on the ground. "Some help I was." It rolled away from him, spilling its contents as it escaped his fury. "I saw him." When I just stared at him, he added, "The angel of death."

"I wonder why he was able to see the date of his death." It sounded more like a curse. To know your death date would be scary.

"It was his family that kidnapped several kids for that deamon ceremony. It was the family business in the eleventh century. Easy money, loads of poor kids to be had, and well…"

Oh boy.

"I guess they got on someone's bad side. Did they try to cash in on a king's kid or something?"

"No, they pissed off the coven's leader. Turns out they were price gouging, and the witches didn't like it. Charging too many chickens or something, so they were dismissed. Still, the coven had a problem. No one else wanted the job of procuring children—not because they believed killing is wrong or anything, but they didn't want eternal hell dealing with witches. When the witches came back to Ned's family, it was with an offer they could not refuse. They promised them something money couldn't buy."

I had a bad feeling about this.

"Eternal life. Except it wasn't quite the eternal life they expected. If they could avoid their death on their appointed death day, all twenty-four hours, they would live for eternity."

"Oh, so the only way to do that was to know their death day, right?"

"Yeppers." He shrugged. "Some help it was. Thus far none of them have survived twenty-four hours of their day yet. His family finally gave up the business and went into the business of catching the bad guys at the beginning of the twentieth century. I guess the prospect of hell wasn't all that appealing to them anymore."

"Especially when it seemed they have their own little hell going on." Also, they probably didn't believe that what they were doing was real anymore.

"Ned's the last of them. He never married, and he was an only child."

That was the missing piece of the puzzle then. He knew his death date, and he knew that the curse would end with him. Therefore, he let it happen. I liked Ned even more now.

"That will be five tickets."

We stopped. There before us was a tall, bronzed man. He wore a silk jacket that was a little worn. He pointed to a colored structure that had macabre pictures on the side. A skull, a hanging body dressed in a blue robe, a dripping knife, a screaming clown lady. Behind them all was a blurry figure in red.

"Can we?" Velma asked in excitement. It was hard to say no to her pretty brown eyes. Sophie looked a bit hesitant, but Velma was firmly holding her hand. "Don't worry, Sophs, I got you covered."

Phoebe was all for it. Even Barney seemed amused. So my date went and bought thirty-five tickets, and we all piled into the rickety go-carts that were held on a string track.

"Keep your hands and feet in, children, because here the bed bugs do bite."

The door closed behind us as the little train went in. There was darkness and lots of screaming. Sophie was in the car in front of us, and I could see her hazel eyes were wide open in the dimly-lit room. The place was hot. At first, I was glad for it, as it was very cold outside. Slowly it became stifling. There was also a smell. It resembled rotten meat. I knew that smell.

We slammed into a brick wall. I mean literally slammed so hard that the front of the flimsy cart came off. Andy became annoyed and stood up to see if the girls were okay, but he was thrown backward and landed on my lap.

"Uh-oh, Andy boy, you better keep yourself alert. Fooling around right now would be an unwise move." Ned's white hair glowed in the fluorescent lights, and then he disappeared.

"Shut up, Ned!" Andy yelled.

I heard the girls giggling. They thought it was part of the ride. Maybe it was.

The next room was even hotter than the previous one. There were little discs of light circling us. Each one zoomed toward us. The strange part was I thought I saw little faces within. The discs looked almost like the orbs sometimes caught on film that were assumed to be the spirits of the diseased. One particularly stubborn one resembled someone I knew. My mommom.

The little orb was bouncing around me, and Andy started to swat it off. The more adamant it was, the more he persisted. Pretty soon we were surrounded by thousands of bubbles, making the air heavy and muggy. I was having a hard time breathing. We were all swatting off the little spheres—now as thick as flies on a dead body—so at first we didn't notice the next room we entered.

It was a ravine of hot molten lava. The pit itself was immense, and, from the heat it was generating, I got the feeling it wasn't a hologram. Both cars were hanging over it very precariously. I grabbed the girls and pulled them into our seats. Barney was blocking Phoebe and Alexi's descent, although I could swear that the little Greek bugger was trying to climb out to fly into it! I'd have to up my fees if this were going to keep up.

There was a lot of burping going on from below. Forms were popping in and out of the liquid, and then Maxie Sampler came up.

"Andy, do you see who I see?"

Maxie lifted a burnt fist and shook it at us. Then just as he was almost fully out of the firewater and trying to climb on shore, a large bestial finger scooped him up and pulled him back in.

Then the beast came out. What it was, exactly, I was not sure, but it looked familiar. Not a dragon, but something like that. It was red, dripping fire-colored saliva, and immense. It eyed us for a while, seemingly trying to figure us out. The stench of burning was overwhelming. I knew him—er—it. It had winked at me. Or at least I thought it was a wink.

"Andrew, Theresa?" it said like an old friend who had been expecting us. "Welcome."

His was a deep hollow voice, but also forceful. Don't ask me. It just was, okay? Something occurred to me. I had seen this whole thing before, on a train station wall. He had winked at me then, too. Boy, I had to do something. I was starting to attract the wrong kind of guys.

"Who the—" Andy started.

"Uh, uh, uh, uh..." A clawed fingertip waved at him like a naughty child. "No, profanity, please. We don't want to negatively influence the dearly departed. They already have enough problems on their hands." Then he turned to me and smiled. "Well, young lady, we meet again."

A black shadow slithered between us. I was kind of scared, and kind of thankful, because at least the shadow was cool. Well, it gave off a coldness of sorts. I was burning up.

"Oh, I see you have your own personal watcher." The dragon reached toward it.

As he did so, I slapped his hand away. My fingers went right through him. Nothing. The watcher was bold and didn't back down, but I could feel its confusion.

"What do you want?" I asked calmly, or as calmly as a woman on the verge of hysteria could.

"Want? Yes, want. I want the door closed."

"SUD is doing that." That's all?

"No, no, no, I want them all back inside. They are mine!" He came very close to us. I was afraid if he opened his mouth, we would be swallowed up. "You have to close it, Theresa."

"Um, I am not a professional. You see these kids? I am their nanny, not Wonder Woman." As I looked over, I saw that Alexi had escaped and was climbing the rail. I was getting up to grab him when the dragon reached over, pinched his little pants and tucked him into my arms. For a moment Alexi struggled, but the watcher touched him, and he froze. He was blue. "Oh no!"

"Don't worry. A watcher's touch on an innocent is only temporary, even on a little rambunctious tyke like him." Hot fetid air blew my way. "You have to close the door. No one else can."

"Why Theresa?" Andy gritted his teeth in a don't-get-too-close-to-my-girl kind of way.

"Because she opened it!" he spat at Andy, who was promptly thrown back in his seat by the heat of the statement.

"I didn't open it."

He came closer, but the watcher wasn't backing down.

"You can't protect her forever." He touched the black shadow, but withdrew his long-nailed finger immediately, sticking it in his mouth like a child who had burned himself. "So they did send a powerful one." He licked his lips, fangs, and chin. Yes, it was disgusting. "You recognize me. I saw it in your aura a few minutes ago."

"A hallucination. You were a dream—a young lost girl's fancy."

Out of the water came Pig Face. He saw poor Sophie and leaped up to grab her. She gave a little scream. I reached out and pulled her next to us. Andy reached for Velma. We shoved the girls behind us. I was angry now.

"Is he a 'fancy' as well?" The creature plucked him up as one picked lint from his sleeve.

"I never opened any doors."

"You did. You were four years old. You read from a spellbook in your stepfather's school. Some stupid warlock was dabbling in stuff he shouldn't have been and carelessly left it lying about for anyone to see. He had no real talent. He couldn't do anything with it. You, on the other hand, you have plenty of it, just like your parents. You just said that little spell and, voilà. My carefully locked dungeon opened." he growled.

So he was mad at me. I didn't care—I was mad at him too. "If I was four, I didn't even know what I was saying. It probably looked like some picture book to me." My stepfather had a lot of them. Too many. Some I shouldn't have been able to see. No one my age should have been able to see them. Naked tortured souls—I was four years old! "Why don't you get the idiot who left it out to fix the problem?"

He promptly reached out and began to shake both of the carts.

"It had very colorful pictures. As for the moron who left it there, well..." The shaking stopped, and he reached into the massive pool of red liquid, swirled a bit, and pulled out a sorrowful-looking soul that I vaguely recognized. A tall, thin guy with a pointed nose and bones that always stuck out. I remember my stepfather wondering aloud if the man ever ate.

"He went to hell for leaving a book open?"

"No, he came to my realm for other reasons. Namely, killing hitchhikers and writing the book with their blood. For some odd reason, pea-brained humans think that I require sacrifices. And they usually go for the innocent ones, the dummies! They never even arrive here..."

I could see him stirring the waters below again. Heads popped up and uttered silent screams. It was like a nightmarish painting by...oh, you know who I mean. He's famous. He painted hell. I guess he knew what he was doing.

"...they're so stupid. Sometimes I wonder why they don't just put their names in a hat and sacrifice themselves. At least that way, I would actually receive one of their gifts." He began to shake the warlock. "His sacrifice never made it here at all, even though it was earmarked for me."

He opened his jaws wide and popped the man's terrified head into his mouth. He bit it off—the sound was sort of like twisting off a turkey drumstick—and left the body and neck hanging over our cart, dripping blood on my shoes. Nice. You go out on a date with a new guy, take the kids—this was just not what you wanted to happen. I liked those shoes too.

He tossed what was left of the warlock back into the ditch beside the bubbling pool. "Your mother took you away." he whined, like a baby.

Yay, Mom, my heroine. "What could I have done? I was a child."

"She could have given you to me. I would have taught you, and then you could have closed the door from the inside."

Oh, that would have been a fun childhood, wouldn't it? Me, Big Red, and all the happy souls in the below. I was brimming over with joy at the idea.

"You shouldn't have left your spells just lying around for idiots to find and transcribe, Luke." Another cart had entered, carrying my mother and Aunt Vienne, with Melvin in the back. My mother was standing and looking directly at the dragon. Somehow, she looked healthier here. "It was no accident Denton found the cave. You know how to influence the weak-minded. And he was very weak-minded."

"No brains at all," he mewled at her, picking parts of Denton's skull out of his teeth with a rough-edged nail.

"You reap what you sow." She looked at me. "Now, release them. They have no place in your realms."

"She is mine. She opened the door!" He came precariously close to her. She didn't move. Was this woman really my mother? The one who preferred melting into the background to a lively Greek family? Who shrank back when we even mentioned Black Friday and malls in the same sentence?

"No, she is not. She was a child who saw a book and said some words. She was not and has never been evil or even mean-spirited." Vienne looked at us. "Release them, Luke." She was pretty, and her charms seemed to have an effect, even on him.

"She has to close the door. Only her incantation can undo what was done." A little ball came in and floated near him. I had seen that one before. "Get away from me." He was dodging it, not even trying to swat it. "I said leave me be!" he roared. "This is not your realm. You don't belong here!"

"He's right," my mother said, looking fondly at the glowing ball. "Luke, he's telling you to return to your own realms and leave our daughter alone." The sphere materialized, and there stood the familiar pilot uniform that I saw in most of the pictures I had of him. His white light bathed the whole room and cooled it off. He saluted me and smiled.

"Get out of here," Luke said. It was aimed at my father, a weak attempt. The dragon or devil, or whatever he was, submerged instead. The spirit evaporated then, and I felt oddly sad.

The room cooled off dramatically, and the ride started again. We all moved to the next room. It was filled with mirrors, but it paled in excitement compared to the previous one. As we exited, the cold winter air hit us all hard, and I got to the task of zipping everyone up. The same man as before greeted us.

"Again, again!" I heard four voices all at once. The children were flushed with excitement. Oh, that was okay then. Somehow, I thought they'd been scared. Can you imagine what they could have told their mother? What if they had been scarred for life, turned against amusement park rides?

"Did you enjoy your ride?" he asked.

"Aunty Delphi, how did they know your names?" Velma inquired, her intelligent eyes quizzing me.

"The Internet," my stepfather answered her with a swish of her curly dark hair. "You can find everything on the Internet, you know."

She considered this and then nodded at him.

He took Sophie and Velma's hand, motioning for the rest of them to follow him. "Who wants cotton candy?"

A chorus of yeses came at him.

"Andrew, why don't you take my daughter on another ride? I think I can handle the troops here and then transport them home. Vienne, Caroline, and I can babysit them after that."

There were times I could live without my stepdad, but this was definitely not one of them. The kids ran ahead with Vienne toward the concessions. He looked at me, and I was so glad he had stepped in to take them.

Melvin turned toward the ride operator. "Nice try. Go back to your lord."

The man stuck his large, twitching nose out and challenged my stepfather. "Make me."

Melvin touched the being, and it melted in front of us, its colorful clothing emptying of the form that had occupied it. A sulfur smell and wisps of smoke came out of it. Then I noticed something was under it, moving around. The first thing that showed up was a tail: long, gray, and scaly. Then came the little furry body with its sharp little claws and finally the largest, ugliest rat snout I had ever seen, still twitching.

The creature was at least a foot in height. Two long fangs overhung his protruding lips. He stood to his full height and shook a little paw at us. My stepfather took one threatening step forward. The little creature booked it out of there.

"Glad to oblige," my stepdad called after his retreating form. "Luke likes to use rats to do his bidding. That's the basis for the expression 'the rat race,' you know." I didn't, but I believed him. He kissed me on the cheek. "Have a good time, Carrot Curls." He walked toward the others.

Andy didn't need to be asked twice. He thanked him, grabbed my hand, and headed toward the Tunnel of Love. A pretty lady came out and asked if we wanted to go on the ride. Something seemed to be swishing in her skirt. For a second, a tip of a tail showed. Andy took one look at it and shook his head.

"I've had enough dark, creepy spaces, furry animals, and burning flesh. I need some fresh air." He looked toward the Ferris wheel.

Now, I don't know if I mentioned this before, but it was cold outside. I was thinking of mentioning it to him too, but he looked so excited to go on this thing.

As we walked toward it, it occurred to me that the amusement park was empty. There were only the few workers we had seen, some concessions, and no customers except us.

"Where did you get this place's address again exactly?" I asked as he was buying tickets.

"It was taped to my door. It looked kind of cool so I thought maybe we should go." He did look like a kid in a candy store. "Then when you said the whole gang was coming, I thought it was just good karma." Then he stopped. "Well, if it hadn't been real." He motioned to the funhouse ride we had just left. "It would have been a cool ride, right?"

He was smiling. There were really nice dimples on

that face. I was sure there was a sweet, compassionate guy in there that I was just beginning to dig out.

"Yes, it would have been a great ride." And it was nice to be with him. Besides, I saw my birth father, and he looked great too. Actually, I was with both my dads. That was the best part of it all.

We entered the Ferris wheel and let the man snap the door shut. "Have a nice ride," a handsome older gentleman with a striped vest and a handlebar mustache said.

"Do you notice how many dead people there are around here?"

I did notice it. In fact, as I looked down, there were only shining white lights below. They made a soft glow. He seemed fascinated by it.

"I think I could get used to this," he added as his arm slipped around my shoulder.

It was a nice ride too, it really was.

CHAPTER 25

After a few rounds on the big wheel, a hundred games of skeet ball, a scrumptious corn dog, a large order of onion rings, and about ten extra pounds, Andy drove me home. I got a gentlemanly kiss on the cheek, and, as he was about to walk me to the door, I heard her.

"Theresa."

At first, I thought it was the wind, but then I realized it was my mother. Among all the stuff that was polluting my brother-in-law's front lawn, she was practically hidden.

"Mom?"

She walked out from between a pair of Santas. She was wearing a white coat with a fur-lined hood. She glanced for a moment at Andy. "Oh, I'm sorry, Andy…"

But she let it trail. He apparently got the hint so he said his goodbyes and asked if he could call me. I gushed a yes that was equivalent to a schoolgirl's "gee whiz," and he left.

We watched as he put the pedal to the metal and disappeared in a spray of gravel and dirt.

"Boys and their toys," Mom said. Her voice was far

off, in another world. In all the Christmas lights she hardly looked like the woman I grew up with. She looked kind of magical. "I need to talk to you."

"Who am I, Mom?" I had often wondered that. It was something she avoided. "Or more to the point, what am I? Did I really open some portal to hell?"

"I tried to protect you. We knew you were powerful. We just didn't know how powerful. Melvin had taught you to read, and you just loved it." She touched her hood and stroked it. "The souls flew to your light. To one who has the sight, it looked like you were always blowing beautiful iridescent bubbles."

I remembered something like that—shimmering spheres of flashing energy. I'd run, and they would follow me into the forest. The forest: the spices of the earth, water, and life. I could just barely picture it. Had I suppressed it? Or had my mother done it for me?

"Who is Luke? Is he Lucifer?"

She laughed out loud. "It's our pet name for them. Lukes are based on the fabled devil. They are the masters of the underworld. Hades." She came close to me. Her dark eyes, light-brown hair, and painfully thin face made me think that if a strong wind came, she would blow away. She didn't resemble at all the woman who had faced up to the Luke in the funhouse this afternoon.

"Fabled?" I wondered aloud. "I thought there is such a thing as the devil."

"Yes, there is one in all of us. It is something we have to conquer every day."

"No, Mom, I mean the fallen angel, Lucifer." I had been schooled in the Bible my whole life. It surprised me she didn't have one in her hands now.

"There is no such thing as an actual fallen angel, Theresa. All angels have a purpose, one task they were created to do. Lucifer was created to watch the underworld. I used the word "fabled" because he is always painted as the evil one. He's not evil. He just lives off the evil of man. The Lukes guard the below. If you talk to one, you have talked to them all."

I thought of the wall that had gathered up Pig Face and the flying dragons I had seen circling the pit of orange liquid fire.

"How it is possible that I could have opened any doors magically—especially one that was guarded by dragons?"

"Dragons."

She whistled it into the air. Her breath gathered up and made a cloud. Out of the cloud came a dragon made of breath. It was amazing to see. It flew around us, and then it dissipated.

"Do you know JRR Tolkien?" she asked.

I knew of him, sure. Everyone who reads fantasy knows of him.

"I showed him the gates of hell. He based Smog, the dragon, on the Lukes. Not just his looks…even his voice." She looked dreamily at the moon. There was a certain glow to her now.

I was surprised. "He talked to him?"

"Yes, he did. That was why he was so possessive of his characters. He knew they were real." She actually chuckled, at this thought.

I could tell something was changing.

"What am I, Mom?" I repeated. I knew I wasn't quite human.

"You are your father, you are me, and you are even a bit of Melvin." It was said almost in a whisper.

"Was my father a warlock?" I knew so little about him, but from what I knew he was an ordinary person.

"He could have been. His people have power in a book called the Kabbalah, but not all are allowed to access it because it can corrupt. Your father had studied the Kabbalah and became a learned person. He could have been a great Kabbalist, but he chose to run away from it." A glimmer of a smile crossed her face again. "I ran into him, literally, in the forest. I was being chased by a lion—well, sort of a lion. It was a Leo. They are much more vicious than their feline counterpart because they're part human. He was on a training maneuver—your father, I mean—and the Leo had gotten very close to us when this man stood up and commanded it to leave us alone. At first, I thought it would attack this guy, but it turned on its heel and ran away. I was impressed, very impressed."

A look I didn't understand crossed her normally pinched features. Were fond memories passing through her normally closed mind?

"Did he know what it was?"

At this, she burst out laughing. "He thought it was a man in a lion's costume. He had no idea he had commanded one of the most dangerous creatures in the magic kingdom to stand down and leave. The beast could see the power radiating from your dad. I then had to take a step backward and look myself. He was so..." She was now definitely lost in a memory for a moment. "When I look at you, I see the image of your father."

She took one of my curls in her hand and stroked it. This was a rare thing as my mother was not overly affectionate, ever.

"Mom, did you and Melvin train him?"

"No, he didn't want it. He said he grew up his whole life with all sorts of things he didn't understand, and he preferred it that way. You remember your mommom, her red strings against the evil eye, or how she cut the way for your cousin who still hadn't walked by the age of two?"

I did remember my cousin Rachel. Her mom,

mommom's oldest daughter, took her to an important doctor who claimed she would be unable to ever walk. There was such sadness in the home. Mommom pooh-poohed the doctor's words. She got on her hands and knees in a hallway, placing two fingers on the wooden floor, and said some kabbalistic blessings. The entire family watched as young Rachel was placed where Mommom had just traced. Miraculously, she stood up and walked.

"I didn't mind your dad's aversion to magic. I was tired of the magical types, as well of the creative types. I wanted someone different. Someone who just wanted me. I wanted—please forgive me—a real man. Your father was all that and more."

Tears started to run down her face, and I could sense that seeing him today had had its effect on her. I did something impulsive and unnatural to me. I hugged her. We stood there for a while, not talking, the quiet of our embrace comforting us both.

"You will have to close that door," she said. "I see that clearly now. No matter what I promised your father and grandmother, you will have to make things right." She looked even sadder than before. "I once was very powerful myself. Full of vim and vibrancy. Protecting you from the Lukes by myself has drained almost all my energy and most of my magic. I resented your father, both of them. One for dying, the other for deserting us. I have let things go, let myself go. I'm sorry, my child—"

"It's okay, Mom." It was. I didn't know why, but I knew she had done all she could. "I am untrained. How will I do that?" Talking to the dead was one thing, but fighting an army of darkness to close some door I left open at four years old? Well, that was a whole other ball of wax. You are probably wondering why I was not abso-lutely shocked by all this, right? Well, if my dad grew up in a house full of Kabbalah, I grew up with a bunch of witches, warlocks, and other weird goings-on—like dead people all around me. Nothing could shock me, not even Santa Claus.

"Melvin can help you. He's head of that witches and warlocks academy. I'll do what I can, too, but you are the only one who can activate Garrett's little device. He was a talented inventor in life and an even better one in death," she said fondly.

I got the idea she knew Garrett Morgan the inventor more personally. Then I wondered how she knew he was involved in all this.

"He'll show you how it works and then you will have to leave right away." She put her bone-thin hands on my shoulders and looked into my eyes. "Do you understand, Theresa? Just stay there in front of the open door. Don't let him entice you anywhere near any other part of his realm. *Don't*—and I mean *don't*—go into its domain!"

"I thought only the marginally good could be sucked back down there. Don't they have to be dead too?"

Her expression was a bit unnerving. "Technically, one has to be living to die, but you are different. You are not really alive, and you aren't dead either."

And? Was that all she was going to say? What was I? What was she saying?

"You are part mortal, but you are also part natural, and that's why the dead flock to you. They see your light. Being so close to the portal could be very dangerous for someone like you. It's not that they could harm you, because you're good, but Garrett's device is meant to close the door. Permanently." She looked terrified and half the woman she was even before we started talking.

How does she do that? Do I do that too? Is that what makes Sophie so nervous about me?

"Mom, what are you?"

A shimmering light gathered around her, and she was suddenly encased in a bubble and rising off the ground. She was so beautiful. I just stared at her. She resembled my mother, but she was—

"Pure magic." Melvin was then next to me. "I was worried about you girls." His thin face and long pointed nose turned sharply toward me. My mother spied him and then floated away from us.

"Melvin, help her. She needs your help…" Her voice trailed off, and she disappeared.

"She was Lyman's inspiration for the good witch Glinda in *The Wizard of Oz*." He still watched an invisible apparition in his mind's eye.

"Lyman?"

"The L in L. Frank Baum stood for Lyman. He was crazy about your mother. He was a sick little boy, and your mom was his nanny. Had a weak heart. I guess she showed him at some point who, or rather what, she was and, voilà—Glinda was born." He smiled. "She's not a witch, of course, but, in those days, how could you explain to a child that she is a Twylyth Teg?"

"A what?"

"One of the fairy folk. A sort of fairy, but a bit different than the ones you've read about. The first time I saw her, she was magnificent."

I could see there was still a fire burning for her.

"What am I, Daddy?"

He looked hard at me. "You are special." He stroked my cheek tenderly. "Your father was different, too. Not an eternal, but powerful. Your mother and he were only together one time. I mean in the biblical sense. They knew each other for months, but, well, army pilots are busy people."

I'd heard of such things before, and that made it a

terrifying thing for the mother of near-teenager like me.

"I adored him immediately," Melvin continued. "We became fast friends. He was so easy to like. Just like you, Carrot Curls. You both have the same personality."

Yes, this was the part I had heard about my father often. This was my stepfather's most frequent statement.

In many respects, I felt Melvin considered him his best friend. This was even stranger, now that I knew that Melvin was much, much older than my birth father.

"Mom said she's scared the door to hell will close with me inside."

He cast a despairing look at the ground and then over several inflated Santa mickeys that were dispersed across the lawn.

"Daddy?"

He breathed deeply. A long stream of smoke exited his mouth. "She's correct. The Lukes may want you there, but I'm not sure they can really keep you there."

"Why would they want me there?"

"Because you opened the door. All sorts of entities escaped his realms. He doesn't take too kindly to that."

"I was four years old, a child. I don't even remember doing it." I didn't, really! My stepfather had all sorts of those books around. I was a curious kid, and I read early."

"I don't think they have a case, and they do have Denton already so that should count. They do torture that boy, don't they? I think I've seen his head eaten at least three times now, and it's really painful to grow one back in the below realms."

I shuddered. The Lukes were something quite unknown to my worldview. Would they torture me, too? I rather liked my head. Did it ruin your hair to have it sucked off so many times? Did I really want to know this?

"You need to go with Andy to the opening, but not yet. You have to wait."

"Wait for what, Daddy?"

"I don't know, but don't go there until I tell you to. I'll work things out. As best I can." He put his arm around me. "I spoke to SUD. Dr. Prescott is the acting director. I told him not to involve you until I work things out. It will be too dangerous for you, otherwise. They have wanted you since you were a child. I told him no way then, and that's what I made clear now." He was quiet. "It was nice to see your father, wasn't it?"

It *was* nice. I only knew him from pictures. "He is taller than I thought…"

I didn't know why the tears came. It was silly, really. My mother, I could understand, but as for me, I hardly knew him. My stepfather wrapped his long arms around me, and I heard low sobs. I realized now that I was feeling their loss and pain. I didn't always appreciate this talent of mine, but it helped sometimes. You thought of your parents differently when you knew what was inside. I was a fairy, right? Because my mom was a fairy and Aunt Vienne was one too? Were we part of Grimm's nightmare world? This was way too much for me. I needed some time to digest this. What would I tell Sophie? And, hey, could I ride a bubble too? Did I even want to? I was a bit of a wimp when it came to heights.

"I love you, Daddy, I really do. You know that, right?"

His tear-stained face looked down into mine, and he smiled sadly at me. "I know, my sweet little Carrot Curls. I know. You are my little girl."

I was and always would have allegiance to him. He brought me up, wiped my rear, and sat through several broken hearts.

"I will never ever let anything happen to you," he

said. "I will find a spell that can prevent them from keeping you."

"Daddy, tell me the truth. Why do they really want me there permanently?"

"Power, my darling. It is simply about power." He turned me toward the door of the house. "SUD and the Lukes have been at it for years. Denton was playing for both sides. They're a tricky bunch, though I'm rather fond of Samuel. He's kind of an independent—a medical examiner, formally of the FBI, but, well, the last guy in charge…"

As we entered the house, I looked to the side for just an instance.

He was there, Redburn. He didn't have the Santa suit on this time. Next to him was the powder blue truck. He gave a slight wave, like, "Hey, do you see me?"

"Ignore him. There's nothing he can do now to you. He's just watching because he's afraid you're going to close the door, and you will." Then Melvin looked back and morphed into his true form.

I wasn't sure I would ever get used to a ten-foot lizard being my stepdad. Still, it did the trick. The blue pickup truck started to move away without its arrogant boss. The leering Hell critter landed on his rear because he was leaning on it. He got up and started to chase after it. Melvin and I both burst out laughing.

"Well, it seems he has lost his ride, my sweets."

At that moment, all the lights went out.

CHAPTER 26

S o how was it?"
I didn't hear Sophie creep into my room. It was bedtime, and a candle flickered on my dressing table. Her face radiated a pure light and, for a moment, I glimpsed what my very pretty daughter would look like later in life.

I should mention that when we got into the house, there was pure pandemonium going on. Barney, whom I just barely made out by the magic hues he gave off, was on the mantelpiece, grinning in delight as all the adults chased one six-year-old in the dark—a six-year-old who had the remote for the Christmas lights, little train, and everything else electric. The mite had decided to see just how many buttons he could push at once, shorting the whole house's electricity.

A series of "I got him" resounded throughout the house. Unfortunately, the capture was not such a triumph as the small prisoner no longer had the device in hand, and therefore the house remained in complete darkness, and a bit chilly, I might add. I had a hunch a certain nymph had something to do with the disappearance of the control pad, but I'd wait until later to confront him.

Never one to be deterred, Rydia, my ever-calm mother-in-law, pulled out the Christmas candles and assigned each of us a color. I got green with gold trim, and it was here, glowing in the mirror as Sophie came in to talk to me. She was smiling—a rarity for her—and how lovely it was.

"It was nice."

She looked disappointed. "And? Just nice?"

I reached behind me and twirled the chair. She sat on my lap, and we both turned back to the makeup table.

"Fattening."

"And? Mom, I am not a little girl anymore, you know." No, she was a nosy almost teenager now and my greatest accomplishment.

"Great! It was great, okay? I had a wonderful time," I gushed, and she looked positively pleased.

"Wasn't that funhouse just the coolest?"

Oh boy, how was I to explain that to her?

"Didn't that guy in the pilot suit look like Grandpa?" She was turned toward me, looking expectant.

"Kind of," I said hesitantly. I was debating what to say to her. She did speak to her dad, and he was dead, but should I expose her to the idea that Hell was real? Should I not? Was I crazy? Wouldn't that make any teen remain on the straight and narrow the rest of their lives? Yeah, right, in fantasy land maybe.

"It was Grandpa, right?"

I nodded. I had never lied to Sophie, and I wasn't going to do it now.

"That's so neat! I told Velma it was, but she said it was a hologram. It wasn't. She doesn't believe in ghosts and stuff."

We remained silent. Four sentences from my reticent daughter was a world record. I touched her face and realized how much she had grown up this year.

"I am glad she doesn't."

"Why?" I asked.

"Because that means I can still protect her from them." She got up, leaving me speechless. My Sophie was protecting her little cousin? She really was growing up too fast, wasn't she? "Goodnight, Mommy." She pecked my cheek so fast I couldn't catch her to return it.

"Goodnight."

She must have night vision, because I didn't hear her bump into anything.

For a moment I sat brushing my hair. The wind had made the entire curls one big tangle. It was then I felt him rather than saw him. Oh, and I smelled Mrs. Claus's sugar cookies and pine scent on him. I turned the chair to face the red suit, white mane, and big belly. "It's almost your big day, Santa."

He laughed and really it did make me feel merry. I wished that Sophie could have just stayed one more moment to see him by candlelight.

"It is, young lady, but before I do my business, you have business to do. I hear you have finally been given your assignment."

"Did you know I opened the door too?"

"Yes, I knew, but I didn't think it was fair that you got such a bad rap for it. After all, you were a child and Denton was a grown man. He shouldn't have left those books around. Kind of like leaving a loaded gun where kids can find it." He wagged a chunky finger at me. "You were meant to open it, of course. No accidents in this world. The Boss doesn't make mistakes. He wanted that door open."

We watched the candle burning down for a while.

I thought of Sophie. "Am I going to have to stay there?"

"Like I said, the Boss makes no mistakes. You have

a lot of people making sure you get out okay." He reached into his pocket and pulled out two sacks. One was white with a black smudge, and the other was red with gold trim. They were both the size of a palm. "Don't go with SUD until your father tells you it's the right time to go." He handed the bags to me. "I thought you might need just a little extra help, though. I know SUD often has other ideas so, just in case, I prepared some protection." He winked. I felt the two bags. The red bag was light and almost floated out of my fingers. He smiled and shrugged. "A little magic never hurts even when a master warlock is involved."

I weighed the other bag and looked at the black smudge.

"Coal?"

"Yes, coal, my dear." He laughed a rich ho, ho, ho. "If he tries to drag you into his realms, and he will, drop it in the pit and then head for the North Pole. Once you've reached the door and activated Garret's little device, throw the Christmas dust and get as far away as possible, young lady." I looked down at the bags again and then up at him. "Remember your promise to Sophie."

"My promise?" I thought about that for a moment. I had promised I wouldn't die too. I suppose being locked within Hell might be considered dying. It certainly sounded like a slow death to me.

"SUD can be rather persuasive. I'd avoid them altogether until your father tells you it's okay…" He was out the window now. However, the look he gave me made it quite clear he meant it. "Not even a cup of coffee with them." He was gone.

CHAPTER 27

All night long, I had tossed and turned. My dreams were a mix of Ferris wheels flying off their hinges with Lukes chasing me around fire pits. The whole occurrence happened on a Christmas tree ten times the size of the one in Rockefeller Center with Redburn calling up to me to lose some weight because I was ruining the tinsel.

Then, to my horror and Andy's pleasure, I vomited up all the onion rings we had eaten.

When I finally woke that morning, I was face to face with Barney.

"Boy, you look lousy this morning."

"Gee thanks, just what a girl wants to hear first thing in the morning."

"Your boyfriend is downstairs again. The guy takes you out on two dates, and he suddenly thinks he owns you."

Was that a hint of jealousy I heard from Barney the nymph? I didn't know whether to be flattered or to shape up real fast. "Um, Barney, do you mind?"

I got out of bed a little self-conscious. I knew these guys were naturals, but still, I was a girl, he was a guy...

He looked at me then at the door. "I can't just walk out of here, you know."

He didn't look too upset about it. Before I could say or do anything, Andy was standing at the doorway too.

"What is this Grand Central Station or something?" I looked from him to Barney and then back to Andy, who looked real good. I peered up into the vanity mirror and realized I looked like a morning head. Not good at all.

"Get out!" Andy put his thumb out and pointed down the hall.

Ahh, my hero.

"I can't just walk out of here, you know," Barney said again. Then Andy stepped in and picked him up. I heard Barney squeal, "Hey put me down, you brute!"

Then, football-style, Andy tossed him down. "Yo, Sophie. Here, catch."

Over he went, a little man the size of a doll. Andy turned around, and there I was.

I hit his chest. "How could you?"

"He's a natural, he can't get hurt," he said, catching and holding my pounding fists. "Besides, Sophie caught him. I'd be more concerned that she just handed him to Alexi, the little Loci."

Oh boy, I have to agree with him about that.

He chuckled. "I hope Barney wasn't all that attached to his legs. It looks like the kid is trying to figure out how to take them off."

I turned on my heel, went into my room, and slammed the door. I looked in the closet then the bed and, finally, in my drawers. A sweatshirt, jeans skirt, and a pair of boots would have to do. I tied the rat's nest up in one of Velma's hairbands meant for a nine-year-old with thin hair and burst out of the door and down the stairs, just in time to grab poor Barney out of the nymph-wrecker's arms.

"Hey, Auntie Delphi! I was checking out how they sewed him together."

Alexi jumped up to grab him when Andy swooped up the blond little munchkin and placed him on the couch. "How about a card trick, sport?"

That got all the kids' attention, and suddenly Andy was entertaining the whole crew. Phoebe had landed on the couch and rescued Andy from her brother as he sat fascinated by the magic of this man's fingers. Even Barney seemed interested. I placed him on the shelf, wagged my warning finger at him, and went over to them. Andy looked up at me and smiled. After about ten more minutes, he revealed one of his secrets and then exited the company of his adoring fans.

"You ready?"

For what, I wondered, was I supposed to be ready for, exactly?

"My nona wants to meet you so I thought breakfast would be good for you. I already okayed it with your brother-in-law. They said I could have you, as long as I returned you by two p.m."

Great, now my Greek family was now in charge of my social calendar.

"What's happening at two p.m.?"

Alexi jumped up, all excited. "The lamb's coming!"

Oh boy, the lamb. I remembered the lamb. Every year, two days before Christmas, the family purchased the most adorable little creature. All the kids got to play with it until it practically screamed to be slaughtered and then Uncle Origene came. He was the community butcher, a big mountain of a man. This was all done in the middle of the night, of course.

After all, no one wanted to tell the kids that the next day's dinner was the same playmate they nearly murdered themselves.

My Sophie always asked where the lamb went. Paulo always told her it had to get ready for Easter.

"The lamb?" Andy asked.

"Don't ask. I need to change to something more respectable."

He took my hand and shook his head. "You look great, come on."

He pulled, and I followed because I was rather attached to my fingers. Besides, how bad could I look if he thought I looked great? As we passed the mirror, I saw the lines from sleep still on my face, the uneven bumps on my head, and that I didn't have a lick of makeup on. This guy needed his eyes examined.

"Sophie, you ready?"

I frowned. "It looks like the two of you are in cahoots."

She fell in step with us as we headed to the little Camaro.

He courteously opened the door for both of us and drove the speed limit, looking in his mirror every so often. I was becoming very paranoid too. Was old powder blue behind us? No, I didn't see him, but I did see a very strange flock of birds above us. To my very untrained eyes, they looked like they were following us. Also—and don't think I'm nuts or my dreams have invaded my reality—these avian creatures looked more like flying monkeys. Okay, so Oz was on my brain, can you blame me? My mother did ride a bubble. On further inspection, I realized they were more insectoid.

"Don't worry," Andy said reassuringly, but he did a fast switch, zooming across three lanes of traffic, to the tune of honks, curses, and screeches of tires, then he took the exit. "I lost him."

"I think I lost yesterday's dinner, lunch, and any meals I might eat in the next week."

Sophie, in the back seat, was smiling, as only a kid who loved roller coasters could. I thought she was disappointed when it was smooth sailing from then on. I looked above us. Yep, they were still there.

We came to a small row home on the edge of northeast Philadelphia. These houses looked old and solid. They were attached, all built with orange bricks and rounded doorways. I noticed that Christmas decorations were few and far between. He saw me looking around.

"The neighborhood is changing. A lot of Asians and Muslims." His own lawn was empty, with only a wreath on the door and a few lights in the form of candles. "Nona doesn't really do it up on the outside, just keeps a few eternal flames going for my parents, my grandpa, and the soldiers in Afghanistan."

I looked at them, and they seemed to blink for a moment. The white curtains moved, and I saw a young girl standing there. She began waving frantically at Andy who smiled broadly and gave a high five back.

"Sarah, my sister," he said.

She didn't look any older than Sophie, though I had noticed a lot of Down syndrome children seemed not to age. When he smiled, I thought I could spend the rest of my life with this guy. He seemed to really love his sister.

The door opened, and there stood a tiny, dark, round woman. Her long, gray hair was wrapped and piled high on her head. "Andrew! Come in, you will catch your death of cold." It sounded more like "Andrew-a Coma in a you willa catch your deatha colt." Her thick accent was not unlike my husband's family's lilting Greek. As he led us in past her, she took me in her arms and kissed both cheeks. When she caught hold of Sophie, she embraced her wholeheartedly and looked deep into her eyes. "You are a good girl!"

Sarah came up from behind. She was the same height

as Sophie, but wider. Her flat nose, little eyes, and big smile greeted us. She had thick black hair and was holding one of those large heads that girls can style, brush, and put makeup on.

Sophie's eyes instantly went to the doll head.

"You wanta play?" Sarah asked Sophie.

Sophie looked at me, and I nodded. Sarah took her hand and off they went.

"She is beautiful!" His grandmother clapped her hands, and I had to agree. Sophie really was. I was so proud of her at this moment.

"I know, Nona."

I turned to see they were staring at me. I thought they must have both needed contacts.

We went into the living room. The furniture looked ancient. There were burgundy velvets, rose-gold-trimmed chairs, and a deep red carpet that felt as if I was walking on the red sea, it was so thick. I could smell breakfast, and I was suddenly reminded of how hungry I was. Unfortunately, so was my stomach, which made itself known in the quiet of this moment.

"I'm sorry." I blushed the same shade as the walls. "I didn't eat yet." I looked at her grandson who shrugged.

"I am sorry too, an old woman forgetting her manners. Andrew, get her an espresso!" she barked at him. He jumped up and left us. "Andrew says your husband died in the war. My husband died in the war too. He was a good man."

She showed me a picture of a young pilot who stood next to an old plane. I gauged the time to be World War II. Next to that was another picture with several pilots. There was her husband, a man who looked just like Andy, but—there were a few surprises, because there was Giles, Dr. Sam Prescott, and Melvin! She picked it up and pointed to the one that resembled Andy, and I could see the love was still there. She pointed to the picture of a blond little boy. "My oldest, Tony, he is a lawyer, lives in New Jersey." Proud mama. "He helped a lot with Sarah and Andrew when they were little." Then she pointed at two wedding pictures, Andrew's grandfather and another one, Tony and his wife. This one looked recent. He was a handsome man in his fifties. I could see the strong resemblance to the pilot. The lady with him was around the same age. She was blonde, fair-skinned, and had blue eyes. His mother picked it up. "She is a nice girl too, but too old to have babies." She looked at my stomach, which acknowledged her stare with a growl. "Andrew, where's that espresso? A person could die out here!"

"Coming, Nona." He came in from, where I supposed was the kitchen. He had a silver tray with three tiny cups, an aroma of dark coffee following him. The plate also held a bowl of poppy seed cookies. Sarah and Sophie came out, as if on cue, and Sarah looked at the tray.

"Choco?" she asked.

"Coming right up." He disappeared and then reappeared with two mugs of hot chocolate topped with mounds of marshmallow fluff and chocolate chips. His nona nodded approvingly. Andy disappeared again. He came out making the sound of a foghorn. The girls giggled uncontrollably. I could see Sophie was enjoying this show.

Each girl was handed a cup. Andy held Sarah's while she put her chubby hand on it too. Together he led them to a small children-sized table set just for two.

"Mademoiselles—" He bowed like a waiter. "—cocoa is served."

Both girls clapped. Andy took a bow and smiled broadly. It was almost a Yaniv-sized one, but only the Doberman himself could put in full wattage.

"He's a good boy, most of the time." Nona smiled at

him lovingly and patted his hand. "Sit, Andrew. We talk, yes?"

He sat, we talked. It looked like sweet little Nona ruled the place. Eventually, the girls were corralled, and we all had a breakfast that consisted of thousands of calories from tons of great foods with names I couldn't pronounce without getting shot.

"Prima calzone," Nona announced solemnly.

"Breakfast is served." Andy smiled at me. He had gone back into the kitchen to get more coffee. "Café al' latte, coffee with a thick milk."

No wonder Andy was wired so tightly—look at how much coffee these Italians drank. The cup was overflowing with a thick white foam.

He took a sip, and when he lifted his head up, he had a white mustache. "Got Milk?"

The girls were in stitches and, frankly, so was I. I liked this lighthearted, sweet Andy. I wished he would stay and play a bit.

Next, Nona got up herself and brought in a very crusty bread that was also sweet. Andy called it brioche. She had several different kinds of jellies and preserves, each served in a crystal bowl with a fancy cover and its own silver spoon.

"Nona makes her own preserves, and they are the best." He kissed his grandmother's cheek, and she made a playful gesture, swatting him off.

She then went back in and brought out skewers of fried pepper and sausage slices. The spicy scent along with pepper's sweetness was delicious. Next came the cookies, which included three kinds of biscotti—cranberry, chocolate chip, and pistachio, my personal favorite. The girls pounced on more than the jams and jellies. It was a different generation, I guess, and soon, I feared, preserving fruit would be a lost art altogether.

"So when are you two getting married?" Nona intoned as the last bit of bread entered my mouth.

Everything was going just grand until then.

"Nona, we only went out two times and—"

"Your grandfather and I got married as soon as he returned from the war. He wrote my papa that he was going to take care of me. He came home, and Andrew and I married. No dating at all. We had a good marriage."

She crossed herself as most religious Catholics did when stating the absolute truth. Not that I doubted Nona for a moment. I believed she would stand at the airport waiting for her newly minted husband in her wedding dress, priest in tow.

Andy winced like a kid. "Nona, things don't work that way nowadays."

Her eyes flew open dramatically. "No?"

"No."

Uh-oh. It seemed not everything was hunky-dory in the D'Souza household. To his credit, Andy was keeping his temper in check.

Nona, on the other hand, seemed to be just beginning. "You want better the pimpled girl with the toilet mouth?"

"She didn't have a foul mouth, Nona."

"She said 'damn.' That is a foul word." She said it low in hushed tones, looking from side to side.

"'Damn' is a word commonly used now, Nona."

Did I feel the temperature rising in here?

"You want a bar of soap in your mouth again for saying it, Andrew?"

That got him quiet real fast.

"Or the girl with the big…" She motioned to her chest. "You think I not know what community relations means?" Then she added slyly, "*These days*?"

"Damn, damn, damn…" Sarah started, but the words

withered on her lips at her grandmother's sharp glance at the bathroom.

Sophie seemed oblivious to the antics around her. This was probably nothing, compared to the noise we lived with.

"Or the girl who spent all your money and no let you call her at home? Is that what goes on *these days* too, Andrew?"

If the table could have swallowed him, I thought he would have jumped in.

"Those girls are not nice girls. This girl is a nice, normal—" That was debatable. "—good girl!" Then she looked me over and thought for a moment. "Are you Catholic?"

"Um, no, ma'am, I'm—"

She shrugged. "Okay, so she is not perfect!"

"My mother is Catholic," I started. "I went to Catholic School almost all my childhood—"

"Oh, see? There is hope." She clapped her hands. "And besides, how are you going to get to know her if those men are coming here?"

I looked at him. "Men? What men?"

"The bathtub men," Sarah put in genially.

"Who?"

"SUD. They wanted us to go with them to the Mint."

Sarah looked all excited at this prospect. "Oooh, candy."

"No," I said, getting that feeling I got when I knew things weren't going to be turning out quite right. I told you I have these feelings, right?

His eyebrow popped up. "No?"

"My dad said I had to wait for him to tell me when to go to the, uhh…mint." I didn't know what he had told his grandmother yet.

"They know that, but they need for you to see it

anyway." He was trying to evade the evil eye that Nona was throwing him.

"She is a good girl, listening to her papa," Nona put in as if to protect me.

I was suddenly very nervous. If Melvin told me to stay away, I was staying away! I got up and motioned for Sophie to do the same. She complied, and we headed for the door. I turned around and tried to look as gracious as I could. "Thank you so much for breakfast, Mrs. D'Souza. It was delicious."

We backed out of the door as Andy came after us. "Where do you think you're going?"

I didn't know where I was going, but I knew I had to be away from here before SUD came.

"Santa also said not to go there until my father gave the go-ahead." I tried to whisper it so I didn't sound crazy in front of his family.

"Santa?" Sarah had followed us out and picked up on these words immediately.

"Really?" Andy wasn't as excited as his sister. I could see his temper rising.

"I need to get home, fast." Then I looked toward the car and back at him. "Could you take us home, please?" I had Sophie with me. What was he thinking?

"They will be here any moment. Why don't you just talk to them? Drink a cup of espresso—"

More coffee? Wasn't he already hyped up enough?

"Santa said not even a cup of coffee with them." I stamped my foot. "I'm going to go with them—just when my dad says to—that's all."

"Oh, come off it, lady!" There it was, his temper, full-blown. "Do you really know anything about your dad?"

What was he saying?

"According to Yaniv, your dad and SUD have been on the outs for years."

"And?" I remembered differently. Wasn't he working with them at the train station?

"Don't you think that it is suspicious that he's telling you not to go there before he says—when he's the one who just happened to leave a book of power lying around for a kid to find?" His eyes were focused intensely on mine as he hissed this at me.

"No." It seemed perfectly normal to me. Really. I mean, I had grown up with a lot of strange things. Books with weird writing in it could totally be a part of my childhood. Anyway, I trusted Melvin. More than I did Andy, certainly. Why didn't he understand?

"You are an impossible, woman, you know that. I don't even know what I saw in you in the first place," he raged at me.

"I guess the engagement is off then!" I steamed back, more hurt by his comment than he could imagine.

His eyes were daggers. This was the cop in him that I totally disliked. "The only way I'd marry you, lady, is if hell froze over.

"Good, then that should be your sign," Nona said. "When it happens, Andrew, you make sure you ask her right away! After all, a gentleman always keeps his word."

What did Nona just say?

She was gathering in Sarah and Sophie, who were looking truly distressed at this point. "You both come inside, let the lovebirds work this out."

He looked truly horrified at her statement. "Nona!"

"What? You want these children to catch a cold?" She ushered them in.

He cast her a glare.

"You think your grandpapa and I never had little disagreements?" She matched his glare with an extra look of soaring broomsticks. Boy, these D'Souzas could cast those eyes. She then closed the door behind us.

"She's adorable," I said, meaning it. I laughed. It was just too funny.

"Adorable? You ought to have seen the day I played hooky from school—" He started to chuckle, rubbing his backside at the memory.

"Yeah, I can see she is a stickler for rules and regulations."

"Mostly regulations. If she got a note that a report was due, I started it that day and finished it the next one. It didn't matter that it was a six-week project. I had to do it right away."

He was smiling, but I wasn't biting. It would take more than white teeth and dimples to get me back. Maybe hell freezing over was what I needed.

"Well isn't this cozy?" a deep voice boomed behind us.

"Captain Breenan?"

The huge police captain man was standing at the curb. Behind him was a powder blue pickup truck.

"You have been causing a whole lot of trouble, D'Souza." The captain's dark eyes gave us a hard look. "Couldn't you have just been a good grieving partner, done some desk duty, and then let us handle Ned's unfortunate demise?"

The doors opened, and a bunch of little Barneys hopped out.

Andy took my hand and pulled me near to him. He moved his head from side to side, trying to see an escape route. I got his drift—there was his family to think about, and Sophie was in there too. We made our break toward the bushes, and the little mites sprang after us. We dashed down the sidewalk toward a neighbor's house and then to the lane behind it. As we turned the corner, Andy came to a halt. There was Redburn. He was just standing there, but next to him must have been at least fifty little flying creatures with very sharp fangs. Uh oh, those guys looked real familiar.

"Loci," the deep voice behind us said. "You ever seen them, Andy? Rather nasty fellows." The captain came to a halt behind us. It was then that I noticed he wasn't quite right. Not crazy looking, just fuzzy. Worse than when I had first seen him, though. Now he was truly not clear. A dark cloud seemed to be surrounding him.

"You're dead," I said as the revelation hit me.

They all stared at me, except Redburn.

"I told you she was dangerous. We should have killed her when we had the chance," Redburn hissed at him.

"I don't kill kids." The captain's voice became hollow as it had when I first saw him. "Get them!" He signaled the Loci, and suddenly we were grabbed and in the air.

Now, I knew everyone had had these dreams, at one time or another, of being able to fly, but flying, while held in the talons of Loci, was not quite the ride of the century. It was truly terrifying, not to mention nauseating and disorienting.

I could see Andy was struggling, but one good kick from the little, spurred boot of the Loci who held him, and there wasn't another peep. He was out cold, with a gash across his head to show for his trouble.

As the blood dripped down from his head wound, several of the little creepy-crawlers made a dive for it, smacking their lips as they caught one or two of the droplets.

I, myself, could feel the talons of the one carrying me digging in just a bit too hard. I gave him a smack to warn him. Just as his spur came toward my face, I heard a very angry voice.

"The master wants her whole and unharmed," Redburn said.

How had he sprouted wings? He took out a sharp object and stuck it in the heart of the thing that was carrying me. I was released, only to drop downward alongside a very dead Loci.

Don't ask what got into me, but I grabbed at the silver thing that was embedded in his heart, pulled it out, and shoved it into my jeans pocket. I was grabbed by another Loci, only to watch in horror as the rest of the flock lurched toward the dead one, ripped him to pieces, and ate him in midair. There weren't even any bones left to pick.

CHAPTER 28

I must have passed out then because, when I came to, I was in hell. Or what only could be described as hell. We were on a cliff overhanging a lake with lots of bubbles burping up red lava. In the distance, I could see the Lukes flying. Any occupant that was able to pull themselves out of the fiery waters onto the very jagged shore was picked up in a large beak, flown to the middle of the fire lake, and dropped back into it. The noise here was so deafening at first that I didn't hear him.

"Theresa," Andy croaked at me.

His wound was red and angry-looking. As I examined it, I realized it had tiny little worms in it.

"My face is killing me." He went to touch it, but I stopped his hand.

"It's infected." What was I going to say—he was being eaten by little black scavengers that would probably devour the rest of his face? "Let me clean it, okay?" I reached into my pocket for a tissue and felt Santa's bags. Well, that was a plus. Okay, so I was sort of the glass-half-full type of girl. It didn't matter that I didn't have Garret's little device or that I had no idea which way was out, much less the direction to the North Pole. I checked the other pocket and felt Redburn's trinket. Should I do surgery? No, I tried for a tissue again. I did fish out a tissue, only a little used. Compared to what was crawling in his cheek, this was a veritable antibiotic salve.

"Don't bother," Captain Breenan said.

He didn't look too good here, dressed an old-fashioned uniform that had been burned quite badly. His feet were bare and mostly bones, with worms of their own crawling around on them, eating what little flesh he still had.

"Who are you?" Andy struggled to get up, but the other shoved him down.

Andy only avoided being hurled into the abyss by my desperate grabbing at his belt. Don't get any ideas. I was a good girl like Nona said I was, just not in the habit of letting people drop into fiery lakes.

"I was a pretty good cop at one time, but I kind of figured what the hell—all the criminals were getting richer and us flat foots? We were being picked off one by one. I saw my two friends' corpses in a car. They had just been mowed down like animals by the people—you know, the ones we were hired to serve and protect—they were marching with signs that said 'Kill the Pigs!' The lovely sixties." He kicked Andy onto the ground and smacked his head with a wayward, bony backhand. Andy was out cold again.

Breenan shook his head, and I saw he had a hole in the side of it. Several little creatures stuck their little bald heads out of the wound and smiled at me. Then they waved. Automatically I waved back, and Captain Breenan looked behind him to see what I was waving at. A big Luke flew up out of the pit behind him, at that moment, and stuffed him into his mouth. I could hear Brennen screaming.

"Put me down, you! I'm supposed to be rewarded by the boss!"

He was fighting it all the way, flailing and carrying on. Then the Luke did let him go, right in the middle of the lake. Brennen went in with a splash that washed over the creature, who seemed to not even notice the burning liquid.

"Such a shame. He was a good cop at one time," Redburn hissed. He was floating right off the ledge and flapping his black leather wings. "How are you, Theresa?"

Did I know him? He did look vaguely familiar to me. Who was he? He began to morph. Not into a man or a Loci, but into a pig—or at least its face. "Pig man!" Before I could stop my mouth from rolling, it was out.

"Don't call me that!"

He spat swine saliva at me. I knew him. He was the ghost from my past in Dodgersville, the one with a taste for kids.

However, I wasn't a kid anymore. "You don't scare me." I looked directly at him. "What did they promise you if you helped them?"

He scratched the lone hair hanging from his chinny, chin, chin. "The train station and all its contents."

He smiled evilly at me. I could only picture poor Abraham's face. How many times would he have to die a horrible death?

"And for Sonny, all the meat he could trap."

Just great. Two pieces of garbage being let loose on the most vulnerable members of society. I really hated pedophiles! They were truly the lowest of low. I stood there, contemplating this new revelation, when I felt the little silver disc in my pocket.

He looked at me, and I looked at him as he aimed himself at me, talons out. I knew it was now or never. As he made his way toward me to shred me to pieces, I threw it. The disc landed true, splitting his ugly face in half and sending him back into the pit below. He squealed as he fell.

"Shut up!" The Luke with its dragon face came up on the ledge, trailing waves of red lava. "Good help is so hard to find these days." He smiled a long-fanged grin at me and laughed as I veered back from his acid breath. "So, Theresa, darling, you are home. We can do so much together. I plan on being very good to you." He gave me a look of, what I assumed was, his best attempt at sincerity. "As long as you cooperate, that is."

Conditions? I had only just met the guy.

"Then we can work together as a team," he said.

Oh, really? Like I was just going to work for him. Maybe he wanted to offer me a train station too?

"We'll get married. I heard of your recent loss."

Now I was being proposed to? Again. Well, that was a record—twice in one day.

"I can't marry you. I'd burn to death here."

Without as much as another word, he knocked me into the pit.

"Theresa!" I heard Andy scream.

What a time to finally come back to life just as I was flailing my way into the fires of hell. I did the only thing I could think of doing. I cried. Okay, so I was a woman, and I was getting hysterical. I wonder what you folks would do in my position? As I did so, I splashed into the fire. Strangely, the flames cooled off as soon as they touched me. I didn't feel any burning. Even more surprising, I flew out of them. Not really flew out—I kind of developed a bubble. Just like Glinda the Good Witch in *The Wizard of Oz*—or, to be more precise, just like my mother.

"Neat, huh?" The Luke was face to scary, ugly face with me. "I told you she was the one." \

Who he was talking to I had no idea, but he seemed to be a bit of a schizophrenic to me.

"You see?" he called out to no one in particular. "You will marry me, my dear, and then we will live happily and hellishly ever after." He leaned over to me. "How about a smooch, lover?"

A large snout came at me. Yes, I said I was desperate, and, yes, he was a big muscle-bound guy, but…well, lizards weren't my thing, you know?

"Hey, get your grimy mouth away from my girlfriend!"

Was Andy waving a fist at him, a dragon that was ten times his size?

"He's the Devil," I wanted to scream at him, but he was so far above us.

"Shut up!" Luke soared upward, leaving me stranded.

How exactly does one drive one of these things? I pushed and shoved at the bubble I was in. For a moment, I just stood there, and then I started to roll over and over. Unfortunately, I didn't know where the brakes were on this particular mode of transportation. It was so disconcerting, especially with all those hot flashes coming up through the bubble, and me not even thirty-nine yet. It was then that the nausea started to rise up.

Now, for all you bulimics out there, there is a sure-fire cure to hold back barf. Just picture yourself in a magic bubble, rolling around hell. Then think of vomit spreading all over your clothes, your hair, with two guys…well, one guy and one whatever…fighting over you.

I mean, this was better than a pill.

I did stop, though. I hit a wall and, to my own shock, it popped the bubble. I was now falling. *Oh my, this is fun, Not!* I landed—not so gracefully, I might add—on a pile of hay. What was hay doing here? Didn't they know this stuff was flammable?

I saw one of the Lukes flying very erratically. There was a lot of screaming going on above me. It was amazing how Andy's voice could carry.

The man was fearless. He was riding the back of the very same Luke! The dragon was going crazy. In fact, I got the distinct feeling that it was Andy doing the hurting. They were really going at it.

It was like a rodeo—the creature was twisting and turning and trying with all its might to get its rider off. It was quite a show, and the occupants of the underworld were starting to take note.

All movement, sound—and even, it seemed, suffering—stopped, as the spectacle above continued.

Up from the depths came a massive creature that looked like all the Lukes combined. As he rose, bodies followed him, flying all over the place. Three landed near me. One of them was Maxie. He looked at me, and I looked at him.

He smiled his charming grin at me. "Hiya, kid."

"Good morning, sir."

"Is it Christmas yet?" He looked hopeful.

"No, sir. Two more days until it arrives."

"Oh, this must be an early gift from my little girl then, huh?" He looked at the great creature that put Peter Jackson's Smog to shame. "You know my kid? Annie's her name."

"Yes, sir, I met her. She's lovely." A sad look crossed his face. "She loves you a lot and waits by the pit in the Moxi for you to return."

I didn't know how I knew that, I just did. Or maybe I wanted it to be true.

"Yep, she was beautiful."

We were rudely interrupted by the massive being.

"What is going on around here?" he boomed, and all inhabitants cowered and held their ears.

I even had the urge to do so, though I was too busy gawking to actually comply. Just at that moment, I didn't know whether from shock or from determination, the smaller Luke was able to unhook Andy from its back. Downward he fell toward the bubbling lava pit. Before he reached it, though, an amazing thing transpired. Wings sprouted from his back, big gray bird wings that resembled what I had seen on the walls of churches.

"A nephilim? Who let one of those in here?" the massive being screeched, trying to bat Andy away from him. "Which one of you idiots did it?"

The one, that had been playing horsey before, dove into the waters and pulled out a very crispy porker with a split head. The pig came out and, for one moment looked relieved, until he saw who was awaiting him.

"You? *You* brought one of those into my realm?" The massive being grabbed the pink body in his fist. The man looked like a tiny doll encased in knuckles of steel.

He was literally squealing in agony. "Your magnificence, how was I to know that he was a…was a…a what is he again?"

Yeah, what was Andy exactly? I liked to know what a guy was before I turn him down.

"Nephilim. He is an angel, you idiot! You brought him into my domain. No other angel is allowed here, just me!" he roared, and I could see his breath burning off the little man's face.

Boy, I was going to do everything I could to avoid this place. It looked brutal. What if I burned his dinner? Well, here, I guessed that would be a good thing.

"He is only a half angel, boss," one Luke put in.

The other flew over to him. "Actually only quarter angel, boss, at least by now."

Three others came over, hovering near their master's hand. In aggravation, the big monster opened his mammoth hand and threw the burning body at them.

They went flying backward—rolling, swirling in somersaults—until they could stop themselves mid-air.

"He is an angel! He is here in my place! No others are allowed here!"

He reached out and gathered them up. Then he stuck them to his body. Each struggled to be free as his mass seemed to absorb them.

It was creepily fascinating. Then he spotted me on the shores next to Max Sampler.

"You," he shouted. As he waded over, the other two poor souls on the shores jumped into the burning water. "You are the root cause of all this. Opening up doors when they should remain locked."

"I was four years old." I stood on the now-burning hay that had ignited from the molten liquid dripping from his body. "I didn't even know what I was doing."

As it neared me, Maxie stood tall in front of me. I was impressed, but I wondered what one dead gangster could do against the Lord of Hell itself.

"Leave the kid alone. She didn't understand squat!" He put his face up as a drip of lava fell, landing on his skin. To his credit, he didn't even wince.

"Get out of my way, Sampler." The creature put two meaty fingers together and made to flick him away when Andy dove down, distracting him.

Maxie then grabbed my hand and led me toward the side of the mountain we were standing next to. He kept fingering the sides, looking for something. Something he definitely knew would—or rather, should—be there. He was a crafty one.

"Yeah. Here it is." Just as the creature dodged Andy's next attack and was about to grab me, Maxie shoved me into the crevice. "You leave this little girl be, you hear me!"

I couldn't believe what I was seeing. Max Sampler had saved my life. Or at least saved me from extreme pain and hurt to my physical body.

"Mr. Sampler, which way is the North Pole?" I figured he was a regular in this place, and he might well know.

He looked around and pointed across the lake of fire. Oh boy, how was I going to get there?

The Luke gnashed its teeth at him. "Move away from her, Sampler."

I pushed as far back into the wall as I could. I could tell someone had been hiding here, as there were remnants of a straw bed. Probably it was Maxie's own hidey-hole, clever man that he was. The Luke must have grabbed him then and thrown him into the river of lava. I heard him yelling in pain. A large red finger with a very sharp fingernail poked in at me. Then it retracted, and a bloodshot eye was looking at me. "Come out, come out, wherever you are…"

I tried to ignore him.

"We can do this the hard way, girlie, or you can come to me. You are staying here, in any case, you know."

No, I wasn't. Burned wasn't my color—it clashed badly with my hair.

"Come on," he whined in a not-so-attractive way. "I am a real angel, at least, not a quarter one." With that, he reduced himself in size and was in the cave with me in human form.

To tell you the truth, as a man, he wasn't so bad looking. I mean, I could have done without the fangs, the horns, and maybe I would have preferred blue eyes. Red ones, somehow, didn't put me in a romantic mood.

"Now, why don't we come out, aye?" he boomed as if he was out in his own realms.

I was thinking that I should tell him to use his indoor voice like I always told Velma when she and Alexi were arguing in the house. However, I wasn't sure this guy would appreciate the criticism—or any suggestions at all, especially from me. He reached his hand out to me, a hand tipped in short, ragged, dirty fingernails. So Lucifer was a nail-biter, huh? I had the urge to veer backward as he neared me.

"I will make you very happy. Together we could rule the world—" He was shoved over by a set of wings.

"Yo! She's my girl, and neither you nor your mini-mes are going to have her!"

Andy. My hero. The devil rose and turned to him.

"Now you see why I don't let other angelic beings into my realm. They come in for five minutes, and they think they can rule the joint."

Boy, it seems he had a power issue.

"I have all of your brethren under a mountain in the Middle-East. I am not sure how your great-grandfather got out, but that is one mistake I intend to fix right now."

He attacked Andy head on. Nephilim against the master of the underworld. It seemed that Andy had enormous strength down here. As they battled, they fell out of the little cave. They rolled around the beach, sparking hay as they went by. Smoke and fire began to rise. I was choking and coughing, with nowhere to go. I looked out and saw that Andy was now on fire too. They were fighting, and he didn't seem to notice. I didn't have anything to quench the flames with, and he was really burning! Then I felt in my pocket. There were Santa's little bags.

"Well, this is an emergency." I edged toward the fiery hot liquid. Then I opened the little bag and out came a few snowflakes. They started out just as flurries. "Some magic."

Things started to really get going when cold heavy flakes fell down on the hay, the water, and poor Andy. He began smoldering, and the stink of wet feathers wafted in the air. Pretty soon there was a full-out snow storm going on.

"No!" Luke shoved Andy away and went to the now partially frozen lake. "What have you *done*, Witch?" He made a mad dash toward me, knocking me down, and grabbed at Santa's bag. I held it tight and managed to pour the rest of it on him.

He froze. Not just figuratively, either. I pushed him off of me. He crashed to the ground and shattered.

"Ho, ho, ho."

Looking up, I saw a sleigh with reindeer heading toward us. On it, along with Santa, were Melvin, Dr. Prescott, and Yaniv. Santa landed the vehicle on the bank and motioned that I should get in. Andy made to come aboard, too. "No room, but you can fly, Andy." Santa pointed at the wings. Then he pulled out a little green bag with gold trim and poured its contents into his hand. The substance looked like shiny white sand. He sprinkled the dust on Andy's badly crisped feathers. The dust shimmered in mid-air, and then Andy's wings were suddenly healed and whole. Andy spread them out and looked hesitantly upward. "You can do it, Andy. You were born to fly." Santa started the sleigh. "Come, Dancer, go, Vixen…" We were off. "Off, Dasher and Prancer, go, Comet, on, Cupid."

I looked behind us. Andy was still standing there. He looked so sad and as forlorn just as the place was starting to look like a Christmas card. I realized he was freezing along with it, so, impulsively, I jumped.

"Carrot Curls!" I heard my father call as Donner and

Blitzen were ordered upward and onward. A bubble enveloped me and, this time, I was able to control the rolling. I actually managed to hover near him.

"Take my hand, you."

I reached for him, and he hesitantly took it. His
wings began flapping, and up we went. I was glad he
took the lead as I really was a new driver and didn't have
much control yet. We soared over the pit that was now a
veritable ice rink. Its occupants were slipping and sliding
happily around. We reached the side of Santa's sleigh.

"Take this." Dr. Prescott handed me a strange device.
Melvin nodded. We had reached the northernmost part of
the cavern. The exit was small, but big enough for us to
fit through. We were in the Franklin Mint. Money machines lay dormant, and the place was silent.

"Go ahead, Carrot Curls, activate it."

I looked at it. The thing looked old fashioned, and I
had no way to know how to use it.

"Just touch it, darling," Melvin said. "Take back
what you did years ago."

They all looked expectantly at me.

"Hurry! Yes, yes, yes," the Greek statue uttered.

He looked a bit panicked, though it was hard to tell
under that sunlit smile he always seemed to wear.

"Take it back? How do I do that?" But as I said those
words, the book that I had read years ago appeared in
front of me. There were strange symbols on the page. I
reached instinctively out to touch the letters. I heard a
voice in my head that pronounced them clearly. I repeated each one carefully. The device ignited and emitted a
green light. The massive door we stood in front began to
close slowly behind us.

"No!" I heard the roar before I saw the clawed hand
come out at me. The massive thing grabbed me around
the waist, talons digging in, and snatched me back. The

door was closing, and I could only picture my Sophie, my useless promise to her. A wave of panic was invading my already constricted body.

"Why have her, when you could have the real thing, Luke?"

He whirled around and there she was, my mother. She was in Glinda the Good Witch mode now. Bubble, crown, and all, shimmering in white. I couldn't believe the transformation. She looked like a goddess.

"You?" He was as enamored as any male would be by her. Yep, she was Aunt Vienne's cousin, pure siren.

She floated near him. "Yes, me, Luke. I will stay here with you if you let her go back to where she came from."

"Mom, no—"

She put her finger to her lips and mouthed, "Sophie." It was the hardest silence I ever kept.

"Luke?"

He looked at me and then at her. Well, what can I say—there was no contest here, okay? She was radiating femininity, and I...well, let's say shimmering butterball turkey would be an apt description.

He let go and, for a moment, I forgot I could ball up. I fell with a thump on my padded rump, and then I blew the bubble up around me. He grabbed at her, and she popped. There in his hand was my mother. He relaxed his grip then submerged into the molten lake below with Mom.

"Just follow the golden road out, sweetie."

And the last air bubbles stopped along with my heart.

I looked behind me. I'll be danged if there wasn't a golden road. In fact, it looked just like yellow bricks. The one problem was I still didn't know how to maneuver this darn bubble I was in. All right, so there were two problems. I could see the door was almost closed. So, in desperation, I rolled myself, not too gracefully, down the golden path toward the last crack of the door, which closed just as I got to it. I did what any red-blooded American woman would do. I began to sob. I had failed—I had broken my promise. Sophie was officially an orphan now: no mother, no father, and no grandmother. Okay, so she had Paulo's parents, but let me have my moment, will you? The tears fell, hitting the edges of the glittering sphere I was in, and the bubble then really burst. I fell unceremoniously on my hiney again—boy, that smarted. As I got up quickly, hoping no one was looking, I noticed an emerald door. There was an old-fashioned, rusty drawstring. Hanging on it was a sign that read, *Bell is broken, use knocker*. I peered upward. In fact, there was a bell hanging there. It was a big black cast iron thing hanging way up high. The chain was broken and lay limply, attached to the wall by equally rusted hinges, but not connected to the instrument it was meant for. I then looked for the knocker: there was none. I was beginning to feel panic again. I began to bang on the stone portal. Then to add insult to injury, I broke a nail! I was taking all my frustrations and pain out on the hapless portal when something occurred to me.

The ringer was eye level. There was no door-knocker, at least from my vantage point. *How would a crafty devil do things?* I peered to the side, around the corner of the door, and then I looked down, and there it was, at knee level. I was just about to kneel and use the knocker.

"I knew you could find it." He was not standing on the brick road. He was hovering just above it.

"Papa?"

"Do you know how Luke keeps the masses in here?" He was still in his pilot's outfit just as he always was in the pictures Mom had of him. I shook my head. "The door. Most people get stuck in hell because they are always looking up and are just too arrogant to see anything that is a bit below them. Rarely do they look down." He came over to me, kissed my cheek, and smiled. "So Luke keeps the exit very low to the ground where humility always lies."

"Can you help Mom, too?" I looked behind me and noticed the road was crumbling as I stood there. "He took her below."

I hadn't realized it, but my mother was a terrific lady. How come it was always after a parent is gone that we see what they really are? She had protected me for so long, and I had not really appreciated her. Now she had sacrificed for me again, and it was too late to say thank you.

"Knock on the door, my little girl. Quickly." He waited, but made no move to help my mother. I knocked. The road was disappearing, turning into molten lava under my feet. The door opened and a thin, white hand poked through. I knew that hand—much stronger than it looked. I glanced behind me, but my father was gone as were most of the yellow bricks.

Melvin pulled me through the opening. How I fit I'd never understand. He hugged me tightly and very close. Over his shoulder, I could see Yaniv and the doctor conversing heatedly.

"Mom was there, and Luke took her instead of me!" I started to bawl.

"He did?"

Melvin's chest caved in, and I could tell he was sad beyond measure. I felt it through his very being, just as I could feel his age now. How he had aged.

Andy stood to the side watching Melvin and me. His wings were gone, and he looked ready to pounce. Every so often he glanced over his shoulder, and, whenever he did, he had that uh-oh look. Melvin released me. Andy hastened over and took up where he left off. I was speechless. It felt good to be in his arms, but very odd, as I wasn't really on speaking terms with him. Yeah, even after all that, I was still mad at him. I told you about the pride part, right?

"Well, we have a problem here, don't we?" It was the doctor's voice, and he wasn't happy. He looked sideways at me and then at Andy. "Normally, we are in and out in these situations, but there were other considerations."

Melvin turned to him viciously, but the doctor didn't wince. I supposed I was the consideration.

"We would use our true forms and just bowl our way out with these little fleas..." The doctor trailed off and, behind him, I saw a sea of little, pointed hats.

Nymphs. Not at all the cute and cuddly Barney types, either. These were growling and hissing like peeved cats in heat.

"The coal in the other packet I gave you."

I heard the whisper in my ears. I looked around and realized Santa was missing. I reached in and pulled out the white velvet bag with the gold trim and the black smudges.

Yaniv spotted it in my hand and smiled, ever hopeful. "Nick said he was sending backup."

The gang was headed right at us when I heard Santa again.

"Throw it into their midst." The words were barely audible.

I pulled out the round, smooth, shiny black piece. To my astonishment, the thing began to grow. It became very big and terribly heavy, the size of a bowling ball. I thought of the doctor's word "bowl"—and took my best shot. The round ball rolled and hit the lead man, knocking him down and causing the group clustered behind him to trip over his body. Melvin, the doctor, and Yaniv turned into their reptilian selves and gave chase. Andy grew wings and charged alongside them. Me? I stood by that little emerald door and waited. After all, I wasn't a superhero or anything. I wasn't sure what I was.

"She is gone." He stood there again, my papa.

"Can she come back, Papa?"

"No, she can't."

A wave of sadness hit me.

"She loves you and Sophie very much." He was fading away. "She did it for you both."

"You coming, hot stuff?" called a voice I recognized.

"Barney?" I was so glad to see him, really I was. "What are you doing here?"

"I am Santa's helper, ain't I?"

I looked beyond him, and all I saw were nymphs hanging off of big dragon-like forms.

"Backup? Didn't he tell you he'd be sending backup?"

"You're his backup?" I stared at the little nymph and then at the hordes of them overwhelming Melvin and his friends.

"Yeah, sister, watch this." He stood on a chair and whistled. Not a loud piecing one, just a minor sort of airy half-blown affair. No one and nothing noticed. "I got to change my brand." He gave his best smokers cough and whistled again. Little caps looked up. Then they peered at Barney. He gave a little wave of his hand and, poof, the whole group stopped what they were doing and came to stand before him. "Hello, guys."

They started bowing. As they did so, each one hit the one in front of him, then some rolled over, others fell backward, and still others fell flat on their little faces.

It would have been quite comical to watch if I didn't know they were here to cause us trouble.

Barney tapped his little, booted foot in annoyance. "Hey, what's the rule out here?"

A little one with a royal purple hat had come forward. He seemed to be in charge of the hoard. "No bowing, my lord."

Barney looked at him sternly. "And none of that 'my lord' stuff, either."

"Sorry, sorry." The nymph pulled off his hat and began wringing it in his hands, which reminded me of poor Abraham.

"It's all right, kiddo, just don't do it again." Barney winked at him. The other still seemed to be cowering in front of my Elf on a Shelf. "Look, boys, we came, we played, had a little girl time."

They all laughed raucously at this. I wondered just how many girls they actually all got.

"Now, it's time to get back home."

The others just stood there.

"You understand what I am saying?"

Nope, no one moved.

"Scram!"

They scattered in all directions. It happened so fast that I blinked and they were all gone.

"My lord?" Doctor Prescott came over to him in his human form, one real nice green orb wide with a perfect eyebrow cocked at Barney, questioning.

"I got a little clout back home, that's all. It ain't nothing." Barney jumped off the chair and scrambled behind me for protection.

The doctor came toward us. "Clout? They were bowing to you. Nymphs don't bow to just anyone—if anyone at all. Exactly who are you?"

"Barney, Barney the nymph, at your service." He

bowed to Sam, trying to appease the man, and, as he did so, he somersaulted forward on the doctor's shoes.

Must be a problem with their balance or something.

"I don't mean your name. I meant your station, sir."

Barney had come around the front end and now was in between my legs again. I wondered if that was because he was scared or simply that he was still a nymph. Andy took notice of this and yanked him out, holding him high off the ground. I felt flattered—three guys in one day wanted a piece of me, a virtual world record. I blamed the thrill I got from this on the hysteria.

Barney waved his arms and kicked his shiny little boots in the air. "Put me down, Feather Butt!"

It was Yaniv who rescued him, making a grab for the little man. "Andy put him down. Sam, leave him be. He is who he is." He whirled around just as Andy was about to say something. "Yes, yes, yes, we understand each other?" he growled real low, Doberman all the way.

Andy and Doctor Prescott both nodded, if not willingly. Melvin didn't look the least bit interested, but I suspected he had known Barney's rank from the beginning. I suspected he knew a lot more than anyone here.

Yaniv turned to Barney, bowed low to him, and winked. "Thank you for taking the time to help us, your lordship."

Barney winked back at him. "And back at you. Thanks for clearing up that little trouble I was in."

Yaniv flashed his pearly whites once more. I wondered if it was the stolen charms or girl trouble that the six-foot-something Doberman had fixed. Probably both. Barney seemed a handful and the type who needed things fixed on a regular basis. Since we were so caught up in our own little drama, we didn't hear the buzzing at first.

"Loci!"

I looked up, and the little, fanged beasts were flying

toward us. The three reptiles transformed again. Andy grew wings, again. Barney got on a chair and kept smashing alternate fists into his palms. What the little guy thought he was going to do, I really didn't know. And little ole me? I just stood there, again.

"Come on, you flying ferret faces," Barney called out to them.

Truth be told, he did look a little tough. Maybe that was an exaggeration, but he sure was cute. I would feel bad if the kid's Elf on the Shelf was damaged or killed.

Hearing the entreaty by the nymph, the flying daggers pointed themselves toward us. Just as they were upon our little gang, the purple-hatted guy came back. He was still scrunching up his hat in his hands. The other nymphs were kind of hanging back behind him, so, at first, I didn't see them. I wondered just how much clout Barney had that they were afraid of him.

The purple-hatted guy seemed oblivious to the oncoming attack. "Um, sir…"

Barney turned his attention toward the voice.

"There's the matter of our pay?"

It was then I noticed this guy was on his knees, crawling over to the chair where his "Lordship" stood, looking rather miffed. The others also went to their knees and began crawling forward. Barney looked at him, then at the onslaught. He held up a small hand and, to our astonishment, the entire company of Loci stopped. Then they all fell to the ground like stones. I guess these guys had no hovering modes like helicopters.

"Business is business." Barney jumped off the chair, kicking a couple of the fallen razor faces to the side so he could address his people.

As the Loci smashed into the wall, they burst into green liquid.

"Excuse me for a moment, please." Barney walked

right up to the kneeling nymph and looked him in the eyes. "What's this about payment?"

"Well, um, sir, your lor..." The words died on his lips with Barney's withering look. "Well, his...um... Redburn, sir. He promised us payment for our service to him."

"And what does that have to do with me?"

The little guy prostrated himself in panic mode. "In your name, sir."

"Oh, I see. Hmm." Barney started to pace and, as he did so, Andy signaled I should follow him out. My father had transformed back to his human form. He went over to Barney, stepping on quite a few of the Loci's small bodies along the way. These guys crunched like locusts. Green liquid oozed out.

Melvin put his hand on Barney's shoulder. "Looks like you have a problem, my friend."

The small man looked at him. "Can you imagine the nerve of this guy? Using my name?"

My father tsked a bit and then got down to where the little nymph cowered. "What did he promise you and your companions here?"

"Er...one hundred gold pieces and one hundred magic charms, per head."

"One hundred!" Barney, in his rage, started stomping around, crushing more Loci cockroaches than I could count.

I had to step back, as the innards were splashing around. I didn't really like the smell emanating from them and was afraid it would make a permanent stain, not to mention stink, on my clothes. He stormed, crushed, and squished with his little nymph boots. Each crunch brought more and more cowering from the poor little nymphs on the ground. They were all prostrate, not to mention shaking violently.

Barney's face turned beet red as he got eye level with the little fellow. "Per head!"

"Per, per group!"

I didn't think it was possible to lower oneself into the ground, but he did. In fact, all of them followed suit. I only saw half the body of each of them. His head popped up, and tears poured out of his crinkled eyes. "We only got fifty left, sir. Er, my lordship, er, your, uh uh...what should we call you again?"

"Never you mind!" Barney snapped at him.

"Yes, Never You Mind."

"Two per head? How many when you started?"

"One hundred, sir."

"Two per head!" Barney shouted once more. He walked around into the corners, smashing a couple of Loci that had gathered on the wall. Guts went flying into his face, and he sputtered in anger. The little guy and company sank even farther into the flooring so only their hats could be seen. And, by the time Barney got back to them, only the pompoms of those hats were visible.

"One and a quarter would satisfy us though, your lordsh—" The purple-hatted guy's head popped up, and all the other little heads did too, hopeful. "—Never You Mind, sir."

Barney was there in a moment, making sure to crunch on all the Loci that hadn't already been pulverized before. "Oh, that's different."

By then the stench was unbearable. My eyes were watering, Andy's were as well, and the little purple-hatted guy's were leaking rivers, though I wondered if that was just for effect. Melvin and his crew seemed unaffected by the acrid mists entirely.

"It is my...um...sir?"

"Yes, I will give each of you one gold piece."

The purple-hatted guy's eyes got wide, and the others disappeared into the ground again.

"The quarter is for me, because you didn't examine my signature on the document thoroughly enough."

"There was no signature, my—er—excellency." The faces came up. "Er—Never You Mind."

"That's right!" Barney turned to us all for confirmation. "See what I mean?" The little men were gone again. "Do we agree?"

Now back to the floor of pompoms. A muffled agreement could be heard from the ground.

"Good." Barney signaled the attack to continue. Ten stray Loci he had missed started to advance from different parts of the room toward us.

"And the charms, sir?" the purple-hatted guy put in.

"Halt! Business again." Barney pushed his hand into the ground and picked up the little guy. Now a whole petrified nymph was standing in front of him. "Now what? I have a battle to conduct here…" He swept a hand over the carnage. The other nymph looked around at all the mess and gulped hard. The purple-hatted guy tried to descend into the floor once more, but Barney caught him. "Enough of that! You move even a hair, and I'll crush you like a…a…a…" He eyed what the other was staring at behind him. "Like them." Then he dropped the little man and hopped toward the approaching Loci, using his hand like a fly swatter to crush them. He returned to the statuesque nymph covered in stinky guts. "Now what?" he sneered between gritted teeth.

"Mmmmm."

Yes, the little purple-hatted guy was affected by the fetid fumes. His nose turned red, and his eyes were literally dripping.

"What?"

Melvin pointed to the whiskers on the face of the

very frightened nymph. "You told him not to move a hair. I believe that includes chin hairs."

"Oh, speak."

"Charms, charms," he coughed at Barney, finally breathing.

"Those were not mine to promise so therefore you need to go to the one who promised them. Who did promise them to you, by the way?" Barney knew. We all did of course.

"Redburn, sir."

"Well, then we go to accounts payable, Devlin, and we will take it up with him. One charm per man."

"Two." But that was swallowed up real fast. "Never you mind." Then he added. "One per man."

"Good. I will collect the unused ones for safekeeping."

I wondered just whose safekeeping it would be.

"Now let's go to the down below and collect, shall we?"

All the nymphs in the room headed to where I had just come from.

The doctor caught Barney in his hands. "Wait a second. Aren't you forgetting something?"

"Let me go." He was dropped unceremoniously. "What?"

All of them stopped where they were and proceeded to drop on the floor as Barney had just done. He got up, they got up. What a scene.

"The little fight we are currently engaged in?"

Barney shifted his gaze to all the carnage surrounding us. "Oh, yeah, I forgot. Proceed!"

His hands whooshed upward. One lone Loci got up and started to fly toward him, then peered around at the carnage—at that point, fifty-one nymphs, three fully formed deamons, one nephilim, and little old balled-up me. He peered behind him, then beside him, and then once again in front of him. He then proceeded to turn tail, revved up, and smashed himself against the wall in a burst of green and yellow liquid. All the nymphs looked with awe and wonder at their glorious leader.

"My prince." They all bowed to him on bent knee. "The conqueror of the dreaded Loci army!"

Barney grew ten feet in his own eyes—oh, and in theirs too, not to mention my own.

"He glared at them. Who?"

They all cowered in unison. "Never You Mind!"

"Exactly." he harrumphed, but I knew he loved it.

Then on a signal I didn't see, they all got up and once more headed toward the door.

"Yeah, well, it ain't nothing compared to what I'll do to the Lukes if they don't give me my charms—" The little army stopped and stared at him. "Our charms, our charms, okay?"

They again began to move and popped through the walls of hell. We watched until the last one vanished.

"Who is Devlin?" Andy asked as the last one disappeared.

"The accountant," Yaniv said.

"Another Luke really, but he feels he is more important than the rest of them so he chose a name for himself," Melvin elaborated as he popped my bubble for me.

I landed with a thump, but on my feet, at least. "Devlin? He chose Devlin?"

Melvin shrugged at Andy. "It's a good name."

"An accountant in hell? Really?"

Boy things down there were so official. Maybe my mom would like it.

CHAPTER 29

Exiting the mint was not nearly as dramatic as all the things we had just been through. The fact that Yaniv popped all the locks, the doctor restarted all the disabled cameras, and Melvin knew exactly which invisible laser beam to step over in order to avoid the alarms should have bothered me, or at least bothered Andy, but it didn't. My stepfather wanted to take me home, but Andy insisted on calling a cab and doing it himself. I acquiesced since I knew that I had to break off this relationship before it got out of hand. Not that being dragged to hell by Loci wasn't at the bottom of the relationship barrel, but you know what I mean.

By the time we got out of there, it was night. Andy stood next to me, waiting for the cab. I could feel him there thinking. "I am so sorry. I didn't know just how dangerous it would be." He sounded sorry about it too.

"Did you not know that Luke wanted me there?" He nodded that he knew. "Permanently?"

"They told me the risks. I just thought I could outwit them."

Arrogant, but humbled now? I doubted it.

"Have you ever been to hell before?" Tears had

started to roll down my face. "I have a child, Andy. I need to be here for her. You didn't outwit them."

"I have a family to take care of too, you know. Everlasting lava is not exactly what I envisioned for them."

Heat was rising in his voice, and I decided to call it quits.

"It's not the same, Andy. Sophie would have no parents." At the rise of his very cute eyebrows, I realized it was the same because neither would Sarah. "Okay, it is the same, but I promised Sophie I wouldn't die. And the truth is you are just a newbie to SUD."

"Look, I said I was sorry."

Then he faced me squarely. Oh man, was this guy good looking. One peek at him, and my belly went jellified again. "Okay." I just couldn't forgive him so easily. I knew all some girls got was popcorn and a movie. I got to live the whole script, but what a script! He looked like he was thinking real hard, too hard. "What is it?" I asked.

"Listen, why don't we call it a day and just get married?"

He was kidding, right? I mean I knew Nona did this, but did all D'Souzas just go for broke?

"I thought you said you wouldn't marry me until hell freezes over?"

At this, he started to laugh hysterically. "Did you just see the same thing I just saw? It is frozen over."

Yes, I had, and I had seen it defrost just as my mother went into it to save my life, which was indirectly his fault. He saw my expression change, so I told him about my mother and what had transpired. He got quiet, really quiet.

"I don't think we should continue, Andy. I am obviously not ready to go out into the dating scene yet, much less marry you." He looked crestfallen, and I really did feel terrible. He took out his cell phone and called for two cabs. This just about killed it for me. *I mean at least walk the girl to the door, will you?*

"How about you think about it? Take a day to sort of mull it over. Come to Nesti Festa Dei Sette Pesci." When I looked at him strangely, he just smiled. "The feast of the seven fish. It's an Italian thing. My nona puts out a great spread."

As the cabs pulled up, he gave one driver money and sent me packing with a kiss to the lips. I had to say my heart relented a bit, but then the door shut, and I was being whisked back home.

"So you broke up, aye?" I looked at the driver.

White fluffy hair, snowy sideburns and a big puffy beard to match. "Santa?" What job didn't this guy do? "Yes, I did. He is not my type. Rash, risk-taking, hot-blooded... " I did admire his body, though I wasn't about to mention that to old St. Nick. I felt miserable, and tears started to flow. I know, I know, he was charming too and could be sweet on occasion. He was a responsible provider and did still live with his grandmother and his disabled sister.

"Yes, I know he is Italian, but so what?" he said, a bit amused, but gently.

"Look, Paulo is dead, and I just am not ready to go out." What was so hard to understand? I was lousy with self-pity and the next available candidate, though totally hot, had an anger-management problem.

"How many tears have you cried since Paulo died?" Millions. He knew the answer. "Sophie will be very disappointed."

Then it dawned on me that Sophie had written him with a Christmas wish this year. A flash of anger went through me. "I can't just marry a guy because Sophie wants a father for Christmas!"

We sat in silence for about five minutes. I was looking out the window crying. Again.

"She didn't want a father for Christmas," he whispered, then paused to make sure I had heard him. He waited for me to focus on him. "She wanted a mother."

"She has a mother." Panic was beginning to rise in my chest. "I am her mother!"

"She wants her mother back." He was quiet. "You didn't die, you know."

"I know." But I had. I had died the minute the two soldiers showed up on my doorstep and died again when I went to the plane to meet his casket.

My lifeblood had left my soul as the bagpipes played, the honor guard folded the flag, and taps echoed in the cemetery. The sad notes blasted the last of my heart beats out of my chest. I had packed up my bags, run straight to his family, and never went home again. Had I become like my mother? A shadow of my former self? Had it taken this trip through hell to bring me back? Was I back? Maybe I would have to remain here until I lost myself to it as my mother had.

Then it struck me. "Will my mother be able to return?"

"No."

I supposed I knew that already. "Will he hurt her?" Concern was growing in me.

"Your mother? No way!"

That was good, I guess.

"And Barney..." Oh boy, had I become attached to that little troublemaker.

"Barney is a nymph. He'll weasel out as many charms as he can from old Devlin." He ho ho hoed it up.

I could feel my spirits rising. "I can do it."

"What?" His cherry red round nose filled the mirror, but he knew already. A smile crossed his face.

"Oh, my gosh! I didn't buy any real gifts this year!" I finally processed who I was with. I had gotten used stocking stuffers, but not the real deal.

"Don't worry. You will have a great gift, on the house, that the kids will never forget. There's no problem with the adults—they all know what you have gone through. They understand." His voice was gentle. "You're back, ma'am."

Oh boy, I must be getting old if Santa was calling me ma'am. Lights, animation, and loud voices filled the lawn in front of us. There were policemen, my family, and every neighbor on the block. "Looks like you were missed."

I got out of the car, and Sophie broke free of Velma's embrace. She ran right over to me and gave me a great big hug. We stood there for quite a while. I didn't even notice that the taxi had driven away.

"You are okay, right?" she asked.

She looked at me with such concern I wanted to cry, but I smiled instead. I had cried an ocean. It was time for me swim free of it and give one of those Yaniv smiles.

"I am fine, Sophie." I had a smile pasted as wide as I could on my mouth.

"And Andy—is he okay too? Sarah and I were so worried about you both." I had to laugh at that. "We saw them follow you," she whispered real low.

Well so much for protecting her from the supernatural and all that.

"Yes, Andy is Andy," I said. She looked at me curiously. "I mean, he's fine. He invited us to Christmas Eve dinner tomorrow night." A big smile, one I had missed severely, crossed her face. "Do you want to go?" I asked. I wouldn't tell her it was fish, *all* fish. She practically lived on cucumbers and cereal.

"Will Sarah be there?"

I nodded.

"Can Velma go too? She wants to meet Sarah."

I looked at my little niece and back at Sophie. Best of friends, worst of enemies crossed my mind. I hugged her close again.

"Of course." I didn't mention that Alysia might not approve. Let her be the baddie.

CHAPTER 30

Barney returned the next morning to be seen under the tree along with all the presents. Next to him was an invitation from Santa to go to the roof that night. As far as I knew, this was his last day with us, but I was relieved to see him and hugged him close. I wasn't sure what my family thought. I probably looked like I had lost it because I kept saying how glad I was to see him. A stuffed doll? Yeah, I looked kind of kooky.

My sister-in-law had put an unsurprising kibosh on Velma joining us, but she did invite Andy and his family for Christmas Day lunch, so Velma would be able to meet Sophie's new friend.

That night Sophie and I did go to the feast of the seven fish. To say things started off a bit uncomfortable would be an understatement. I mean, I did just break up with the guy. Or at least I thought I had...

Nona greeted me at the door. She was wearing a very colorful dress of greens, reds, and oranges. Interspersed were strands of gold thread that were intentionally shagged. The streetlights danced on them, and they lit up in greeting to all who came to her front portal. She stood, waiting for us to step into her domain and giving Sophie a warm hug, and then turned to me. "Hell froze over, no?"

At least she didn't say "When's the wedding?" She winked and pulled us in.

I couldn't quite describe the smells, but let's just say, though I knew the night was supposed to be all fish, it didn't smell it in that house. In fact, it smelled wonderful. Fresh bread scent permeated the halls as we hung up our coats. Tomatoes and basil wafted into the living room as the first course was served by none other than Andy himself. Decked in a red Santa jacket, white fuzz, and a nymph cap—yes, it was definitely nymph. He saw me eying it.

"One of the little buggers left it there. I thought it would be bad for business if the mint opened and there it was." The cap was purple and had a bell at the end that jingled all the way as he served. He handed me trout bruschetta on a melba toast. I took one bite of this basil, olive, and fish concoction and, man, was I hooked.

I should tell you I was not the only one there. Believe it or not, Giles the elf was also a guest. I wasn't sure my friend Andy was so happy about that. All through the meal, Giles kept complimenting Nona in French. He was wearing his host's outfit and, every so often, made to get up to help serve.

Nona repeated a definite "No, no," swatting at him to remain in his seat, and then promptly ordered Andy to get the next course. I might add that like a "very good boy" he complied without complaint. Sarah also complied, but she was much more interested in playing with Sophie than serving, so after the third attempt at getting the girl into the kitchen, to my shock, Nona gave up.

"Sarah has her wrapped around her little pinky." Andy's shrimp scampi breath whispered in my ear. The garlic did not smell so bad on him!

Let me just tell you that while most people ate fish to lose weight, here at Nona's there was no option but to gain it.

Between mouthfuls of fried octopus, tossed in a green salad, Giles regaled us with the misadventures of the SUD, primarily those of Andrew Senior; it seemed that the old elf was his partner at one time.

As Nona served the crab fettuccini with a cream sauce so rich that I gained ten pounds just smelling it, the girls finally made their break from the table. Sophie had mostly picked, but then again I hadn't expected much more. She would be back when the dessert appeared. I had a feeling Sarah would help serve that.

Andy asked the question. No, he didn't ask me to marry him again, thank goodness, he asked the nephilim question. "Nona, ummmm, you know how hell froze over?"

Okay, so they kept hinting, but that was not exactly asking. "I...kind of..." He looked behind him to make sure that the girls were out of hearing distance. "Turned into an ummmmmmm..."

"An angel?" She stood up, also peeking behind her as well, then promptly grew wings. Not gray, dingy wings like Andy had, but glowing white ones that spread out and filled the room.

"Oh, my!" Giles gasped and clapped his hands in excitement. "*Mon ange, vous etes vraimont belle!*" He got up and bowed to her.

"Watch it, that's my grandmother you're talking about!"

I pulled the guy down before he lost it to an elf's charm. "That only means 'My angel, you're very beautiful,' Andy."

"Yeah, well, she is not his anything."

Not yet, but I could see she might turn out to be very soon, so he better get used to it.

"Very much like your grandfather. For some reason, he had an aversion to French too."

Andy laughed, and Nona retracted her wings.

"You get it from my side of the family. It seems my father was a Nephilim. He was very old when he met my mother. She was a mortal and truly had no idea what the man was. They were married for a long time, but when she died, he tired of living." Her soft Italian-accented voice was sad. "I was close to him, but he missed her terribly." She turned her round, soft face away from us. "He said it was time to go home. Then he was gone. Where home was, he didn't say, but he did tell me what I was and that he couldn't return from where he was. Ever."

We sat quietly and ate clams drenched in butter and toasted almonds.

"Nona, how long have you known I was one?"

"I never thought you were one. I hoped not at least. My papa was so lonely, and I had hoped that you wouldn't have to suffer like he did." When Andy just stared at her, she added one last detail. "Because we live a long, long time, *caro*."

She looked at Giles as the old elf stared back at her. I thought about all the friends that they must have lost to time and death. Okay, so this was getting real depressing.

"Do you mean we don't die?" It dawned on Andy finally what she was saying.

"Technically you can be killed, Andrew, but no, you probably won't die of natural causes," Giles put in.

It seemed he had been looking into this lately and as he stared at Nona, I could tell why.

"SUD had suspicions you might be one. They didn't know for sure, but they certainly guessed it."

SUD seemed to have a lot of guessing going on.

"The last director was quite a character, and not very popular. He was not big on privacy. He opened files that had been guarded by some very heavy charms. Your grandfather had been in the witness protection program for a long time. As you can imagine, he had some major history going back to Adam." Giles looked uncomfortable saying this. "He wasn't always such a nice fellow, *mon chère.*"

"Again with the French," Andy mumbled.

Nona looked rather amused at her grandson's discomfort. "Yes, I know. He told me he had been in some trouble years ago."

Some trouble? Did he mention teaching man the art of war, or the raping, pillaging, and murder that was going on? No, I supposed Paulo would not have told Sophie that either, had he been an angel. Which he was now, technically, playing a cello. And what about this witness protection program? How many others like Andy's grandfather were in it and did I live next to them? Then again, they probably moved away from us years ago. Nobody wanted to spend eternity next door to us, it seemed. It might be my imagination, but as soon as someone moved in, they put out a for-sale sign the very next week.

"Sam has been trying to fix a lot of dis-origination that was caused. You could call it a cleaning house." Giles looked at me and blushed. "That includes mending the rift with Melvin and SUD. It seems that the last glorious leader was not as fond of honesty and integrity as he should have been. Melvin informed him of some fraud and less-than-favorable methods that had been employed of late." He tapped his long fingers together as if contemplating something. Then, when it seemed he had made up his mind, he said, "Coincidentally, that is when Denton happened to leave the book open, and the gates of hell were opened. It was then that Melvin was dismissed from

SUD." He licked his lips nervously. "They claimed he had been reckless, but I always suspected it was for not turning you over to the Lukes."

"Geez, you SUD guys sound like something else," Andy growled.

"Like I said, Doctor Prescott is mending the problems as fast as he can. He really is an erstwhile fellow. He was a Minuteman, you know."

Yes, he was. He was also the only Minute Man to make it to Concord and warn them the British were coming since Paul Revere had been arrested in the early morning. It was rumored Prescott had died very young, but I now saw that was not entirely true.

"Yeah, well—" Andy started

"Dessert!" Nona intoned. Not surprisingly, two girls appeared instantaneously. Nona sent them into the kitchen to get a very familiar dish.

She called it struffoli, but my mom-mom called it taiglach. It was little round balls of fried dough that were covered in colorful sprinkles and drenched in honey. My Greek side of the family also served this, but only on Easter. Then Andy went in and got hot chocolate and cappuccino. To my surprise, Giles took a hot chocolate. We all used our hands pulling out the little balls as strands of honey dripped and dangled from our mouths and fingers back onto the plate.

Andy showed the girls some more card tricks, but I could see my Sophie was anxious to see what the surprise was on the roof tonight. It was really nice being there and I thought that Andy knew it.

He looked hopefully at me. "My offer still stands."

I was sorry to say my answer still stood, as well. It was still very much a no, but it was nice to still be wanted. He shrugged, and I could see he was a bit hurt. Maybe hurt was too strong a word, perhaps just worried.

"Then it's off to the roof. Girls, your sleigh awaits." Andy stepped out of the house and pulled out a remote. The side of the house opened as he entered it. What came out of it was not the hot little Camaro, but a Camaro dressed like a Christmas tree. There was tinsel and garlands galore on it. Shiny blue, greens, and silver were topped with balls of all colors.

"Oh, wow!" both girls cried, running to it.

Andy pressed some button inside and the door opened for them.

"You coming, mon petit? See, Giles? I can use French too."

Giles had stepped on the front porch to watch the spectacle. He looked at Andy then at Nona next to him, then he did the unthinkable—he kissed her!

"Why, that—"Andy leaped from the car, but before I could wedge myself in between them, Nona stopped him.

"Andrew! Get back in that car and take my daughter-in-law and grandchildren to go meet Santa! I can handle this guy myself."

Yes, but could poor Giles handle Nona? *Wait—did she just say daughter-in-law?*

CHAPTER 31

I hadn't had time to do much Christmas shopping, but the invite did say to meet Santa on the top of our porch on the roof Christmas Eve. I was there with Phoebe, Sophie, Velma, Alexi, and Barney. Santa had invited Andy and Sarah too. It was midnight, and nothing was stirring, not even a mouse, not to mention my blood circulation which had frozen five minutes before the Big Guy arrived.

"Santy!" Sarah called out as eight reindeer landed quietly on the soft snow that had just started to fall. She ran to the nearest reindeer and hugged it.

"Sarah!" Andy reached for her.

"It's okay, Andy. They're friendly."

Alexi looked at the old man and then at the animals. He reached into his pocket, and to my surprise, he had nine baby carrots. He showed Santa, who nodded approvingly at him.

"One at a time, boys."

A little hand reached up as the polite animals took one carrot each. Leaving one carrot slicked with reindeer saliva. Alexi went up to Santa and handed it to him reverently. "For Rudolph."

The others turned their heads and stamped their hooves.

"Boys…" Santa's voice was that of a loving parent being forced to discipline misbehaving kids. "Thank you, Alexi, he will be thrilled." Then he moved over some sacks of toys and motioned for the kids to join him on the sleigh. As they piled in, he whispered in my ear. "They are a bit jealous of old Rudy. Getting his own movie sort of put them in a bad light. Serves them right. It wasn't nice to make fun of people—er—reindeer." A ho, ho, ho was uttered.

There wasn't enough room for Andy or me.

Sophie started to get out. "There is no room for my mom."

I was touched she was getting up for me. "No, Sophie, this is your gift."

She sat down again, and both Sarah and Velma took a gloved hand in theirs. I knew the three of them would get along just fine.

The sleigh had started to rise when Santa leaned over to my ear. "Your mom sends regards. She says not to worry about her. She might be out of touch for a while because she has a lot of cleaning up to do. Apparently, Luke is quite a hoarder." And they were off with another hardy ho, ho, ho. "He might not have bargained for your mother. She is quite the neat freak."

We watched for a while as they disappeared into the night sky.

"Well…" Andy turned to look at me, holding my two handsicles in his warm mitts. He took off the gloves and put my appendages in his pockets. He then hugged me.

I let him. *What's a hug between friends?* "Well, what?" It felt good to be alive. It really did.

"What if I asked you, again, to marry me?"

The guy was persistent. I did have to say it was romantic. Snow, starlight, reindeer...

"I'd say that we needed to get to know each other better, first." That was the best I could offer him. I wasn't a marry-on-the-third-date kind of girl. Or it could have been that Paulo was standing off to the side. Was he nodding his approval?

"Move on, Eros," he whispered again and again.

I wanted to say Andy was rude, gruff, and had landed my mom in hell.

"And he's not even Greek," Paulo added mischievously. "Then again, neither are you. See? No one's perfect."

Oh, that was a low blow, mister!

"However, he has a kind heart and a good light surrounding him." Paulo was now winking in and out. "Besides Sophie likes him, and he will be a great papa."

Then he was gone.

"Umm, now that your late husband has given me his approval, not to mention has stopped peeking over my shoulder at us, may I kiss you already?"

Somehow, he managed to persuade me to kiss him. Maybe it was his dimples, or it could have been that ridiculous nymph cap he was wearing that made me think there might be another Andy somewhere under this rough exterior. Or maybe it just was time to move on.

To say we were distracted was a bit of an understatement, but the thumping of hooves a half hour later interrupted our kisses. Was it that long? Really? Five beaming passengers exited the sleigh.

"Did you have a good time?" Andy broke off and helped them all out as Santa jumped out to assist him. Mr. Gallant was great with his sister Sarah. Sophie seemed at ease with him too, and Alexi didn't seem to frighten him in the least.

"Yeah!" Sarah was so excited.

Velma's round eyes looked up into mine. "This is not something we can tell our parents, right?"

I wasn't so sure my in-laws would approve of this. They would definitely think I was filling them with tales.

Santa smiled at us. "I have to be going and you kids need to go to sleep."

They all nodded, whispered goodbye to Santa and ran inside. You had to hand it to old Saint Nick.

When they were gone, he stared at us both. "I will sprinkle some Christmas dust on them while they sleep. It will be a dream they will remember forever." He hopped back in his sleigh, spry as a twenty-year-old and started to rise into the air. As he did so, he called out over his head, "Merry Christmas to all, and to all a goodnight!"

And quick as that he was gone.

"That's my cue, I guess." Andy took Sarah's hand and then kissed me again.

They left, walking down the porch steps to the decked-to-the-hilt Camaro.

"Are you still here, Paulo?" I knew he was. I could always feel him before he entered a room when he was alive. A warm embrace went around my neck and shoulders. We stood there for a while in the silence of the night. "Merry Christmas, Paulo."

"Merry Christmas, Eros." I could feel him pulling his energies back. Fading. "Tell Sophie that I gave you her Christmas present."

Boy, that child was working overtime this holiday season, and all I had gotten her was reindeer leggings, slightly faded.

"I am saying goodbye, my love."

I had regretted one thing when he passed away so suddenly—I never said goodbye to him. I began to think hard. Had I told Sophie this? Yes, I probably had or told it to someone within her earshot.

"It is so hard because you drive me to mania!"

"You fresh ghost." I could still sense him, waiting. "Goodbye, Paulo."

He was gone now, really gone. Yes, I cried, but only for a little while. It felt better now. I was letting go, and he was letting me do it. Sophie was right—I had always known he was near, there for her when I couldn't be. Now it was time to return home and be the mother she needed, the one I needed to be for her. Maybe even the one I had had but didn't appreciate until she was gone.

Eventually, I did sneak into the house. At first, I didn't notice the form on the chair.

"Welcome back, Delphi." It was my mother-in-law, Rydia. Her face was wet with tears. "Paulo has finally gone to heaven." It was then, I realized she must be a sensitive too.

"I am sorry, Mama." I was sorry for her, I was sorry for Sophie, and I was sorry for me, too.

"Every mother wants the best for her child. He served his country, gave his life, fighting terrorists and murderers. He had a good marriage and produced a wonderful daughter that I treasure. I just want him to be at peace, for you both to be at peace with your lives." She kissed my cheek and held me in her embrace as I kneeled on the floor there by her knees. "Sophie needs you. It's time to live again, child."

We stared at the tree as the lights twinkled. For a moment, I could swear I saw the angel at the top of the tree light up. I knew that Rydia saw it too. She breathed deeply, and I saw a tear slip down her face.

"Another angel was just brought to heaven. War doesn't take a holiday, I am afraid, ever. May the good

Lord end this war soon, and may there be peace on Earth already."

I put in my hardy Amen. Just as suddenly the tree twinkled in a spectacular light show of dazzling colors lighting up the whole room.

"And another soul has come into the world."

She smiled and…you know?…so did I.

About the Author

"Me?" says author Arcey Dear. "I'm just an ordinary boring person who likes to shop in thrift shops during the holidays—it's probably the thrill of the bargain, or being able to push people out of the way to get a really good deal. (Yeah, my shrink says I have an aggression issue. You got a problem with that? I mean, the shrink part.) Or it could be the fact that, even with a few nicks and dents, the item might pass for new—if I gave it in the dark."

Dear has been told she's a bit quirky, though that's mostly by her kids. Her life is totally weird, and the things she writes about really do happen: things like finding a passport in the Goodwill and trying to hand it off to a cop who wouldn't touch it, totally real. Nymphs…well, that was just a really short Goodwill clerk…she thinks. A Warlock for a dad, real. Him being a deamon, not real. Etcetera, Etcetera…Just believe her when she says her life is odd. The stuff she writes is meant to be laughed at while eating hot fudge sundaes. Readers, you can lose weight later when you play Pokemon Go, but not until the final page is read or the last drop of fudge is licked!

She hopes you enjoy reading her books as much as she enjoys writing them! Visit her on her website: www.arceydear.com